VICTORIA C. JOHNSON

IMMORTALS IN LEATHER

GODDESS ASCENSION BOOK 2

Thank you to my family for providing me the support needed to follow my dreams. You make me stronger, better, and braver. A special thanks to my husband for being my first reader. I love you!

CHAPTER 1

W HY DID HE PICK SOMEPLACE that's so damn hot?" I complain as we walk up to the large building that resembles a dorm.

"I know. My leather is chafing," Apate says as she waddles ahead of me.

Things have been a little odd in the last few weeks. For one thing, one of our partners in crime, Peitho, has totally lost her goddess-given mind. She's suddenly got some parasite growing inside her and doesn't want anything to do with us anymore. There have been no concrete studies that show if an immortal drinks ambrosia while pregnant, the baby will be born without the ability to shape shift. Absolutely none!

I guess none of us thought we'd see the day when Peitho seriously shacked up with someone. I mean, like happily and without cheating or anything. We kind of have to buy it now that she's spawning his scaly half-dragon child, though. Not that I'm not looking forward to the baby and everything, but it's a lot of change.

Now we're in the middle of hell—I'm sorry, Florida—about to meet with a god who's a few drops short of a full chalice. What Ares thinks he's doing as the leader of a werewolf biker gang, I have no idea. It's not for profit or anything. One must therefore assume that it's the thrill of it. Feeling the heat of the sun on my back and looking at the rather ordinary building in front of me, it's hard to believe there's any serious fun to be had.

"The leather is chafing because you forgot to use that powder I told you about," Enyo advises Apate.

"Or maybe it's because it's hotter than Apollo's right ass cheek," Apate grumbles.

I have to admit, she's not the only one more than a little fed up with Enyo at the moment. Hell, I think even Lyssa is starting to get annoyed, which is saying something, since they're usually stuck pretty firmly up each other's ass. Ares is Enyo's brother, so everything must be oh-so-perfect for this little Immortal Representative mission. This includes us looking the part. When we first went to the shifter convention some months ago, Peitho had us do the same thing. We put on togas. Which is not quite the same thing as all of us being clad in skintight leather in upper ninety-degree weather.

I'm currently standing out here in the middle of the day after catching a plane back from England, dressed in a black leather miniskirt and a matching bustier. I can feel sweat not only trickle between my ample breasts, but also down my back, getting dangerously close to dripping down my crack. Overall, I could be in a better mood. When the minor goddess of ruthlessness, shamelessness, and unforgiveness isn't happy, not too many others are.

"Come on, Anaideia, baby, if we're lucky we'll find some randy werewolves," Apate says to me.

I shrug. "I've been with a few. Some can be kinda hairy."

"Ah, either a hit or a miss. I hear they can also be possessive but aggressive and satisfying in the sack. I, for one, will be taking what I can get." Apate winks at me, looking like a perfect angel with dimpled cherub cheeks, honey-blonde hair, and big brown eyes.

"How many people are in Ares's little group anyway? We may have to fight for 'em," Dysnomia points out.

Enyo speaks up with pride, "I believe he has twenty or so underlings. It is the largest gang in this area."

"Isn't there only one other wolf one in the area? Though how werewolf biker gang popularity started, I'll never understand," Dys says.

"Agreed. From what I understand, most of them don't even have bikes. They just walk around in leather and bad attitudes.

Whoever told wolves that it's attractive when they grow out their hair and let the sweat drip, should be shot," Apate agrees.

"I swear you can smell them within a mile radius around the house." I wrinkle my nose at the heavy wet dog scent lingering in the air.

Nemesis, standing a little in front of us all, says, "Since we've already paid the cab, have our bags lying about, and have gotten a good dose of complaining in, maybe it's about time we knock on the door?"

The seven of us all trade looks with one another.

Enyo sighs. "I'll do it, but because he is my family, not because I am your servant." She lifts her fist and bangs on the flimsy door as if she's trying to break it down.

We all stand patiently back, suitcases in front of us, eyes on the door with cold expectancy. When it opens, I'm not quite sure I can put in words what I had been expecting, but this certainly isn't it. There's a man standing there. He's, well, sort of short for a wolf. He has shaggy brown hair, and even from here, I can see great big brown eyes. With tan cargo shorts and a light green polo shirt, he couldn't be any preppier. Clearly not one of the hulking wolves we're looking for.

He smiles warmly, but it dims considerably when he actually looks at us. "Can I help you?"

"Damn, we must have actually gone to a dorm house! I knew that cabby didn't know what he was doing. Sorry, kid, we'll get out of here," I tell the boy.

The girls all nod, and start grabbing their things.

"Ares will fillet some asses when he hears we were given bad directions," Enyo says excitedly.

"Hold on, did you say Ares?" The kid at the door asks with distaste, "You're not the Immortal Representatives, are you?"

I can tell that we're not exactly what he was expecting either. From the way that his eyes trail up and down my lace-up leather hooker boots and Apate's red leather bra/shirt, I know he's a bit disturbed. Though really, I don't know why. Maybe he thinks we're going to beat him up for his lunch money. Sure we may look badass but we also look hot. Like always.

"*You* work for my brother? Normally he teaches more manners, but I will forgive this instance," Enyo sniffs regally.

He gives her an unimpressed look. "Right. I can take you to Ares if you want to come in."

"Of course we'll be coming in. Dear brother has invited us all to stay here while we help with the little mess. Though if this is the sort of company that's to be expected, I don't know how long that will work out," Enyo's eyes light on him.

He shrugs. "Whatever."

I step in, moving forward a little, "What Enyo is trying to strategically say, is if you continue to act like a disrespectful dick while we're staying here, she'll probably kill you. Well, her and Lyssa. Oh, and make no mistake. Ares won't mind."

The boy just looks at me blankly. "That it?"

"Shit, does he have balls of steel or a death wish? Maybe both?" Apate asks lightly with an impressed whistle.

"Who let you answer the door?" Comes a booming voice from just inside the house. The famed Ares makes his appearance. He doesn't look old, but he does look mature at early to mid-thirties. He has a closely shaved, dark beard and short dark hair. He actually looks very military. Well, then again he is dressed up in leather chaps and a leather vest without a shirt under it. With the God of War, it's not a bad thing to see some extra flesh.

The preppy guy looks at all of us as if extremely bored. "No one else was around to answer the door, so I figured it would be better for me to then just stand by and let them wait."

"You know the rules! I told you that you were under no circumstances to be around when my sister and her colleagues got here. Hell, you were supposed to be at the pub! Not scouring the foyer looking for an excuse to get snippy with new prey," Ares booms at the kid. "Max, if I knew you'd be so much trouble ..."

"Yeah yeah, you would have never let me stay. Do you want me to help carry bags in?" Preppy Max asks.

Ares just sighs at the boy, utilizing more patience than I've ever seen. "Might as well. You know where to take them."

"Super," He says the word with so much sarcasm, I'm thrown then Ares doesn't punch him into oblivion.

Ares finally turns to our merry group, all of a sudden smiling and turning on the charm like he does so well. He gives us a bright, somehow joyously surprised smile. I don't know how he manages to convey surprise in there, since he's known weeks about us coming, but other than that, the smile is perfect. So perfectly fake.

"Nemesis! I hope you've been taking care of my girls," He says, shaking a finger at her.

"I do what I can," She acknowledges.

"Anaideia, Apate, Dysnomia! You all look as lovely as ever," Ares says, eyes barely looking at us even as I somehow feel caressed in their light.

"Looking hot yourself, old man," Apate nods.

He shakes his head at her in mock disapproval.

"Aergia, glad to see you're still awake."

"Yeah, hopefully not for much longer," she says dryly.

"Oh, and here's my Lyssa. How are you, my darling? Starting any . . . fights?" He says the word fight like an addict says their drug of choice.

Lyssa does something we don't get to see too often. She giggles like a schoolgirl and throws herself into Ares's arms for a hug. For his part, he holds them wide open and ready to catch her. It's almost a touching moment, when you forget that they've bonded over bloodshed and mayhem. When she steps away, they're both smiling.

"Enyo?" Ares turns to her with a question, then opens his arms as he did with Lyssa.

I am about to laugh, expecting her to give him the finger and tell him there's no way that's happening. The girl I've thought of as the most badass, cold, unfeeling woman in the immortal world, squeals and throws herself at her brother. They embrace and finally let go after a long moment, faces flushed and eyes shining.

"I've missed you greatly sister! Things are just not the same without you. None hold a torch to your shine on the battlefield," Ares says.

"I should hope not, brother, since you taught me yourself," Enyo points out.

Ares laughs, "Indeed, though you have a thirst for blood and war that rivals even my own. I hope you've been well satisfied in your travels?"

"Oh yes, you know humans!"

"They can't last seconds without starting another fight! They're truly marvelous creatures, though I prefer the older ones more than modern. They had much less rules. Besides, I really do dislike guns. They take so very little skill," Ares says with a little pout of his lips.

"As do I, brother. It's all over so quickly," Enyo nods a little sadly.

I sigh with some annoyance, "Yes they're just so stingy with their lives nowadays. Can we move this pow wow inside or what?"

"Of course, my eager little immortal. Hopefully Max is coming back to gather more bags, but knowing him he'll forget. I'll send some others for them. Follow me!" Ares says, leading us all into his home.

We'd been told it was built like a dorm, but I didn't realize to what extent. There's a big living room in the middle of the building with a kitchen connected to it. There's a stairs leading up where I know there will be rows of apartments. I suppose it's the array of leather jackets, shoes, blankets, pillows, plates, etc. that's strewn around the room that gives it an authentic look.

"Jordy, Skip, there are some bags that the girls brought out front. Bring them to their rooms," Ares says to two werewolves walking by.

Honestly, Jordy and Skip? Just what has the world come to? At least the two of them are dressed like... well, they're supposed to be. At least it's better than Max. They're even better behaved, just saying a quick affirmative and then moving into action. What well trained dogs.

"Come everyone, have a seat! This is your home now for the next few weeks," Ares says with a smile, motioning at the large couches in the living room.

I toss a shirt out of my way and pop a squat. "So, what's up? We heard you were having a few problems."

He coughs a little. "Yes, well, it's all been blown out of proportion, really."

"Uh huh, how so?" Apate asks, being a professional liar, able to spot one.

"Let's save business for later! I want to show you around the place then take you out. We're going to have a great night!" Ares says with a grin.

"I really think we should focus on this as soon as possible. The Olympians did send us here, after all," Nemesis points out.

Ares rolls his eyes like a sullen child. "They are always nosing into my business even when I'm here in the mortal world! It's so irritating. Come on, one day won't make a difference! I haven't seen you all in so long I just want to have a little fun before we go and get all serious."

I shrug, it's a valid point. Plus I don't want to focus on his petty problems.

"Nemesis, I haven't seen my brother in centuries. Give us this day to catch up," Enyo says, as close as she comes to actually asking anyone anything.

Lyssa nods vigorously behind her and backs up her argument with a, "Yeah!"

Nemesis finally sighs. I bet she gets tired of the one that's always telling everyone no. "I suppose we can go out tonight. But tomorrow I want all of us to focus on why we're here. That means you, Ares, are going to tell us everything that's going on and not keep out a thing."

"Agreed," He says easily enough, though who knows if he really means it. "That means I can show you around the operation tonight!"

"What do you do? Sell weapons?" Lyssa asks.

"Drugs?" Dysnomia throws out there.

"Are you assassins?" Apate says excitedly.

"Have a garage?" I ask, since they seem to be into bikes.

Ares waves all of our guesses away and says, "We own the pub and restaurant across the street."

"Wait, so you don't even get to roll around town on your big, hot motorcycles and do shifty business?" Apate asks, never one to know boundaries.

"Well, we sell ambrosia," Ares says.

I have to nod at that. "At least that's illegal, by immortal standards."

It's one of those pesky laws that the all mighty Olympians decided to bind us down with, those of us that have gone mortal bound. If we decided to take lovely ambrosia with us, which is the drink of the Gods and makes us way tipsier than mortal alcohol, then we can't share it. It makes mortals go mad and possibly die. Mortal immortals can handle it in small doses, but it makes them way, way out of it.

"I've never been one for rules," Ares says modestly.

Considering he's only selling some illegal booze that just gives supernaturals a bigger buzz, I'm not too impressed. The eight- now seven- of us girls have been traveling around the world for thousands of years. We've gotten in a lot of shit and done a lot of bad things. The fact that I feel not a smidge of shame from him is somewhat admirable, but he's not doing much in the first place.

"So, to get this straight, we're going across the street to your pub, where you sometimes sell ambrosia to the mimmortals?" Apate asks.

"Mimmortals? What is that?" Ares asks.

"Mortal immortals," Dysnomia chirps up.

"Or minor immortals. Basically all those shifters, dragons, griffins, and stuff." Enyo shrugs.

"Huh, I like it," Ares says before turning back to Apate. "On Sundays, we also hold street fights between mimmortals in the pub basement. You have a problem with going to the pub?"

"Is there dancing?" she asks.

"Yes, there's a dance floor in the back," Ares says.

"Sweet, I'm in. Ambrosia, dancing, and supes. Sounds like fun to me." Apate smiles. "Even if it's only Friday and not a hopping, fighting Sunday."

"Wait, there'll just be supernaturals there, right? No humans or followers looking for a thrill? You know I have absolutely no patience for that kind of thing," Enyo says disdainfully. "When they ask me for an autograph written in blood, it's always so gauche."

Ares gives her a slightly amused look. "Of course, sister dear. No humans ever enter. We've had the place spelled to keep full humans from noticing the pub or wanting to enter. So far it's held beautifully. Though if a person has a hint of other back in their genes, then they'll be able to enter."

"Even if they're weak, I suppose it's better than nothing." Enyo nods.

"Nothing, meaning human," I join in sarcastically.

"We've taken the bags up." Jordy and Skip appear, empty-handed and lurking just in the doorway to the living room.

Ares turns to them, seeming pleased. "Yes, yes, very good. I'll have them shown up so they can freshen. Tell everyone that we'll be going to the pub in two hours. I'll expect everyone to be there. Oh, and tell them to be dressed for a celebration."

I can't help but cough a little. "Um, I remember in the good old days that could mean a number of things. To get naked, wear your best toga, or throw on the hoop skirt and corset. You're going to have to clarify to me what dressing for a celebration in this day and age means to you."

Ares gives me a practiced amused smile. "What you're wearing is fine, very sporting in fact. I like the boots. The red ribbons . . . very alluring."

"Old pervert," I snort.

"Please, the amount of time we're talking about is nothing. Any man you choose, unless you find him in Olympus, will be young compared to you." Ares laughs.

How long I've lived compared to the supernatural and human men I've been with, yeah, I can't help but agree with him. I mean, the last guy I was with was a one-night stand werewolf. I think he might have been one hundred fifty or so. If I'm with a supe then I like them at least a century old. Considering I've got thousands of years on me, it takes cradle robbing to a new level.

"Um, we'll go tell the others," Skip and Jordy say and quickly retreat.

Ares turns back to us. "Don't mind the guys. They're just a little shell-shocked to have you all here. I don't think they know what they should be expecting yet. I've been pretty lax with them, so they probably think you guys are . . . nice young women."

Enyo just laughs and laughs at that.

"If anyone is liable to whack anyone, it's probably Enyo or Lyssa." Apate shrugs. "They're badass."

"Yeah, people these days are getting kind of soft. They think violence and murder are kind of supposed to be frowned upon or something," Ares says.

"So, what? They think we're pretty little goddesses who are afraid to throw down and kick some werewolf ass?" I ask.

Ares smiles. "You have such a way with words. Yes, that's what they're thinking. Modern-day werewolves think they're just so tough. It's pathetic, but the amusement of it keeps me around. So if they start a pissing contest, you'll . . . ?"

"Lay 'em on the table and measure! We'll make them our bitches," I say with enthusiasm.

Ares's eyes widen and momentarily dip down to my waist.

"No, I'm not packing heat. The whole dick thing was just a figure of speech." I roll my eyes.

Ares grins. "I really did miss you all. Follow me upstairs."

All of us troop up the stairs, laughing and pushing around like we really are just kids messing around. When, in fact, we're some of the most powerful beings on Earth and have lived almost as long as the planet itself. It's funny how things like that work out.

"I've set you up with three rooms. Each room connects with a bathroom that you share with the room next to you. In the rooms you're staying in, there are two full-sized beds. One of you can either double up with another person or stay in the living room, it's up to you guys," Ares says, after pointing out a hall bathroom to Apate.

On either side of the long hall is bedroom after bedroom. Which means all the wolves are up here too. In the middle of the hallway, there's a small sitting area. On either end of the hallway there's a bathroom I assume is public. There also appears to be closets spread out here and there.

"So, there's not a lot of privacy, huh?" I point out.

"Well, everyone has their own room," Ares says a bit defensively.

"Yeah, but everyone's room is right here next to everyone else's. If anyone has a late-night visitor, you can probably hear everything that's going on," I point out.

Ares kind of shrugs. "I haven't had anyone complain about it. Then again, there's also two rooms downstairs that are masters. They're supposed to be used for guest rooms, but they've kind of turned into love chambers."

"I hope they remember to clean up after themselves," Apate says, the rest of us snickering.

"I'll wait downstairs while you settle in. Come on down at seven and we'll go over to the pub. We can have dinner and catch up. I can pull out karaoke, even if it's supposed to just be for Saturdays," Ares says.

"Ooh, fun!" Apate claps happily.

"This just gets more bizarre the more I learn." I sigh.

Dysnomia bumps my shoulder. "Sure to be a story, though."

CHAPTER 2

———— ∾∾ ————

I T'S HOURS LATER THAT I find myself, the minor goddess
of shamelessness, ruthlessness, and unforgiveness, sitting in
a pub. Not just any pub, but the pub that's owned by Ares
and run by his hardcore werewolf biker gang. It's not enough
that I'm leaving out ambrosia for the night, since I'm around
people I can't trust, but there's a decided chill in the room.

To be blunt, it's not every day I'm surrounded by about
twenty werewolves sporting leather and scowls. It's not every
day that supernaturals are rude to women like us. I guess the
goal right now is to try to hold down the "ruthless" part of my
powers. The ones that make me pretty impulsive and . . . well,
kind of bitchy and violent. The ugly side of my personality that
likes to hold a grudge and make you pay.

"You're a cute little girl. What did you say your name was?"
the guy sitting next to me asks.

I wish that I was sitting in the middle of my girls. No, we've been
spread out among the werewolves. I'm not too sure if it's so we can
divide and conquer, or if it's so they can. Actually, I'm not quite sure
how it happened in the first place. All I know is this kind of sucks.

"I'm Anaideia," I repeat. "Who are you?"

"Jordy," he says with a big, confident smile.

"Oh yeah, you carried in our bags." I nod.

"Yep. Man, you're just a little thing, aren't you? I was
thinking since you all are immortals, you'd be big and beautiful.
But you're just a little gal," Jordy continues to babble.

I can't help but sigh. "How old are you?"

"Fifty-four," Jordy says, looking confused.

I turn in my chair so I can face him head on. "Huh, I figured you were young, but even I didn't think you were that young. Look, dude, I'm so far out of your league it's pathetic. Take your 'little girl' shit to some pretty little mortal who might even give you the time of day. All you're doing right now is bugging the fuck literally right out of me, and when you're as old as I am, ripping off someone's balls isn't as big a deal as you'd think."

Jordy just looks at me with a frown. "No need to be such a bitch."

"Honey, I'm not the bitch. Your kind have that covered, wolf boy." I finally grin.

Jordy, pleasantly, has nothing to say and just moves on to another part of the table. That leaves two werewolves to my left and an empty spot separating me from Enyo. Hell, I'll even move closer to that freak if it means avoiding these losers. When I'm about to make my move, someone slides into the place.

I can almost feel a growl make its way out of my throat when I recognize who it is. That gives it the final push it needs to release. It's Max. The smartass who opened the door when we first arrived. Great, his idea of freshening up was to put on artfully ripped up jeans instead of shorts. This small man looks ridiculous here in the middle of a table of overbearing shifters.

"Well, well, well, look who's here. Had a lot to drink? I hope you're a happy drunk," I tell him dryly.

Max turns toward me and our eyes meet. His are unbelievably big and brown. The kind of brown that can change. Turn from liquid chocolate full of warmth and love to something dark and lifeless. Pretty much those doggy eyes that can turn you to mush with either guilt or affection.

"I haven't had anything to drink, so I'll have to keep you guessing."

"Neither have I, but I'm starting to regret my choice. Your friends can be damn annoying. Keep giving me the 'little lady' talk." I roll my eyes.

Max looks around as if confused that I'm talking to him. "Yeah, well, not everyone here is my friend. It took some convincing to be let into the group, and not everyone was too happy about it."

"Why not?" I ask in confusion.

"I'm a wild dog shifter, not a werewolf," he says as if it's obvious.

I look at him. "Huh, I just thought you were a small werewolf, but yeah, that fits. I suppose I should have smelled or sensed it, but you just stink like wolf to me. You know, living with them and everything."

"Yep, well, I'm a dog not a wolf, so they weren't too happy."

"I'm the smallest immortal in the group. I look like a sweet, adorable little girl in her twenties. Can you imagine how many times I've been jumped by people thinking I'm an easy mark, or worse, a good piece of ass?" I ask him.

Max frowns at me a little. "You've been mugged?"

I can't help but laugh softly. "I've been mugged, attacked, pretty much all you can think of. Luckily, I'm not just what I look like."

"Yeah? What are your powers? I already know that Ares's sister is a warrior goddess. Oh and her friend, the creepy one, is apparently madness," Max says.

I shrug. "I have a few gifts."

"Yeah, what are they?" he asks me directly.

"I'm shamelessness, ruthlessness, and unforgiveness. So when someone does me wrong, I not only don't forgive them but punish them ruthlessly. Oh, and I guess I can pull shamelessness into that by saying I feel no shame after punishing them. Anyhoo, if someone attacks me, they get what's coming to them," I say with a small grin.

"Man, that smile is creepy." Max shakes his head at me, but he's smiling a little too.

"Yeah, whatever. I'm getting a bit bored with this immortal representative thing. It looks like we'll just been hanging out with shifters until our term is up, no offense. On our last assignment some shifters and a vampy mortal went nuts and started killing/abducting people to sell as slaves. Not to mention we lost one of our own."

"You really do like to overshare. When you say you lost one of your own, do you mean they died? I didn't think you guys could die. Or was the other person another sort of supernatural?" Max asks.

"No, it was another immortal. My close friend, Peitho, the Goddess of Seduction and Persuasion. She was with me for centuries!" I say with a frown.

"She died?" Max asks bluntly.

"Nope, it's even worse than that. She's gone totally insane and thinks she's in love, with a dragon nonetheless. He even stole her away and lied to her about the beginning of their relationship. Actually, all of that probably made her feel comfortable. Now she's all pregnant and ready to have a half-immortal and half-dragon prince baby," I say.

He blinks at me. "That's a lot. That's really a lot. I've never even met a dragon. I guess that makes for an odd couple?"

"They're a reclusive bunch. Eh, not as odd a couple as one would think. She has this amazing gold skin. Since dragons like treasure, that works. Plus, he's a big softy. Totally adores her. He may even be wild enough to keep her," I say with a little grin, thinking of them. "I bet their kid will be a total demon."

"You're kind of random," Max points out.

I sigh. "Are you listening, or just judging me? Either way, I don't mind, just put on a good face and pretend like you care about what I'm saying."

He blinks at me, shrugs, and says, "I can do that."

"Super duper! Now distract me from the pain that is my life. Tell me about yourself," I suggest. "I'm sure it's pathetic enough to make mine seem better."

Max just looks at me then sighs and says in a practiced way, "I'm almost five hundred, and I don't have much family. My sister lives here too and is a member of the gang. We became members because we like pack life without having to be with our pack. Well, that and my sister is a chef."

"Does she have to go back to school every few decades to learn about new technology and cooking styles?" I ask.

"She's only seventy-four, so she hasn't really had to worry about that yet. But I guess she will when she reaches that age," Max says with a shrug. "I don't usually settle down. I'm more of a loner. I like to travel a lot, but Sophie needs me here, so here I am."

"When I was seventy-four I was leading men on the battlefield," Enyo says, jumping into our conversation.

Max looks at her wide-eyed.

"When I was seventy-four I was tracking down all the people who looked at me funny and torturing them. By the end of their training, they'd known better. They treated me like the goddess I am," I say with a dreamy sort of smile. "I reached my full powers at twenty-two. You can imagine how immortals and mortals alike treated one such as me. Without all of my skills, I didn't stand a chance. But look at me now? Totally kickass."

"Did you eventually kill them?" Enyo asks.

"They eventually screwed up," I explain.

Max sighs. "You guys are really messed up. I thought Ares was joking when he said to expect you to be even worse than he is. I can honestly say that he was right. You guys are totally wrong."

"Stop your whining, it was a different time." I wave him away.

"Yeah, and Ares is just as bad as us!" Enyo says in her brother's defense.

I point out, "He does seem to have mellowed out a bit."

Enyo shakes her head rapidly. "No, he's just mainstreaming. He has to pretend that he isn't all blood, killing, and mayhem. I'm sure it's still in there. You can't change what you are, and that's literally what we are."

I shrug a little; she does have a point. We are personifications. She's war, literally. Just like I'm literally shamelessness, ruthlessness, and unforgiveness personified. It's not like we can just flip a switch and change our very nature. When that's no longer what we are, we'll no longer be here. That day sure isn't today.

"You're probably right. I mean, look at him. He obviously wants to rip out someone's throat and bathe in their blood," I say.

The three of us turn to look at him in unison. Ares is at the end of the table on Enyo's side. He's in the middle of some werewolves, with Lyssa randomly thrown in. If you look closely, you can see Ares's smile is more a clench of the jaw and his hands are clasped into fists.

"Yep, a good clean kill would do wonders for him," Enyo agrees. "I hear virgin blood is the best to bathe in."

"Maybe we should suggest Apate, then?" I ask her.

She looks at me before bursting out laughing.

"What?" Max asks, confused.

"Um, he won't have a lot of luck looking for virgin blood in our group." I wink at him. "A kill is definitely what he needs. Maybe we can find a bad guy for him to take out."

"Murder can be so refreshing," Enyo agrees. "He is in dire need."

Max speaks up, "Of getting laid."

I turn to him and just look. With that somewhat wimpy, snobbish exterior, I didn't think I'd like him. Then there's the fact that he was a total bitch earlier. But now, with that one comment, I decide I may have to rethink my stance.

"You know, I think you could grow on me," I tell him.

He raises a brow. "Like a fungus?"

I giggle, then say somberly, "I would be honored to be the host to your parasite."

Enyo just looks at the two of us blankly. "You said that my brother needs to get laid? Have your gang females not been attending to his needs?"

I speak up, "I don't think this is really that sort of gang, Enyo. I think the girls pretty much get to pick who they do or don't sleep with. Or heads will roll."

Enyo looks completely confused. "What on earth does that mean? They are his underlings. They are supposed to see to all of their leader's needs, and that leader happens to be my brother. It's not a complicated issue. I will speak to them if I need to, so they understand their duties."

Max speaks up quickly, "I wouldn't, if I were you. Besides, Ares kind of wants to keep things professional. He doesn't even want gang members to see each other, let alone him."

"That makes things more complicated. What an inconvenience. I don't see how that would take away from business. It's just sating needs," Enyo says with an annoyed shake of her head.

Max and I trade a look.

"Is she for real?" he whispers to me.

"You have no idea," I whisper back.

Enyo suddenly snaps and smiles, a scary sight indeed. "I've got it! I'll just have one of you sleep with him. Since Peitho is gone and she was probably the most openly sexual, I'll have to pick someone else. I doubt Ares would like Dysnomia's brand of love. I'm not sure I want my Lyssa to be with him. Nemesis would never. Maybe Apate. Wait, how about you, Ana?"

I just look at her. "Are you really trying to pimp me out to your brother? Like, really?"

She gives me a blank stare, blinking her creepy violet eyes at me. "I don't see why not. You're not attached to anyone right now, and my brother is quite attractive. I'm sure you would both find the situation mutually beneficial. I'll go tell him you'll meet him in his room."

"Hold up!" I say, blocking her with my arm. "I am not sleeping with Ares just because Max said a smartass comment about him needing to get laid. There's no way it's going to happen!"

"I don't know why you're protesting like this. You've never been that picky in the past," Enyo says. "Unless you and Apate are together, like I've long speculated."

I ignore the blatant insult. "That's it, Apate and I are together. There's lots of steamy, lesbian sex going on. So you can see why I can't go fuck your brother so he can better control his animalistic urges."

"Was that so hard? I swear, you sluts are so damn dramatic. I guess I can take Apate off the list too. Though why you didn't tell us, I just don't know. Shameless my ass. Hmm, well, there are many women here . . ." Enyo says, walking off without saying another word to us.

"Did that bitch just question my shamelessness?" I turn to Max. He just raises a brow. "I do whatever I want and answer to no one! Never do I feel bad about myself for anything I desire or do. I embrace it."

"Yeah, sure."

"I could tell you stories that would make your little doggy tongue loll," I say with a sneer.

Max turns to me with a grin. "You were so lying to her."

"What clued you into that? The fact that Apate was behind her laughing?" I ask, watching as she comes closer to us.

"I hope you're happy," Apate says between giggles. "Now she's going to tell everyone and they'll be insufferable."

"Wait, it is a joke, right?" Max asks, looking between us.

I say, "Yeah, but they'll be insufferable either way. You don't want to know the things we've done to significant others that the others have had in the past. It ain't pretty, my friend."

"So true. Plus, there's a rule that we aren't allowed to date each other. Not a problem for Ana, since she's strictly into men. Actually, not really a problem for any of us. We get along great and we're total soul mates, but lusty love so isn't going to blossom there." Apate laughs.

I nod. "Of course, if I were into women, I'm sure I'd find your form simply delectable. As it is, can't change my preferences."

"Ditto, baby." Apate grins. "It really is inconvenient we're all mostly into guys. So much more competition!"

"Right, you're both mad hot, but don't wanna bang one another. Back to the punishment thing?" Max asks.

"There was some question of what was going on between Lyssa and Enyo a few centuries back, but turns out nothing was happening. Kind of a letdown. We were all ready to punish them for breaking the rules." I sigh.

Apate nods. "Turns out they just have a totally weird, close, co-dependent friendship. Like those don't pop up just about everywhere."

"Now we'll be attacked, questioned, and punished. I mean, we'll be punished whether they find out it's a lie or not. Enyo will kick my ass if she learns I lied to evade sleeping with her brother." I grin.

"Man, you get pimped out more than actual prostitutes." Apate laughs. "What about you, Max? Any special lady or nice gentleman in your life?"

"I'm into women, if that's your subtle way of asking. Nope, I don't have a girlfriend or anything. Kind of hard when you live with this group," Max says.

"I feel you, Max. Relationships are so overrated," I agree.

"Especially relationships with big fat dragons." Apate sighs.

Max smiles. "You two really are the jealous types."

"Uh-huh, whatever. We just worked out. Now that we don't have Peitho, everything is sure to go to hell. She was like the lube that held us together," I say drearily.

"The lube?" Max asks.

"Well, the girl sure wasn't glue." I shrug.

Apate nods. "She did always have a steady supply of condoms to give out. One year, she even got us all our own special monogrammed ones."

"I can tell you guys have led odd lives." Max just shakes his head.

"Ooh, I just caught something delectable in my line of vision! Come on, Ana, I have some pretty boy friends that you just *have* to meet. They're conveniently located right next to the cake," Apate says, a girl on the hunt.

I turn around as I'm tugged away. "Talk to you later, Max."

"Sure thing," he says, but doesn't sound overly sure of that.

"You have to see this guy. He's, like, so hot." Apate grins at me, pulling me deeper into the crowd.

I'm highly doubtful of that, since we have pretty different tastes.

"Are they part of the gang?" I ask her.

"Yep." She grins. "Which means we'll have easy access to them. Never a bad thing. We could set up dates with them in fuck rooms."

"What are you saying? Of course that can be a bad thing. Like, if you end up not liking them and they're always right there. Knowing exactly where you are too!" I point out, it actually being one of Peitho's hookup rules.

Apate waves away my concerns. "When you see these two, you'll see my point. Ah, here they are. Go on, take a look before the time comes to strike."

"I swear you go after men like a bloodthirsty piranha that's caught a scent," I say to her before turning to gawk.

For once, she wasn't lying. As the Goddess of Deceit, that's saying a lot. Both men are tall and built like typical shifters. One has black hair that's been cut all ragged with a razor. The other has straight white-blond hair that falls around his chin. The one with the dark hair has black eyes, while the other has very pale blue eyes that are offset by his tan skin. It's like the two are opposites of each other. Very hot opposites.

"They must have nymph or merman blood hidden in their gene pools," I say.

"Who cares? The one with dark hair is Turner, and the one with pale hair is Conrad. I'll introduce you." Apate tugs me the last few steps until we're right in front of them.

"Hey, guys! You remember me, right? I'm Apate, and this is my lovely goddess friend Ana." She gives them a big smile.

"Hey," the one with dark hair says.

"You're, like, a foot shorter than me," the other one, Conrad, says.

"You know, I'm not blind. I can see that I'm short and you're tall," I say with some annoyance.

He blinks at me in surprise. "You're a goddess, right?"

"Yeah, what of it?" I ask.

"I don't know. You're not really what I expected." He shrugs.

I guess I shouldn't really be too annoyed. Most people picture goddesses all tall, thin, and willowy. That's definitely not me. I have long red hair that's the color of blood. I know because when it's soaked in blood, it doesn't look any different. I have gold eyes that rival the shine of Peitho's skin, but are a shade lighter so they look more yellow. Then there's the fact that I'm totally short. Luckily I'm curvy with a nice ass and decent-sized chest. It stops me from looking about twelve.

"This entire situation isn't really what I expected, so I think we're both just going to have to deal with it," I say.

It's a good thing it's not like it was in the past. I could have just ripped out his throat for insulting me and lapped up his blood. Alas, I can't allow myself to get upset over little insults these days. I mean, then I'd be killing random people left and right, with the manners of today's people.

"Come on, guys, I know she's short, but she's still mega hot," Apate says cheerfully, then, with a scheming whisper, "Not bad in bed either!"

Conrad turns to her with a slightly disdainful look. "Yeah, you're more of what I expected. All cheerful and blonde."

I can feel my little fangs lengthen to a more noticeable size, starting to bite into my bottom lip.

Apate finally turns to me with a shrug, completely ignoring both men. "Sorry, they were hotter when they weren't talking."

"Excuse me?" Turner asks in surprise.

"I think you both heard me just fine. The truth is, nice guys end up looking cuter over time because they're nice. While douchebags end up looking fucked up the more annoying they act. You're getting near that dangerous douchebag territory," Apate says, giving them a falsely friendly smile.

Conrad whistles slightly. "I kind of like you more now."

"Adorable. What do you say, Turner, wanna dance with a goddess?" Apate asks, making eye contact and walking sensuously closer to him.

I watch with some interest as she starts attempting to trap the poor boy. He looks surprised at her proposal. When she puts her waist firmly against his, slides her hands up around his shoulders, and begins whispering in his ear, he doesn't look any less shocked.

"Hey, skank, what are you doing with my boyfriend?" A large female werewolf comes up to the edge of our group. She looks pissed. With a big, strong body and smooth predatory moves, I know what this will lead to.

"Skank? Oh, honey, I've been called *way* worse by *far* better," Apate says, turning slightly from Turner, while still holding him firmly.

The werewolf's eyes start bleeding into a predatory yellow color. "I just bet you have. Look, you're new here and you're friends of Ares. I'll give you to the count of three to get off my boyfriend. Either that, or I'm going to enjoy kicking your ass."

"Uh-oh," I say, but no one turns to me.

Apate gives her most innocent smile, which usually means she's going to do something really bad. She turns back to Turner and licks her lips. It's not just that she does that, though, oh no, she presses herself more firmly against him. That leisurely swipe of tongue across upper lip tells of things in the night that he'll definitely want to be a part of.

"You want him? Come and get him," Apate taunts, turning to look at the werewolf as she gives Turner a quick kiss.

"That's it, you asked for it," the werewolf says, stalking forward.

I do the only thing I can do. I move to the table just next to them, take a seat, and get ready for the show. I just hope there's no hair pulling. That sort of thing is so pathetic. Pull a punch or cry on home and don't come back. I hear the distinct crack of bone and see Apate with a bloody nose, grinning manically. Oh yeah, that werewolf has a good right hook on her!

"What did your friend do to Marsha?" Max says, coming out of nowhere to drop into the seat next to me.

"Is that her name? We were never formally introduced. Apate decided to hit on Marsha's boyfriend, Turner. She's never really been one to back down," I say.

We both turn in time to see Apate jump up on Marsha's back, screaming, "Die, giant mutant beast! Die! Good Goddess your feet are *huge!*"

Max winces. "Now them are fighting words."

Some other werewolves catch sight of the action, and soon word spreads. One of them yells out, "Bitch fight!" and we're suddenly surrounded by overly interested mutts.

"Aren't you going to stop them?" Max asks, watching as the two roll around on the floor.

"I wish I could, Max baby—rolling around on the floor during a fight is so undignified. Still, she taunted the wolf and wanted a fight, so no point in breaking it up. She's on her own now. Besides, she's checking her punches so she won't accidentally kill the poor girl," I say, having actually been watching closely to make sure of that.

He snorts. "Right, they're werewolves. They beat most supes strength-wise."

I look at him blandly. Then, and I'm not entirely sure why, but I'm a wonderfully impulsive gal, I punch the table we're sitting at. I easily punch a hole through the wood when I put a little elbow behind the impact. When I pull my hand back my knuckles are a little bloody, but luckily no slivers. It doesn't hurt too much either. Things like this never seem that bad when you can compare them to much worse incidents.

"Oh, man! What the hell are you doing?" Max exclaims, jumping up to grab my hand, glancing at the table.

"I dunno, just showing you what we can do when we're not really trying." I shrug.

"Yeah, and breaking your hand in the process," he snarls.

"Relax, you worrywart. I just broke the skin covering my knuckles. No actual bone damage." I sigh at him. "It'll heal super-fast, so no point in bandaging it, either."

"Because all gods forbid we disinfect and rinse it off, huh?" he asks me.

I turn my head thoughtfully. "Well, no gods or goddesses have ever forbidden me from cleaning a wound, but they also don't condone doing pointless things. Since it would be pointless, I think I win this bout."

Max looks into my eyes. "I'm really starting to think anyone over five hundred is mad."

"Dude, you're about five hundred. Join the dark side! We fuck better!" I grin up at him.

He gives me a reluctant smile before looking down at my hand. I guess it can be kind of interesting to watch an immortal heal. Mostly because you can actually see the process before your eyes, if you're watching carefully. Right now, I can see my skin fuse back together like the good little skin it is.

"Wow, I think you may heal even faster than a shifter," he comments.

I look over his shoulder. "Ooh, you're in luck, Max. Nemesis and Ares are coming on over. Nemesis is like the head of all of us immortal roomies. She's sure to break this little party up."

"That's a good thing?" he asks with a raised brow.

I grin. "You're learning! In this instance, it's a very good thing. A fight with one of us should only last so long. Or we both know how it'll end."

"Apate, back away from the girl *now*." Nemesis stands before the two brawling ladies in all of her stately glory.

"Marsha! How dare you embarrass me like this in front of my sister and all of her closest friends? Get up, now!" Ares fires at the other member of the fun.

Marsha starts first, "Look, it wasn't my fault. I told her that she had to the count of three to get off Turner or I'd kick her ass. I didn't want to fight her, but I can't just stand by and let her slobber all over my territory either."

"I knew dating within the gang would start all sorts of problems. What does it matter if Apate was talking, kissing, or whatever else with Turner? Why would that turn into you fighting her? Threatening a goddess isn't the way to get her to back down, Marsha. Besides, did Turner even tell Apate to back off?" Ares asks.

That's when the shit really hits the fan. Ares, Marsha, Nemesis, Apate, and the interested audience all turn to look at Turner. During the fight, he'd just been standing there calmly watching the two of them. Actually, that's pretty much what he was doing before the fight too.

"Well, boy? Did you tell Apate she could have you when you were previously engaged?" Nemesis asks him with narrowed eyes.

He blinks, probably intimidated by our fearless leader. I can't really blame him. Part of the reason why she works as our leader is that all of us girls are a little afraid of her too. She's very tall and pretty curvy with long, straight black hair, black eyes, and, oh yeah . . . black wings. They're not out right now, as she can furrow them under a layer of skin, but she still looks pretty damn frightening without them. Plus, her aura of authority is a thing to behold.

"Answer her," Ares orders him impatiently.

"I didn't have time to tell either of them anything! One minute Apate was hitting on me, and the next her and Marsha were fighting," Turner says.

"Do you have anything to say?" Nemesis asks Apate.

Considering her nose is moving on its own back into the correct position, it's amazing that she sounds so calm as she says, "Nah, not really. Though I'm totally willing to be the bigger person, put this misunderstanding aside, and accept her apology."

That's when everyone turns to Marsha.

"Don't you have something to say?" Ares prods her.

"You can't be serious. This *woman* hits on my boyfriend, doesn't back down, starts a fight with me, and I'm the one who has to apologize?" Marsha squawks.

"She's new here and was confused. I really don't think breaking her nose was the kind of welcome I told you to give my visiting friends. Apologize, or you won't like what happens next, I can promise you that," Ares growls at her, losing patience.

Marsha turns to Apate grudgingly. "I'm sorry for starting a fight with you."

"Apology accepted, and may I say that you have an excellent arm on you! I'm sure Ares must have taught you some hand-to-hand combat. Now, I'm certain I smelled cake earlier. If you could direct me to it? I hope it's chocolate!" Apate says with a grin, ignoring the blood starting to dry on her face.

The werewolves huddled in a little circle around them just blink in surprise.

"You guys really are off center." Max grins.

I hear a wolf mutter, "She can brawl *and* eat? Sounds like the perfect woman!"

"Told you so, but we're always great fun." I smile back at Max.

Then something odd happens. He had stayed next to me during the fight, standing by my tall barstool after looking at my hand. Not only that, but he'd held onto my hand. Somehow, during the excitement, our hands kind of . . . laced, the fingers now all smashed comfortably together.

I clear my throat. "Wasn't expecting that. Well, see you later!"

He looks just as confused about the hand thing as me, but I don't stick around to talk it out. I make a quick getaway and spend the rest of the night on some quality time with a cake and my friends, trying not to get into any trouble.

CHAPTER 3

W HAT'S THE BIG DEAL? WHO'S after you, and what
do we have to do to stop them? I mean, I'm ready to
take some people down if they're the ones causing
me to be up at eight o'clock listening to you," Aergia snaps at the
room full of werewolves.

It's kind of true. When we discussed hearing all about Ares's
troubles with his late-life crisis, none of us thought he'd go stomping
up to our rooms at seven a.m. and tell us to be downstairs for a gang
meeting at eight. I myself was hoping for a nice leisurely lunch
debrief. So much for that. Now around thirty of us, assorted shifters
and immortals, are now sitting around the dining room table.

"I would love to tell you all about the slight situation we
have going on here. It's not quite as big a deal as the Olympians
would have you believe. It's just a bit of a misunderstanding,"
Ares says from the head of the table.

All of us girls turn to one another. In all of the years
that we've traveled together as roommates, we often have
"misunderstandings," and we often downplay how bad they are.
That's why when we turn back to him, none of us are fooled by
that comforting lie.

"Details," Nemesis says.

For the first time in quite a while, Ares looks uncomfortable.
"Some certain organizations aren't pleased that I'm in the area,
or that I've taken a leadership role in the local crime. They're
causing some trouble for me."

"What other organizations?" Enyo asks.

Darrel, Ares's second-in-command, speaks up first. "Pretty much all of them. Not just organizations either, but organized crime groups. They're completely shutting us out of the business. They also have pretty good leeway with local institutions and are making trouble for us in that respect as well."

"What do you mean other people in organized crime?" Nemesis asks.

"Well, the ones that are supernaturals at least. They think it's an unfair advantage that we have Ares as our gang leader since he's a powerful god and has major magic. That's why they're cutting us out of everything," Darrel explains.

"Just what kind of crime goes on around here that interferes with yours? I mean, you just sell a little ambrosia on the side, right? Plus host some fights on down-time Sundays?" I ask.

"Yes, that's what we do. The fact that we own a business upsets them too, though. They've had their patrons agree not to support our pub. Some of the different groups are a burglar ring led by two fox shifters, another biker gang, a drug ring, money launderers, counterfeiters, and there's a nasty coven of witches," Darrel says.

"Wow, that's a lot for one area, isn't it?" Apate asks.

Darrel just shrugs. "It's a big city, by the ocean, with good weather. It's easy to fit into a vacation spot like this. The point is, they're organized and have all agreed to shut us out of the community."

"Even the groups of individual crime are organized into one larger group? That's kind of clever, to keep everyone in check and everything," I point out.

Ares reluctantly agrees, "Yes, they have a council and everything. They even vote on things. They have representatives come from each of the crime rings to represent everyone. They've voted that I shouldn't be allowed in the crime community with my extra advantages as the God of War."

"I swear, it's all that bitch Felicity's fault!" one of the female wolves spits out.

"Who are you, and who's Felicity?" I ask her.

She pauses in her anger to give me a big smile, saying, "I'm Regina, but you can call me Reggie. Felicity is the leader of the other biker gang. She just doesn't want the competition—plus, we have way better hardware."

"You have better bikes than her and her people, and now she's trying to get you out of the community?" I ask her.

She nods her head, making her dark bob shake. "Pretty much. It doesn't help that she's got a lot of influence with everyone and has been here since, like, forever. She's totally out to get us."

"It's true, that woman is completely unreasonable," Ares says.

"Why don't you just turn on them? Fight it out? I've never been a fan of this new-age 'voting' concept," Enyo says with acute distaste.

Ares smiles at her fondly. "That's what I was thinking too, my dear, but I guess the Olympians caught word of my plan. They want me to resolve this little matter without spilling blood, it seems. That's why they sent you. Now, you know that I adore you completely, but I'm not sure what you're going to be able to do that I haven't already tried."

I can't help but agree with him. This problem doesn't come up all that often. Usually people welcome the help of immortals. This new generation is too bold by half. I wonder if they could be bribed into allowing Ares to be a member of their council. Then he could still play the part of gang leader. I mean, all it takes is one look around here and knowing what their business is to know that he isn't a real big threat.

"I swear, the Olympians are starting to grow so soft! They won't let us take care of anything the correct way anymore," Enyo growls with annoyance.

"I can't help but agree, Sister. Now you all can think of a little plan, and we'll see if that works. If it doesn't, I'll take care of them the old-fashioned way until we have no more competition or boundaries in our way," Ares says with a pleased clap of his hands.

"Hold up there, big guy," I tell him. "When you say they won't let you do business, do you just mean that they refuse to eat at your pub and have told their clients not to either?"

Ares sighs dramatically. "Yes, and I'm really quite hurt about the entire thing, since I spent so much time and energy making the pub a wonderful place to go."

"Sure, but have there been any other threats?" I ask.

His eyes seem to light up. "Threats? Who would dare to threaten *me*? I'm the God of War! No, none of them have threatened me, but I'm sure they have planned something to convince me to stay away from this sort of activity."

"Like what?" I ask.

Darrel steps in, "They can make things difficult for us in many ways. Crime around here is really the basis of the community. We don't want to ruin all of our supernatural connections."

"I see," I say, though, in truth, I really don't.

"Great, what's the plan?" Ares asks us eagerly.

We all turn to him in surprise. Nemesis is the one to say, "We don't have a plan yet, since we just learned about the situation. We'll have to talk about it amongst ourselves and come up with the best course of action."

He nods in a very understanding manner before dropping the bomb. "I hope you talk it out quickly. There's a meeting tomorrow afternoon that I'm supposed to go to. I'm invited as a guest to discuss my concerns."

"There's a meeting with the other crime leaders tomorrow afternoon?" Nemesis asks in a voice that's too calm.

Ares says, "Yep, and I'm sure you all want to come so you can clear this itty bitty matter up. That way I can get back to cooking and selling some light ambrosia to the college kids. They get such a kick out of the thrill of it all. Anyway, I'd really prefer not to make any of the other Olympians too mad at me at the moment, since they fronted the capital for everything. That means it would probably be best if I don't end up having to kill anyone."

"No pressure, though," Apate mutters.

"I really wish you had told us about this meeting and why we were coming here in the first place, so we'd have had more time to prepare," Nemesis tells him.

His eyes narrow at the slight scolding. "It's not my fault you didn't come sooner. I told the Olympians that I'd have to take care of matters myself if you weren't here by a certain time. Luckily, you just made it."

"Yes, lucky indeed. If you'll excuse us for some time, then? We should probably go upstairs and start talking about options for what to do," Nemesis says.

Ares gives a bright smile. "Of course, of course. Don't work too hard! If you need anything at all, just ask one of my wolves or find me. Everyone dismissed!"

Nemesis gives each of us a quick shake of the head, pretty much telling us to save our opinions for when we're in private. She leads us all upstairs, and we go to the room that she's currently staying in with Aergia. Nemesis sits regally on top of the bed, while the rest of us flop wherever there's space. I end up in the floor with a pillow and Apate at my side.

"I'm sure what we heard today is a surprise to everyone," Nemesis begins.

Enyo interrupts with, "I'm not surprised at all. It is understandable that all the weaker supernaturals are afraid of my brother and his considerable powers. If it were me in his situation, I would have killed them all by now. Or beaten them into submission."

Nemesis just gives her a blank look before saying, "You know, your opinion on this matter probably won't be that helpful. It might be more time efficient if you're just silent."

Enyo gives her a scowl. "What do I care anyway? You'll all fail, and I'll be able to lead the wolves into battle anyway."

Lyssa sighs happily. "I can always give the wolves mad rage. Wouldn't that be fun!"

"No, Lyssa, I forbid you from doing that! What I was going to say before I was interrupted, is that this is a very delicate situation. Knowing Ares, he's probably personally pissed off two-thirds of the people who are now fighting against him. So trying to be diplomatic isn't a bad thing at this point," Nemesis says.

"Yeah, so keeping Lyssa and Enyo away from the other organized crime members is goal number one, right?" Apate asks. Nemesis gives Lyssa and Enyo a dark look. "Since they've shown that they can't be trusted to make sound decisions, yes, it is best that they stay out of the matter as much as possible. I was thinking of drawing up a contract stating Ares will not use any of his greater powers against the other gangs."

"A few problems with that. First, how the hell would we get Ares to sign the damn thing? Second, they probably wouldn't accept the contract as a promise that he wouldn't do anything super powerful. I mean, let's be real. He probably wouldn't follow it anyway," I point out.

Nemesis gives a nod at that. "You may be right, since he's already let his nature be known in the community. What else could we do? You know how important this mission is to our end goal."

"It's true, if we fail now we'll probably be sent back to Olympus. No more big power and world domination," Dysnomia agrees.

I huff. "Guys, that's not fair. I finally won Australia in that last game of poker."

Nemesis gives us all a quelling look. "We need to stay focused on what's important. Cleaning up Ares's mess may seem like a ridiculous mission, but if we can't even do that, how do you think we'll take over Earth? How will we become the ruling force of this planet if we can't handle one souped-up immortal?"

Apate gives a little shiver. "Can you feel the juice Peitho gives off, now? She's so much stronger. I want to feel that kind of power coursing through my veins."

Peitho gives off a discernible heat with her newfound strength. Her husband, Hunter, helped her ground her powers through true love and acceptance, the ultimate source of worship. Although it's forbidden by the Olympians for lesser gods to be worshiped, it was a loophole that worked in our favor. We've been able to hide our plan's progress by explaining her added power away as the combination of her magic and her growing baby's.

Nemesis smiles at Apate. "You will have that kind of power soon enough, we just need to stay on task. Soon we will all have power beyond our imagination, and we'll no longer be the underlings of Olympus. We'll be the goddesses of Earth."

"As long as Ares doesn't ruin this for us all," Apate huffs.

"I was thinking we could bribe the other biker gang? They seem to hold a lot of clout with the others. If he has them behind him, then I think he's good," I suggest. "How much money did you bring with you, Nemi?"

"How much do you think they'd want?" she asks me.

I shrug. "Honestly, if I were them, I'd demand a lot. I mean, a *lot*. Since they're pretty much agreeing to babysit the poor old guy."

Enyo growls out, "I'm not sure if I like this conversation."

"You don't have to like it. This is something we can do that might actually work," I say.

Nemesis nods. "You've been no help anyway, Enyo. Why don't you and Lyssa go play swords with Ares? We can take it from here."

"You're kicking me out?" Enyo asks.

"But we can do swordplay with Ares!" Lyssa says excitedly.

Enyo appears to weigh the pros and cons. "It's true that Ares and I haven't fought together in such a long time. Fine, fine, we'll go. Don't get any crazy ideas, though."

"Yeah, because we're the ones most likely to do that," Apate says sarcastically.

Enyo and Lyssa get up and go to the door. I'm about to breathe out a sigh of relief that we won't have to worry about them, but there's a commotion outside of the door as soon as it closes behind them. Enyo and Lyssa come back into the room. Enyo has a pretty little present for us, in the form of Max, held by one hand in front of her, legs dangling in the air as she effortlessly supports his weight.

"I found this lurking outside the room!" Enyo says, smiling like she'll earn a prize. "Shall I beat him?"

Max gives her a disgruntled look. "The penalty for eavesdropping is not a beating."

"I'll be the judge of that," Nemesis, says, though we all know she's just playing bad cop. Well, to Enyo's bad cop. "How much did you hear?"

"I know you plan on bribing the other biker gang," Max says easily.

Everyone sighs and/or curses.

"Did you hear anything else?" Enyo's eyes narrow.

Max shrugs nonchalantly. "Don't worry, I totally tuned out the world domination part."

"Fuck, now we have to kill him." Enyo's smile contradicts the tone of her words, one hand rising to wrap around his throat.

"No, Enyo! It doesn't matter what he heard; he's nobody. He doesn't understand what we were talking about and, more importantly, no one would bother listening to him anyway." Nemesis waves away the concern.

"I don't know about that. I could probably get Ares riled up. Or all of the supernaturals around here who already hate immortals," Max points out.

Nemesis tilts her head at him like a great bird of prey. "What do you want?"

"Let me help with the plan to bribe the others. They already hate immortals—if I'm the one who offers the bribe they might actually consider it," Max explains, suddenly serious.

"Why would you want to help us?" Apate scoffs.

"My sister likes it here. I don't want to have to pack us up and move just because some people are pissy that we're working for an immortal," Max says. "It might not seem like a big deal to you, but finding a place where we sort of fit in means something to us. Just let me contact them about the bribe. It shouldn't be that big a deal."

We all let that sink in. Of all the excuses, this is the one most liable to hit home. We've always been considered misfits back in Olympus. We're the throwaway gifts. Not powerful enough for them to care about and not interesting enough to hold any weight.

"I say we kill him and be done with this." Enyo once again raises her hand.

Nemesis snaps, "Enyo, Lyssa, leave now and close the door. You two will also be keeping everything we said to yourselves because this was a house meeting. You understand that? No telling Ares anything at all!"

Enyo sighs. "Fine. Come on, Lyssa, it's starting to feel like a dagger kind of day."

When Max is finally dropped to the ground and the door is firmly closed behind Lyssa and Enyo, Nemesis says, "The big deal is that if Ares found out we were going to bribe anyone, he'd flip his switch! Right now, he thinks he's humoring all of us and is playing along. If we insult him by offering a bribe, then he won't be so easygoing."

"Wait, so you're not going to offer one? Because I really think that might be the ticket," Max says.

I jump in with, "What Nemi is trying to say is that we're going to be bribing them, we just don't want Ares to know. Get it? Because if he knew, he'd totally trip balls."

He grins a dopey grin that only wild dogs can manage. "Yeah, I get it."

"Will that be a problem for you?" Nemesis asks.

"If you're asking if I have some misguided loyalty complex where I'll go blab to Ares, then no. I know this is all for his own good. Besides, since he's new at all of this, he doesn't really know that we're supposed to be completely loyal and stuff like that. He had us swear fealty to him. That was about it." Max shrugs.

Apate grins. "He's just so used to warriors. Doesn't he know nothing's real unless you have a contract? At least now we have an insider to help out with our plotting! Well, Max, what do you know?"

"About what?" he asks.

"How did Ares piss everyone off?" I ask.

He grins a little. "From what I'm hearing, this sounds like it may be pretty typical of him. Ares rolled into town and thought everyone would bow down to him because he's a major god. He thought he'd take over the organized crime council. Felicity is the head of it, so that's why she's particularly upset with him.

Luckily, he at least didn't play the girl card and tell her to go home and bake."

"Yeah, since he's been around us so long and used to go into battle with Enyo, he has no illusions that we're the weaker sex or some shit like that." I grin.

Max meets my eyes with a somewhat odd expression. That's about when I remember that the last time I saw him, I was running away. Literally running. Mainly because, out of nowhere, we were holding hands, not just holding but with laced fingers and everything! Plus, we did that like it was the most normal thing in the world. I don't think so. Not happening.

"That's why Felicity is mad. What about everyone else?" Nemesis asks.

"They didn't really like him ordering them around and assuming that they'd just give up control to him. Mainly it's Felicity who got them riled up about it. They probably would have gone along with him if she hadn't pointed out how he bossed them around and everything," Max says.

Nemesis considers this. "We need to contact Felicity about the bribe."

"I can go down to their bar," Max suggests.

"You'll need one of us. We can help influence their acceptance of the bribe," Nemesis states. "It won't be overt magic, but even our lesser auras of power can be mesmerizing for mortals and immortals."

"Okay, who's going with?" Max asks.

Apate raises her hand. "Me, me! Who couldn't trust a face like mine?!"

"You're not going to offer them the bribe," Nemesis says with a little laugh. "After you were in that stupid fight last night, do you really think I'd trust you with something so serious? No, you'll be here, and I'll be keeping my eyes on you."

"Are you going?" I ask Nemesis.

She smiles. "I'm told I can be a bit too intimidating. The Goddess of Retribution sticking up for the God of War probably won't endear us to them."

"That's true. If I had a say, I'd suggest Apate since she looks so harmless, but you're right. After the fight last night, she's kind of a wild card. Maybe the other little blonde one?" Max suggests.

I look around for the woman in question, but Aergia has already slunk off, most likely asleep in some closet. Honestly, the woman would be a great spy if she could stay awake long enough. She's quite good at coming and going without anyone noticing.

"She's out of the question," Nemesis says. "How about you, Ana? You're pretty small? Maybe Dysnomia too?"

Dysnomia speaks up, "I'm not sure if that's the greatest idea, Chief. I'm all lawlessness. Right now, all I want is to go there and make them chaotic enough to start a fight with the God of War. My skin itches at the idea. It would be so fun! Can you imagine?"

Nemesis listens to her manically excited voice and says, "Yeah, you can stay here too. I'll be keeping a close eye on you as well. I hope you're happy. I'm feeling more and more like a nursemaid the longer we're together."

Dysnomia shrugs and pops a sucker in her mouth. "At least I warned you that it wouldn't be a good idea."

"True, she wouldn't have in the past," I say in her defense. "Good job, Dys!"

"Everyone besides Ana and Max can leave," Nemesis says with a sigh.

That means that Apate and Dysnomia leave the room together, practically skipping. I'm left wondering what kind of delicious trouble they're going to get into that calls for that level of enthusiasm. None of us leave a super-secret plot happily unless something else is going on.

"Right, I have a duffel bag full of money. It should be enough," Nemesis says, walking to the closet to take the bag out as simply as if it were full of socks.

"How much?" Max asks.

Nemesis gives him a look. "Enough."

"What if they want more?" I ask.

Nemesis says, "Use your judgment and negotiation skills. I have more money here if it's needed. I'd prefer not to have to stop at a bank for our other expenses, though."

"What do you want me to get them to agree to?" I ask.

"I want them to agree to stop fighting to have Ares shunned by the supernatural community. I also want them to agree to speak on his behalf before the supe crime council. They have to agree to support him as the leader of this gang," Nemesis says clearly.

I shrug. "Simple enough. I'll give them an offer that they can't refuse."

"Good girl." Nemesis smiles at me. "Oh, and one more thing? You may want to just say you're the Daimon of Shamelessness."

Max nods. "Yeah, ruthless sounds kind of harsh."

I grin at them both. "All right, agent super sleuth is going to make contact. I'll be back to check in with base soon."

Nemi rolls her eyes. "I'll be waiting."

We're walking away when I say to Max, "You might want to change your clothes."

I look down at his outfit and find that he's wearing a pink and lime green striped polo and those annoying cargo shorts. I'm wearing leather pants and a shirt. How on earth could he be about to go to a real biker gang dressed like a little boy?

"What do you mean?" he asks.

"Dude, you look like a college kid. No one can take you seriously dressed like that. I mean, are those loafers?" I ask, looking down at his feet.

"They're very comfortable!" he says defensively.

"Whatever. Let's just go," I say, unable to avoid the fact that he looks pretty adorable with his angry face, looking down at his shoes.

Max mutters, "It wouldn't kill you to cover up once in a while. You're missing, like, half a shirt."

"It's called a crop top, and it's adorable. I'm sure they'll think I'm lovely. Now take me to your bike so I can go to a bar and give a wolf a bunch of my hard-earned money," I tell him.

"First, I don't have a bike; we'll be going there in my car. Second, did you actually earn the money from a real job?"

"It's probably the porn money." I shrug nonchalantly.

His eyes widen. "You guys . . . have been in . . ."

"No, no, my friend Peitho has a line of adult stores. We've invested in her company and everything. We make a good bit of money from that, but we also have our own ventures," I tell him. "Not like an actual every day, full-time job."

"I'm shocked," he says sarcastically.

I decide that I'm no longer going to talk to this annoying little dog. Ten minutes later, when we're driving down the road in his tiny hybrid, I start to get bored. It's not that Florida isn't a nice little state, but this area they're in is just so suburban. I swear, I'm surrounded by minivans.

"This is my hell."

CHAPTER 4

~∽~

MAX

W HY DID YOU GUYS CHOOSE this location?" Ana asks me.

I turn to her in some surprise. I'd been counting, and she lasted an entire eleven minutes and thirty-four seconds without talking to me. I'm pretty sure it's a record for this girl. It doesn't help that she looks pretty cute sitting next to me. All that truly red hair floating around her and framing things I'm already trying not to look at. Not easy with that tiny white shirt and her rather large . . . assets.

"It was a good place for the pub, plus Ares could buy the building across from it for housing," I tell her.

"Huh," she says, and I wait for more before realizing that's it.

"How do you like being here so far?" I ask in a vain attempt at small talk. "From what Ares said, you all travel a lot. This must be an odd change of pace for you guys. Not very exotic or exciting."

She turns in her seat to face me. "Yeah, so far it kind of sucks. I didn't really want to come in the first place. Ares has gone all rogue trying to take over you shifters. Which would be funny in most circumstances, but now we're here trying to help him? Not an easy job. Plus, I was ready for a vacation after the hell that was our last assignment."

"You're not having any fun at all?" I ask.

"Why do you care? I miss my friend and don't really like that everything changed at the drop of a hat. Now she's having a baby and will probably never be with us again. Our entire group is totally screwed up," she huffs at me.

"Just making conversation." I hold a hand up to her in surrender. "I'm sure it was a big shock when she went off and got married."

Ana frowns at me, her big yellow eyes narrowed. "Married? You mean now that they're together and having a kid they'll want to get married too? That bitch is going to make me a bridesmaid. I can feel it. She'll pick the ugliest thing in creation for me to wear!"

I try to subdue her. "Now, now, we don't know if she'll get married to him or not. Since they're already in a good, stable relationship, they might not feel the need!"

She laughs humorously. "No need to parade around like an idiot? She's the Goddess of Seduction and Persuasion! It's what she does!"

I try not to give in to the panic. "Oh, look, we're here! This is the bar. Um, do you want to take a minute to collect yourself?"

Her eyes narrow further. "Don't start with me, Dog. You're only a few inches taller than me. I can take you down!"

I gulp, knowing that's probably true. "But you wouldn't want to, would you? We're friends, aren't we? Yes, we are. Now we're going to go in there and trick some stupid werewolves into agreeing to set Ares loose on their town."

Ana turns her head at me in contemplation. "You know, I'm really starting to like you."

That sets in the panic even more. Now, I'm kind of attracted to the woman. Okay, who am I kidding? I'm totally hot for her. Not so surprising since she's a goddess, and all of them are the definition of fine. Well, most of them. Plus, Ana isn't about a foot taller than me, which is never fun. She's pretty funny too. I can tell that we're both observers. That doesn't mean it's a good idea to start anything. That's pretty much the worst idea ever.

"I mean, I was totally ready to be pissed, and you just turned it around to the bright side! We get to mess around with the dumb mutts!" Ana grins at me as she retrieves the duffel bag from the backseat.

Oh, she meant that. "Um, yeah. That's what I'm good at."

Ana walks over to my side of the car as I get out. She's suddenly right there at my side, taking my arm and saying, "Escort a lady, kind sir."

I tell myself that she's saying that because I'm the one the bar patrons know. I'm just as likely to get turned away, but at least they know who I am. Still, the feel of her little hand on my arm is startling. It makes me feel . . . masculine to be next to someone so small and dainty. Knowing that she can take care of herself doesn't stop my stupid genes from wanting to protect her.

"Show time, big guy. It's an in and out mission, so let's try not to start any trouble. Don't order a drink, either. I'd hate having to deal with you getting into a drinking game or poisoned," she says to me. "No one likes a ruffled wild dog."

Hah, big guy.

"I don't drink, so no need to worry about that. I'll just keep quiet as much as possible and let you do your thing," I tell her with a little smile.

"Super, then get me in, and I'll take care of the rest," Ana tells me confidently.

I can't help but think these are the last words that some men have ever heard. I still lead her up to the bar door, because that's what every fool in my position does. They listen to the conniving girl.

"What are *you* doing here?" Everett asks me as soon as Ana and I walk in the room.

I just smile lightly. "I have a friend here who would like to meet Felicity."

Everett's eyes turn to Ana, and I don't really adore the aggressive look in them. He's Felicity's second, and if we have any hope of meeting her, then we have to get through him first. The fact that he's huge, with bulging muscles and military training, doesn't help our cause.

"I don't think so," Everett says easily.

Ana lays a hand on my arm, telling me to shut it so she can speak up. She says, "Look, I want to help resolve the little matter you have with Ares. I'm not here to start trouble or anything; I'm here to help."

"Yeah, and what's a little girl like you going to do to help?" he asks her. "You're not a wolf. This is no business of yours."

I can tell she's annoyed, but her voice is unbelievably pleasant while she says, "You're right, this isn't really my business. The only thing is, Persephone got her ass off her great green throne to come and tell me and my friends to try to help. So if the Olympians tell us to try to resolve this issue so they don't have to step in, I kind of have to go with the flow. I'm fairly certain you'd rather deal with me than them anyway."

He frowns down at her. "I'd ask if that was a threat, but we both know it doesn't matter if it is or not. Either way, it's going to happen. Come on, I'll see if she'll see you."

"Super duper! Lead the way." Ana smiles up at him innocently.

Everett just shakes his head, and I can't really blame him. We walk farther into the dimly lit bar, and my eyes automatically adjust. I turn to Ana to see if she's having any problems seeing, but it seems she has good eyesight too. Everett leads us past watchful and not entirely welcoming gang members and patrons until we reach the back room. He knocks on the door and disappears for a moment when he's told he can enter.

"This is working out pretty well," I comment.

She elbows my side sharply. "Dude, you're totally going to jinx it!"

Before I can reply Everett is back at the door. "She'll see you now," he says, and adds in a softer voice, "Try not to piss her off. None of the rest of us want to deal with her when she's in a mood."

"Sure thing, baby cakes." Ana grins at him. "Don't worry your pretty little head."

Everett is rather gruff looking with buzzed dark hair, dark brown eyes, and a fair sprinkling of scars. I don't think she could have said anything to take him more off guard. "Whatever. I'll be waiting out here, so don't try anything stupid."

Ana and I walk into the room. It's a nice little office. There's a desk, some filing cabinets, and a bookshelf. Across from the desk are four ordinary-looking chairs. Felicity is sitting at the desk with a wicked kind of smile that makes my stomach feel a bit queasy. That woman may look all sugar and spice with long blonde hair and blue eyes, but she's vicious when she wants to be.

"Hello, I'm Felicity, and I'm the alpha of this pack," she says with that small, evil grin playing at the corners of her mouth. "Please, have a seat and tell me exactly why you're both here. I know you're Max, the wild dog from Ares's group, but who are you, dear?"

Ana sits down with a little thump and a sickly sweet smile I'm sure is fake. "I'm Anaideia, but you can call me Ana. I'm the Daimon of Shamelessness. The Olympians invited my friends and me to come here and see if we could come up with a solution for the problem Ares is currently in."

Felicity laughs and claps her hands in delight. "That's just precious! They've sent you to make sure the great Ares doesn't embarrass them?"

"Yeah, pretty much. That, and they want to make sure he doesn't kill anyone. It takes a bit of time trying to pin the bodies on natural disasters or other creeps," Ana says with a delicate shrug of her little shoulders.

That seems to sober Felicity right up. "If he's such a loose cannon, what exactly do you think you can say that will change my mind about him being in this area with this kind of manpower? It's not just a matter of business or profit. I also don't want him to get pissed and start randomly blasting people away."

"I wish I could guarantee that he won't do anything like that, but that would be backing him with my word when I'm not completely sure. He knows that he has to abide by certain rules if he wants to stay mortal bound, but if he gets upset enough that he doesn't care about that anymore, then all bets are off. I can't give my word, but I can, however, compensate you for this risk." Ana smiles at her.

Felicity blinks happily and says, "This just keeps getting better and better. You're going to pay us to let him be included in supernatural crime politics?"

"The real question is, are you going to allow me to?" Ana asks.

Felicity gives her a level, measuring look. "I'm not sure you can put a price on safety and the people of this community."

Ana laughs, and it's like the tinkling of bells. It's a nice sound, even though I'm sure the noise is about as fake as her smile. "People have been putting a price on the lives of other people for as long as I can remember, and same thing for safety. I think we can agree this is the most mutually beneficial option both of us have at this point. The more you play nice with him, the less likely he'll get pissed off and hurt anyone. Plus, you get a little coin to take the sting out of humoring him."

"Very true, Ana, very true indeed. How much are you offering us for the care of your god?" Felicity asks.

Ana picks up the duffel bag at her side and throws it on top of the desk with a thud. "Check it out for yourself. I think you'll find the amount more than satisfactory, all things considered. He will likely become bored in a few years and move on."

"What a comforting thought," Felicity says sarcastically before bending forward to look into the duffel bag. Considering it's nicely full of assorted bills under fifty, her eyes widen. "This does appear to be generous compensation, indeed."

"I thought you might think so. What do you say, Miss Felicity? Do we have a deal?" Ana asks her, a playful smile on her lips.

Felicity looks up and meets her eyes. "What specifically would you expect from me if I accept your terms?"

"We'd want you to back his leadership of the gang. We would also want you to speak on his behalf to the supernatural crime council. If you agree to this, then there will be no further problems between him and the others in the community," Ana says clearly.

Felicity shakes her head. "What if something comes up and I can no longer condone his actions?"

Ana sighs. "We would prefer not to hear from you for at least five years, but if a problem comes up, we would be willing to increase your compensation. Only a problem that is real and we approve of beforehand."

"So you're saying you want me to suddenly change my mind and speak well of him to everyone? Basically tell them that he might be the God of War, but he's a pretty tame guy and isn't a threat to us or our businesses? I'm not sure I can do that. My credibility would be shot," Felicity says.

"I know this is a big decision, and I don't mean to rush you, but we'd really like an answer about . . . now. If you agree to accept the money and back Ares, then we'd like you to start at the meeting tomorrow," Ana tells her.

Felicity's face turns dark. "I called that meeting personally for the sole purpose of allowing Ares to defend himself after our ruling that he shouldn't be allowed to be a part of our organized crime community. I can't really show up there and do a one-eighty."

"That's something that you're going to have to deal with if you accept our proposal. That would be your side of the agreement," Ana says.

"I can't ruin my reputation for a few bucks. If I change my mind at the drop of a hat like that, no one will trust me anymore, especially if they learned about the bribe. I've been a member of this community for one hundred eighty years now. I'm not going to throw it away," Felicity says grimly.

"That's a no, then?" Ana asks in surprise.

"Yeah, that's a no," Felicity says with a finality that I know she won't turn back on.

Ana looks confused. "You do realize this is the only offer you're going to get from us that you'll actually benefit from, don't you? Myself and six others have been sent in to look into this matter. If we fail, which we'll do almost anything to prevent, then they're just going to send in people higher up. I really doubt you want to deal with Artemis or anyone else just because you refused to humor Ares for a while."

"You're not going to threaten or scare me into this. I know what I'm doing and not doing. That includes throwing away everything I've built," Felicity says to her with narrowed eyes.

"We're willing to increase the price," Ana says, no more smiles, all seriousness.

"I'm not going to accept it, no matter what it is you have to offer," Felicity says firmly.

"Don't you want to tell your fellow gang members so they can have a say in this matter?"

Felicity gives her a dark look. "No, I am the authority here, and what I say goes."

At that, Ana oddly smiles. "Very well. I look forward to seeing you at the meeting tomorrow. I'm sure it'll be informative."

Felicity looks at her, considering her words. "Yes, I'm sure it will. Would you mind passing on a message to Ares, for me?"

"Ooh, of course! Just tell me what you need!" Ana says, looking excited as if it's a done deal, even as I feel a pit of uncertainty at the bottom of my stomach.

"Tell him I know about Freddy."

Ana looks confused. "What's a Freddy?"

"That will be all," Felicity says with a sniff.

I groan. I knew this wasn't going to end well. I told Ares not to mess with Freddy, yet here we are, and the woman is obviously pissed about it. If one thing's for certain, she won't be letting it go any time soon.

I tried to convince him not to do it. Nope, Ares wasn't having it. His mind was made up on Freddy. Now here we all are, just because of some stupid prank that should have never happened in the first place. Felicity and Ares are making too big a deal about it. Then again, he should have never handled it the way he did. A person can't really blame her for not being all that pleased.

"I don't understand the message," Ana tries again.

Felicity gives her an annoyed look. "You don't have to understand it. Ares will. That's all that I'm worried about. Everett can show you out now."

With that she turns back to the papers on her desk, effectively dismissing both of us. Ana turns to me with a dark smile that makes my skin practically crawl. I'm not used to women who are so . . . odd. Before I can try to do anything, Ana is up out of her chair and on her way out of the room. It's all I can do to keep up with her.

"Hey there, Everett. The boss lady wants you to make sure we find our way out of this place," Ana tells him cheerfully. "You know, because I'm incapable of finding an exit on my own. Plus, then you can be all big and bad, watching us leave away in our car so we feel threatened and put in our place. That sort of thing. I'm sure you can manage."

He straightens up from where he'd been leaning up against the wall. "Follow me."

I say, "At least things ended on good terms."

Ana gives me a grin. "Oh, honey, you don't really think that's the end of it, do you?"

"Um, yeah, I kind of did?" I say it as a question.

She shakes her head at me in amusement. "No way, sunshine. This isn't done until I say it is. She might stomp her feet and give me that bad girl frown, but when the end of the day rolls around, I still have to deal with Ares and the rest of the girls. You see what I mean?"

"What are you two talking about?" Everett says, turning around to eye us suspiciously.

"Nothing you need to worry your little pumpkin head about," Ana tells him cheerfully. "Carry on!"

He grumbles something unflattering but keeps on walking.

"Hey, Everett, were you just talking to Felicity? Did you ask her about approving the list of goods we need to order?" Another male werewolf comes over. I haven't met him personally, but he's tall, built, with dark hair and of Asian descent.

"Felicity told me you need to cut down the budget by fifteen percent," Everett tells him.

"What? We've already cut down the budget. There's no way I can shave off fifteen percent!" the man exclaims.

Everett shrugs. "I don't make up the rules, Kinsley. I'm just telling you what she said. Do what you can, and I'll take the revised list to her."

Ana suddenly steps up to them.

"I don't think this is a good idea—" I try to tell her, but she shushes me.

"Do you two boys see this pretty purse I've been carrying around with me?" Ana asks them both, motioning at the duffel bag in her hand.

Everett narrows his eyes at her. "Yeah, what of it?"

"Well, there happens to be a *lot* of money in this bag. In fact, it's stuffed full of money. I just offered all of it to your gang leader under the condition that she'd support Ares in the supernatural crime community. She declined on the off chance that supporting him or taking the money would ruin her reputation," she tells them both cheerfully.

The man named Kinsley starts muttering curses. "We can't afford to turn down money to save her reputation. Besides, why the hell should it bother us if he's in charge of a gang of wolves or not? They're not messing with our business. They own a restaurant, for God's sake."

"That's what I was thinking, but she didn't agree. Even when I offered to up the price. Maybe you could talk to her about it? Get her to agree to the deal before the meeting tomorrow?" Ana suggests.

Kinsley looks down at her for a moment. "I'm not doing this for you or your god, but we could use the money. So yeah, I'll be talking to her."

"I really don't think you want to do that. We both know it won't do any good. She's not going to listen to you, me, or anyone else about this. Her mind is made up. It would be best not to stoke the fire," Everett says to Kingsley.

"She can't ignore it if I get other people to talk to her about it too. I think we should have a gang meeting. We can all talk about it and vote yes or no about taking the money. It's what she should have done in the first place, with such a big decision that affects us all," Kinsley says angrily.

Ana pipes up, "I did suggest that, actually."

"Quiet, you." Everett glares down at her before turning to Kinsley. "We can talk about this in a minute. I'm going to take these two outsiders away. Don't do anything without talking to me first, you got that?"

"Yeah, sure," Kinsley tells him, but I doubt he really means it.

Ana takes a pen out of the front of her shirt. I'm pretty sure the pen was in her bra. "Here's my number, in case you guys change your mind. Go ahead and call any time! My cell phone is always on."

Then she scribbles on the palm of Kinsley's hand.

"Right, I will," he says, looking down at the numbers.

Everett nods his head at us and we start walking again.

"Ana, I don't think that was a good idea. You know, telling him that," I tell her.

She shrugs at me. "I did what I thought might help. At this point, that's really all I can do. If it doesn't then we're probably no worse off than we were before. Besides, Nemesis and the others won't blame you if things go bad. I'll totally take all the credit."

"That's not really what I meant," I tell her.

She turns to me curiously. "Then what did you mean?"

"I was telling you that for the good of everyone and the situation in general, not because I'm afraid of getting in trouble," I tell her, a little insulted.

"My bad. Most of the people I know think about good old number one. You know." She winks at me.

"Hey, exit's right here, you two," Everett says, going so far as to hold the door open for us.

"Thanks, Everett. You've been such a lovely host. I hope to be coming back soon. Give everyone my love," Ana tells him brightly before sashaying away.

Both of us stand there eyeing her.

"She's a weird one, Max, but I gotta say . . . I don't hate it," Everett says with a little amused shake of his head. "Good thing she's hot. Damn sexy, really."

I narrow my eyes slightly. "She's interesting all right. See you later."

Ana's waiting in my car by the time I make it over there, and I wonder how she got in since I had it locked. Then I realize that she's messed with the radio and reprogrammed all of my channels. I have a feeling with this one, you either love her or hate her.

"How did you get in?" I ask her.

She looks at my slyly from the corner of her eyes. "Without a key, how do you think? I picked the lock. We all have certain skills, huh? Plus, when you get to be the age I'm at, you've learned not to let silly little things keep you from what you want."

I just look at her. "We all do. Most of them aren't something that we can end up in jail for, though."

"Some people are so picky! Where do you think I learned how to do it, Max? I try to make every experience an educational one." Ana huffs. "Got anything you're good at?"

I pull out onto the street and pretend to be too busy to answer for a moment. "I'm good at lots of things, for your information. I have many skills and hobbies."

"Sure, but name one for me," she commands.

I shift uncomfortably. "I guess something I like to do is garden. I have a couple of bonsai trees too. I've kept them for hundreds of years, so a few are really old. It's neat to have a living thing almost as old as I am. Ares had me help him out with a rather large gardening project recently, actually."

I turn a little to see her looking at me seriously. "That's a little weird, Max, but it totally fits. You know? If you kept going on like a normal person I'd start to feel seriously uncomfortable. I'd like to see some of your tiny trees sometime. I like the ones that bloom."

I breathe a little sigh of relief. "Yeah, a lot of the wolves have interesting habits."

"At least your hobby results in something pretty." She nods approvingly at me.

"So you break into places?" I ask her.

"When I need to. Or when I don't really need to. I dunno, I have lots of hobbies. They include shopping, terrorizing the other girls, and all sorts of things. I change them often. You know, I get bored pretty easily," she tells me.

I can't help but give a little laugh. "Yeah, I can imagine that."

Ana grins at me, and for the first time, it isn't one of her little fake smiles that she gives to everyone else. I can tell because her real smile isn't totally perfect. In fact, it's kind of crooked. Her mouth is a bit higher on the left side than the other. It's pretty cute. Like wanting-to-kiss-the-side-of-her-mouth cute.

"Why are you staring at me?" she asks with narrowed eyes.

"Eh? Oh, sorry. I was just thinking, and the eyes tend to wander," I tell her, straightening up to look back at the road.

"Whatever. Let's go give Nemesis the bad news. Granted, they might still call us back ready to deal," Ana says in a self-satisfied way.

I shake my head. "I really don't think your plan is going to work."

"We won't know until we know," she tells me cryptically.

"Sounds like bullshit to me," is what comes out of my mouth.

Ana starts giggling. "Usually only the girls dare to talk to me like that. At least, dare talk that way about me to my face. Don't worry about it, it's refreshing."

I am startlingly relieved. I generally don't make the largest amount of friends with my smart mouth. Actually, most of them leave in a hurry after I've offended them in some way. Still, Ana is pretty funny, and I'd hate for her to get pissed at me too early on. Not when she's been so amusing so far.

"Do you know what the whole Freddy thing was about? Ares didn't do anything to him, did he?" Ana asks, turning to me directly.

I feel uncomfortable, but I promised not to tell anyone about this. "I don't know what she was talking about. Maybe she got confused. I'm sure Ares didn't do anything wrong."

"Ha, that makes one of us," Ana says with a shake of her head, but, luckily, she lets the subject drop.

When we get back to the house a bunch of other wolves are lazing about. Pretty much all of the ones who aren't currently working at the restaurant. They all look at me a bit curiously when they see that I'm with Ana. Some of the werewolves are upset about the immortals being here, especially after the fight last night. Others are eager to get some one-on-one time with the girls.

"Hey, lads." Ana waves at the wolves in general.

They all look to her, but most of their eyes don't make it past chest level. It makes something inside me come alive—my hackles raising and throat tightening in a pre-growl. I manage to keep it back, mostly because Ana is staring at me and hasn't even noticed any of the others past a cursory greeting.

"Nemesis is probably up in her room," Ana tells me. "I'll go fill her in on what happened. Thanks for tagging along, Max. It was more fun than I thought it would be."

The rest of the day is spent around the house and the pub. Mostly the girls try interacting with the werewolves and vice versa, seeing how that works out. I suppose since a fight doesn't break out, everyone's getting along fairly well. I try to keep an eye on Ana, but she runs off to join her goddess friends.

When I see her later that day with a sour expression, I know no one called.

CHAPTER 5

N OON THE NEXT DAY, AND I'm pretty damn pissed.
It's not often that I don't get what I want. I mean, I'm a
daimon! I might not have ruled the streets of Olympus
with the big bad gods and goddesses, but I'm a queen in the
mortal world. So why can't I get one stupid werewolf to bend to
my will? It's insulting, that's what it is.

"Nice shoes," Max comments at me.

I turn around, noticing him standing there in the hallway.
I've got on a jean skirt, a black T-shirt, and red pumps. When I
examine Max, I notice why he likes the shoes. He's got on a red
and white striped polo. Figures.

"I wish I could say the same. Still with the loafers?" I tease him.

He smiles back. "They're comfortable."

When most guys have been teased or plain old picked on by
me or one of the other girls, they tend to change their act. Not
because we mean for them to—well, at least not always—but
usually because they're so intimidated by us. The fact that he just
grins along and still wears his shoes kind of means something.
That he's not a pushover. Which I should have guessed since
he's the only wild dog in a group of werewolves.

"Whatever. I'm sure you'll stand out at the meeting. Are all
you mutts going?" I ask him.

Max looks around like a bunch of werewolves will come
popping out of nowhere. "No, but Ares, Darrel, his second, and I
will be going. I'm supposedly there to show diversity since I'm

not a wolf. I guess we're trying to show that we're not just like the other werewolf gang."

"Course all us girls will be there too! This is sure to be a big cluster fuck, and I'm ready to get laid." I grin.

He blinks at me, obviously trying to understand. "Just to clarify, you mean that it'll be a mess and you're looking forward to having front row seats, right? You don't really think you're getting laid?"

"Dude, I may not be much for organizations and meetings and shit, but even I know they don't usually turn into orgies." I roll my eyes at him.

Max just grins his dopey wild dog grin, all white teeth. I half expect his tongue to come lolling out of his mouth, but, luckily, he seems to have a bit more control than that. I manage to smile back. He's pretty fun. Plus, he's a sarcastic as hell.

"Come on, we don't want to be late," he says, grabbing my hand to tug me after him.

"True. Nemesis would kick my ass," I agree and let him pull me down the hall.

It's when we're down the stairs and with everyone else that I sneak my hand out of his. I mean, obviously we're just kind of friendly acquaintances. If the girls saw it they'd think we've screwed or are going to in the near future. Which isn't going to happen. I'm a one-night stand girl, and Max so clearly isn't. Well, even if he is, I like him too much to mess it all up by fucking him.

Ares turns to both of us. "Great, we're all here! The meeting is at a hotel that one of the supernatural patron's owns. We'll be taking more than one car, of course."

"It's been a while since we had a ride together." Apate winks at me, letting Enyo overhear from the other side.

"I still haven't found someone for my dear brother," she growls at us.

Max smiles with a tight, closed mouth. That's when I realize he's holding in laughter. "Not even going to go there."

"Probably for the best." Apate gives him a sickly sweet smile.

He just gives her a look. "I've already been warned that you're the Daimon of Deceit, so there's no point in wasting the effort in trying to look innocent to me. I know all of you are trouble, no matter what gifts you guys have."

"Whatever. I *am* the innocent one," Apate says, disgruntled.

"Pay attention! Ares said that he'll give us an introduction to the council of supernatural crime leaders and explain why we're here. There should be two to three representatives from each group, so try to pay attention to all of them, and which ones we might possibly be able to flip," Nemesis says, giving each of us the *look*, which means we better be on good behavior. "Don't embarrass me."

I end up in Max's car with Apate, Enyo, and Lyssa. Just my luck.

"I've got my throwing daggers on me just in case, but Nemesis said that my sword was too much to take to a peaceful gathering," Enyo says.

Lyssa pats her back comfortingly. "She wouldn't let me bring my bow and arrows either. Luckily, we can kill them all with our bare hands if it comes down to it. I'm sure Ana can help out. Normally I think of it as cheating, but in this instance, her claws and poison may come in handy."

"Hey, what about me?" Apate protests.

"What about you?" Lyssa asks in confusion.

"I can kill people too, you know. Just because I have this amazingly beautiful face doesn't mean I can't rip other people apart when I need to," she says.

Enyo and Lyssa just laugh lightly.

"Come on, you know you have the worst aim of everyone in the group," Enyo reminds her.

"Um, I'm pretty sure no killing is going to go on anyway, so no need to worry about that," Max says, looking a little worried with this line of conversation.

I add, "Plus, if there is any, Ares will probably call them all. We'll just have to sit on the sidelines, watch, and think of something to tell the Olympians when they call for our heads. Though even they have to understand we can't really control him if he goes into a rage."

Lyssa nods. "Finally, a good point."

"So not comforting," Max says.

I just shrug at him when he gives me a look. "You have to know how to reach your audience, Max baby."

A few minutes later Max speaks up, pulling into a parking lot. "Here we are."

"Super. Shall we sit together so you can tell me all the dirt on everyone? I do so enjoy a good bit of gossip," I say.

"Sure." He shrugs.

"Hey, I thought we'd sit together," Apate says to me, possibly playing the jealous girlfriend.

I turn around to look at her. "After that little stunt with Marsha and Turner, I don't really want to be involved with your brand of gossip. Why don't you keep Dysnomia company? You can stop her from making everyone chaotic."

"Yeah, because that sounds like so much fun," she says sarcastically.

"Come on, Ares is already out," Max says, and we join everyone else who's here waiting for the others to come.

Eventually we're all gathered in front of a cute little hotel. Ares leads the way inside, the receptionist pointing where he should go after recognizing him. Her eyes widen a bit at the entourage, but I can't blame her for that. After a few minutes of walking, we're in a pretty basic conference room. There's a large table full of various people. Luck is on our side, and the room really is quite big, with extra chairs and everything.

"I didn't realize you'd be bringing your friends," Felicity says calmly, hands folded in front of where she sits at the head of the table.

Ares sits down where a group of three seats have been saved. "Yes, my companions in Olympus decided to send their representatives to help us resolve this matter peacefully."

"Indeed. Just how do they consider this matter any of their business?" Felicity asks in a pleasant voice.

Nemesis speaks up, "Our business is anything supernatural. We would like to keep this from becoming messy and affecting the rest of us even more."

"Really? Can you please tell us who all of you are? Artemis, Persephone, Hera, Nyx? Any of those names fit?" Felicity asks.

I can see Nemesis stiffen slightly, though when she answers, her voice is clear of anger. "I am Nemesis, the Goddess of Retribution. There's also Enyo, the Goddess of War, Lyssa of Mad Rage, Apate of Deceit, Ana of Shamelessness, Ruthlessness, and Unforgiveness, Dysnomia of Lawlessness, and Aergia of Laziness. I doubt any of you know references of us from literature."

"Indeed, I can't say that I recognize any of your names," Felicity says smugly. "Which is strange, since you all have such unique natures. I'm curious how you think your particular gifts will be helpful in this situation."

"Our natures do not define us, they influence us. All the same, we're representatives of the higher Olympians and are here on their behalf. For that reason, we'd like to stay for this meeting," Nemesis says clearly.

Felicity says, "By all means, we'd love to have you here. I assume that you know the problem right now is that most of us agree that Ares shouldn't be allowed to be the leader or involved in organized crime. With his connections and power, it gives him an unfair advantage. There's also the fact that he has a strong aura that affects many people and also gives him an advantage."

"To help us understand, is he actually competing with any of you for business?" Nemesis asks.

Everyone at the table kind of looks around at one another.

"Not directly, no," Felicity says. "No one here also owns a restaurant or is involved with illegal fighting."

"It's a pub, actually," Ares clarifies. Everyone ignores him.

"He's not fighting with anyone for their customers. I'm not entirely sure why you all think he shouldn't be allowed to be the leader of a gang, then," Nemesis says. "His being here doesn't appear to be hurting anyone."

"It's the principle of the matter. By giving him permission to stay here, it's saying that any of you immortals can come here and take away our livelihoods," Felicity says with great conviction.

Apate speaks up. "I hate to break it to you, but most immortals are completely content to stay in Olympus. He's an exception to the rule, wanting to come here and start up a gang. In fact, I don't know a lot of immortals who would choose life of crime over what they already have."

"That's almost comforting, but it's hard to believe when here we are, dealing with the exception to the rule," Felicity says with a small smile.

"Yeah, all you immortals don't need to be coming here and stealing our businesses and clients. So many mortals and supernaturals alike are in awe of him just because he's Ares and famous," a werewolf next to Felicity says angrily.

Felicity lays a hand on the werewolf's shoulder and says, "Just like Jo here said, we will lose business. The drug dealers especially, since Ares wants to sell ambrosia. I can't think of any junkie or curious supernatural who would pass up the opportunity for a taste of the exotic drink of the gods and goddesses."

"Hell, if that's what you're after, you can have a case of it for free," Ares says.

Felicity glares at him. "No, that's not what I want. I'm saying that we will indeed suffer from business loss because of you and your little band of misfits."

"We prefer being called a 'motley crew,' " Ares's second-in-command, Darrel, says.

"What is it you and your associates are asking for?" Nemesis finally gets to the heart of the issue.

Felicity says, "We don't mind if Ares keeps his restaurant, but we want him to stop the sale of ambrosia, as well as the organized fighting."

"No way. I have connections now and everything!" Ares says.

"We also want him to step down as the leader of this gang of werewolves. It's not right for him to be in mortal supernatural organizations," Felicity continues like he didn't speak.

Ares says, "So not going to happen. I'm having a blast with the guys. I'm not giving it up just because you all are being conservatives."

Nemesis shushes him like a spoiled child. "Don't you think what you're asking is a bit extreme? The only activity that the gang is involved in is running the restaurant, selling a bit of ambrosia on the side, and holding a few supernatural boxing matches in a basement. It's not a big operation."

"It's still enough, and no, we don't think we're being extreme with our requests," Felicity says, nose high in the air. "I also don't appreciate you sending an associate to my office yesterday to offer me a bribe to accept Ares into our council. I really didn't like when the individual tried to start a fight within my pack by telling them about the bribe offer before I had a change to inform them myself."

Ares gasps dramatically. "You offered them a *bribe*? Just to let me stay here selling ambrosia with my gang of werewolves? I can take care of them without you having to waste money!"

"No, no, we'll take care of it. It's all right," Nemesis tells him soothingly, while shooting Felicity a glare.

"No, it's not all right! I don't want you, or anyone else, to spend money on such a stupid matter. I'll just have to resolve it myself. It's insulting that this has dissolved to such dire straits. The old-fashioned way, since we all know it works well," Ares says. "Everyone back at the mountain will never let me live this one down! Plus the fact that they refused it!"

"Good thinking, Brother. I told them it was a bad idea," Enyo speaks up. "Lyssa and I can assist you, if you need it."

Ares looks pained. "First you try to bribe these idiots, and now you're implying that I can't take care of them on my own? I've killed more people than both of you combined. I taught you how to kill!"

"Yes, but wouldn't you let me be part of the fun? I've never known you to be selfish." Enyo pouts.

"That I can definitely discredit," I tell Max from where he's standing by me. "With multiple examples."

He grins. "Hell, even I can prove that statement false, and I haven't known him nearly as long."

I roll my eyes. "Neither of us are his precious Enyo. Or even Lyssa. Someone should teach him it isn't right to play favorites."

"Enyo, Ares, cut this out right now! We're trying to have a calm and intelligent conversation here, and your bickering is not helping," Nemesis tells them in her scolding voice.

Max leans close and says, "Ooh, they so got spanked."

"See what I mean? Ares is a wild card that can't be trusted not to introduce violence into our community! There's a reason we don't want him to be here," Felicity says, validated.

"Ares has agreed not to harm anyone while he's here living with mortals," Nemesis says.

"He still has the control of a group of werewolves. Even if he doesn't harm us himself, I'm sure he'd have no problem ordering his wolves to attack us," Felicity says.

All things considered, probably true.

"What if Ares could be an asset to all of you and your businesses? The individuals involved in drugs could move product at the fights Ares holds. Also, if people came looking for solutions for specific problems at the pub, he could send them your way. Such as needing to break in someplace," Nemesis points out reasonably.

I can see that she's got some thoughts turning at the possibility for more customers. Especially since they're probably right and he gets good traffic at his pub and fights. If Ares is seen as an asset instead of just dead weight, it helps the cause considerably.

"He's unreliable," Felicity says, and even I can tell she's grasping at straws.

Persephone's ever-loving flowers, why is she being so difficult!

"If you left him contact information as well as what each of you can do, he can send clients your way," Nemesis continues, knowing she's gotten a few people interested, despite Felicity's unreasonably stubborn stance.

A small woman off to the side with white-blonde hair speaks up, "How can we be sure that he wouldn't try to dip into our business? Ares might decide to try his hand at our crafts once he has people willing to pay for the work."

Ares laughs, sending her a small, condescending smile. "Money isn't really a factor in this, my dear."

Felicity smiles triumphantly. "Exactly! He doesn't even need the money, while this is our livelihoods."

Nemesis gives her a cold look. "Everyone here understands and gets the point that Ares doesn't really fit in with you all. He doesn't need the money and is just in the crime for shits and giggles. This means he won't be going after your business because he doesn't *need* to."

"That's almost worse, though. He has money backing him up to get involved with any area of crime that catches his fancy," a woman with long blonde hair, obviously a feline shifter, speaks up to point out.

Ares rolls his eyes. "I'll agree to only keep my greedy little fingers in the ambrosia and fighting pot? That satisfy you killjoys?"

Felicity frowns at him. "Well, it doesn't satisfy me, for one."

"What if he has to pay a . . . 'membership fee' to be included in this community and have a spot on your council? You can decide to do what you want with the fee. Either split it up amongst your groups or use it in the community. Would that appease any of you?" Nemesis asks.

They all look around at one another, suspiciously at that. I think more than one person is a little hungry for money. Well, most people in this mortal world are. Apparently there's never enough, and some hoard it while others go without. Something wrong with the system? Obviously, but we gods and goddesses are a little too busy dealing with one another to bother with mortal governments.

"What exactly would the range of this 'membership fee' be, and how often would it be paid?" a guy from across the table asks.

Nemesis takes a pen and piece of paper from her briefcase. I thought the briefcase was for show and didn't know she actually kept supplies in there. She takes a moment to scribble down a number, fold the paper, then hand it to the man. His eyes widen a little after looking at it, before passing the paper around.

"It would be a sum paid bi-yearly," Nemesis says evenly.

Felicity is the last to get the paper, and she looks down at it with an amazing poker face. "This is all well and good, but the safety of our community comes before some sum, even one this large."

"Oh, come on, we need the money! Besides, it's not like he's going to go mad, raid, and pillage like in the olden days! Ares was here for months before we even knew about it, and nothing happened then," the man protests.

I see Felicity stiffen. "I suppose you're forgetting that we found out about his presence when a shifter overdosed on ambrosia and ended up in the hospital?"

At that bit of insight, all of us supernatural representatives turn to Ares.

"You conveniently forgot to tell us about this," Nemesis says to him in a silky smooth voice.

He looks a bit uncomfortable. "It wasn't that big of a deal. The kid lived, after all! Besides, it was before we figured out the dosage to tell mimmortals to take. Now we only sell that amount per shifter, and tell them not to take more than that if they want to live to see another day. It's a trial and error kind of business."

"Error being the near death of a teenage shifter," Felicity says heatedly.

"Exactly. Now that we have that little kink figured out, things are much more efficient! Almost no one gets sick from it now. Especially if they listen to the rules when we sell it. There's a printed directions sheet included with each vial of ambrosia," Ares says proudly.

"Yes, but if someone doesn't abide by your directions, you'll still be seen as at fault," Nemesis says.

Ares shrugs. "No, I won't. It will be their fault for not listening. And frankly, they get what's coming to them if they don't."

"This is the exact kind of attitude we don't want within our community," Felicity points out. "Luckily, the shifter lived through the overdose, but if he hadn't, Ares would have just seen it as a learning experience. No, I forbid him from being involved with drugs or anything else equally dangerous! He has no place here. If Ares wants to stay, he can continue to run the pub, but he must no longer associate with his werewolves, sell ambrosia, or hold fights!"

"Forbid? *Forbid*! How dare you forbid me from anything, you rancid bitch!" Ares says, standing up and slamming his hands down on the conference table, eyes bleeding red. "I'll blast your ass from the face of the Earth before I let you tell me what I can and can't do! You hear me!"

Ares begins raising his hand menacingly, about to point at her with intent, when Nemesis grabs his wrist. "There will be no striking down!"

"She insulted me!" Ares protests angrily.

"All the same, do you really want to handle all of the paperwork the other Olympians would serve you with, if you struck her down? You know that blinking someone from the face of the Earth includes a lot of crossing t's and dotting i's," Nemesis tells him soothingly.

He does pause at that. "I do hate paperwork."

"Doesn't everyone? Come on, big guy, let's go drown our sorrows in some ambrosia and let the girls handle this one," Apate says, jumping up to his elbow cheerfully.

Ares looks down at her with a little pout. "Fine, but you can bet this isn't over! I'm not changing my business just because of these . . . *conservatives*."

"Damn hippies," a shifter close by mutters.

"Hey, down with the man, up with the people!" I respond.

It's true, these people have a hell of a lot of nerve thinking they can stop someone like Ares just by telling him no. I mean, the other Olympians have their hands full with him when he gets some crazy idea in his head. Legit, they have no idea they've just stoked the fire to his bitch fit, and Ares can be quite the bitch.

"Yeah, we'll get them," Apate tells him soothingly, like he could pop off at any minute, which is well and possible.

Ares follows behind her. "Don't they know who I *am*?"

When they're gone, Nemesis turns to Felicity stoically. "I hope you realize that you've just made him more determined to keep all of his businesses open. He also doesn't see you or your group as an authority, so he won't abide by your ruling that he should be banned from the criminal community."

"Even I know he wouldn't have actually hurt me," Felicity says with total confidence.

Nemesis looks surprised, then says, "I hope you're not honestly this foolish. Sure, the Olympians have told him not to harm anyone, in slightly more diplomatic words. That doesn't mean he can't be pushed into it. Make no mistake, Ares doesn't abide by any laws, rules, or suggestions. If you piss him off, he will not hesitate to kill or torture you and yours."

"Sure," Felicity says, as if Nemesis is just trying to frighten her.

I can't help but chuckle slightly. "Oh, Nemi, you warned the poor sucker. You can lead a hooker to condoms, but you can't make her use them. If the girl gets her dumb ass killed, it is no more than what's coming to her. I do feel bad for her family, though. Ares does hold quite the grudge. He's old school like that."

Felicity just blinks at me. I seem to get that a lot.

"If he dares to continue his illegal activities, we'll be forced to deal with him," another member of the council speaks up pompously.

Nemesis finally gets annoyed. "Right, I look forward to you all trying to stop him."

"I shall scalp you all, remove your brains, and use your severed heads as wine glasses if you persist with this issue and upset my brother," Enyo growls, standing up and looking down at everyone menacingly.

Comments like that just make my head feel funny.

Everyone blinks at her in shock. To be fair, I'm sure they don't hear such eloquent threats every day. "I'll be sure to look out for that," Felicity says.

"We will remain here for at least another week to make sure there are no further problems. I hope you all understand that you have no power here, and Ares will be continuing with his business with or without your pointless approval. Have a great day," Nemesis says before standing up and sweeping regally out of the room.

I turn to all of the silly mimmortals. "What she means, is eat shit and die. Toodles!"

The rest of us leave quickly, making our way to the parking lot. "This is certainly going to be an interesting week." Max grins at me when we get into the car. "I particularly liked your whores and condoms analogy."

"What can I say? I'm one of a kind." I smirk at him. "That Felicity girl sure is annoying. I'm pretty sure she has a stick permanently lodged up her ass. I mean, do any of those people really think that they have any control over what Ares does? I'm surprised he put up with them all for so long. The old Ares would have gotten rid of the problem right quick and carried on his merry way."

"I can believe it. From the stories I've heard, I'm surprised he's so lax," Max agrees, both of us ignoring the intense chitchat between Lyssa and Enyo in the backseat.

"I'm pretty amazed that they aren't more afraid. I won't lie, Ares isn't the kind of guy to pull any punches. He would have killed her and her family if Nemesis hadn't stopped him. Hell, he would have killed her damn cat if she has one," I say.

Max shakes his head as he follows the others back to headquarters. "I don't know either. Maybe there's a rumor going around that he's grown soft?"

"They're fucking idiots if they believe it. People like the God of War don't simply go from being a major badass, into the kind of guy who lets a group of low-level criminals push him around."

"What do you think is going to happen?" he asks.

Lyssa speaks up from the backseat. "Ares is going to continue with his ambrosia and mimmortal fighting. If they get all up in his junk about it, he'll show them who's boss. He's not the God of War for nothing, and while this might be minor, it's still a battle. Not only does he have strategy, but he also has brute force."

"Let's not get carried away with his whole strategy part," I say. "Most of the God of War stuff is about liking war and being able to kill and fight well. He likes to act before he thinks, remember?"

"Yes, and as far as I'm concerned, that's the perfect strategy!" Enyo bursts out.

I turn to Max with a look, and he raises a brow in response. "Like I said, this is definitely going to get interesting." He grins.

"No doubt. Let's go get hopped up on ambrosia and hope he doesn't do anything too rash before morning." I smile back at him.

CHAPTER 6

H OLY FUCK, MY HEAD HURTS. How much did I drink last night?" I ask Apate from where she's sprawled next to me in bed.

Apate looks over at me with squinted brown eyes. "I lost count after my sixth ambrosia shot."

"Damn that concentrated ambrosia!" I groan, thinking back to my excitement when I found out Ares even had a supply of the coveted shot version of ambrosia. "I don't know how I even got home. Better do a clothes check."

Both of us turn down to survey our bodies. I had been wearing a short black dress. I quick peek down tells me I'm still wearing it, even if it is a bit on the rough side. A hand up the skirt says I'm still wearing panties, and they don't even appear askew. A feel at the chest and I know my bra is securely on. I don't feel any dried fluids on my legs, and a pat at my head reveals only bed head. No cum or make out hair. Yes, the thorough body check was taught to us by the one, the only Peitho.

"I'm good, what about you?" I ask her.

She turns to me with wide eyes. "No panties."

I cock my head at her. "The important question: did you actually wear any last night?"

Apate closes her eyes to think. "You know what, I don't think I did. Since I wore shorts I thought that was enough of a barrier on the dance floor and I wouldn't get a surprise 'poke' from behind. Yep, I'm good, then!"

I can't help but smile at her. "So how the fuck did we get here?"

"You can bet your ass I didn't help either of you. I hate sloppy drunks. Some little pack member helped you, Ana, and Nemesis had you, Apate," Dysnomia says from the door of the room.

"Jeez, do you have to shout?" Apate shudders.

Dysnomia cackles evilly. "You two are such a treat. By the way, I drank you both under the table."

"I fucking hate you for your endless stomach and never getting a hangover. If I thought the mortal devil existed, this would be proof that you're it," I groan at her.

She gives a smile to rival the sun. "Oh, honey, ambrosia just loves me as much as I love it."

"Bitch."

"Do you want to know what you two missed since you've slept like the dead?" Dysnomia asks, sitting between us on the bed.

We're both silent.

"I'll tell you anyway! Nemesis is pissed that we couldn't come up with a better alternative to full-out insubordination. You know how relations in a community are so important to a business. Even a shady one. She's also got her feathers all ruffled up, literally, from Felicity. Nemesis is quite annoyed to have her good deed of warning the girl thrown back in her face," Dysnomia says gleefully.

"Is that it? No offense, but all of that was sort of implied after last night," I tell her.

"Fine, I'll give you the gossip, then. Deirdre slept with that prick Skip last night! All of the wolves are talking about it! Deirdre is claiming that Skip doesn't really *size up*, if you know what I mean," Dysnomia continues.

"Eh, I thought Skip looked like a boring lay. I just don't know what's going on with guys these days. They've gotten so bad in bed, which is amazing since it's much more openly talked about now. My professional opinion is they should all watch more porn and try to get a clue." I sniff.

Apate says, "I agree. If I let a guy have a try at me, and he isn't good, I don't reward the fucker back. I tell him to go find someone who won't realize how bad he is. Or to get a diagram and learn which hole is which. I'm not wasting my plethora of amazing skills on a newbie. I'm way too fucking old to play teacher to some amateur."

"Then again, some are very good," Dysnomia points out. "Many more people are open about being a part of the domme community than before. It's easier for me to find compatible bedmates than in the old days."

"I'm sure having a share in the sex toy industry doesn't hurt." Apate laughs.

"Oh, that reminds me of why I came in here. It's Sunday, so it's fight night. Ares decided that, to increase sales, he should have ring girls like in real boxing matches. Since you two were the only ones still in bed, you were automatically elected. Congratulations!"

I fling my head back on the pillow. "Wake me up when it's tomorrow."

"Yeah, right. Ares is already strung tighter than Lyssa's bow. I wouldn't try him on the issue if I were you. Besides, with the lack of the support from the others, they're worried about sales going down. Ares really enjoys playing house, so if no one comes he's going to be pissed," Dysnomia says.

Apate chirps up, "It's just being a ring girl. It's not like they nominated us for mud wrestling."

Dysnomia tilts her head. "Not a bad idea."

"I prefer jello, and blue is my favorite. At least you can fight and have a little snack on the side then." Apate smiles at her.

"Good Goddess, shut up before I find myself in a pool of jello with you!" I snap at her.

Dysnomia just grins. "It's three now, and they want to go over to the pub at six to set up. Since I've spread my joy and cheer, I'll leave you two to your puking."

I watch her leave the room with a little skip. "That there is one thoughtful girl."

Apate just laughs. "I don't know what you're so glum about, this is going to be epically fun! Then again, you've never been one to prance around like I do. Man, I miss Peitho."

"Just not enough for you, huh? Yeah, I miss her too. Then I wouldn't have to be the one up there with you." I wink at her.

"Might as well get dressed and see what's going on around the house," Apate says, getting up to stretch, not noticing the ambrosia-soaked napkin stuck to her ass.

* * *

Half an hour and an obscene amount of concealer later, we look semi respectable. With normal-looking tanks and shorts on, we're obviously not in our showtime fight getup. All the same, I think we're ready to face the respective public.

As soon as the two of us leave our temporary room, there's a commotion. By that, I mean I stumble over a little wolf. Well, actually a hulking person, but a relatively small female werewolf. Those damn shifters are fucking huge compared to me. Therefore, when we tumble down to the floor in an ungraceful heap, I immediately go into the fetal position, hoping not to get a monster elbow stuck in me.

"Whoa, sorry there! I'm kinda clumsy," the wolf says, starting to straighten up.

I uncurl enough to see that it's that wolf I thought was pretty nice. I think her name was Regina. She's pretty, with a sloping dark bob and large golden eyes. The fact that she's giving me a dopey dog-like smile makes her seem all the better.

"It was probably my hangover stumble that brought us crashing down," I joke.

Apate says, "Catch you down there, Ana. I need to go take a piss."

Regina and I both look after her at that blunt and fairly random comment. "She takes a little getting used to," I say.

She just grins at me, both of us still in piles on the floor. "Trust me, a wolf would bail like that if I fell in a heap at their feet too. I'm Regina, but everyone calls me Reggie. Well, mostly."

"I'm Ana." I grin at her.

Her eyes seem to brighten up. "Really? That's perfect. I've heard so much about you!"

"I'm almost afraid to ask."

"Oh, it's nothing bad. You're just the one they're talking about. Well, you and Max," Reggie says, shifting to a more comfortable position on the floor, as if she plans to sit there for a while.

My eyes widen, then narrow. "Just what could there possibly be to say about either of us?"

Reggie chuckles. "Yeah, I guess you were pretty well and gone last night. Max kind of looked after you. Like when a wolf was hitting on you in your drunken glory, he put an end to that little idea. He also carried you in here. I think you threw up, and I believe he held your hair. Everyone is all abuzz about him carrying you in here like some kind of Prince Charming. Since he's so small and everything. Well, you're smaller. Plus, he doesn't really date that much."

I groan. "Great, so I've made a total ass of myself in front of my new kind-of friend."

"I don't think he cares. He's a good one like that. You know, pretty bitchy but loyal like only a wild dog is." Reggie grins.

"Well, it's going to suck running into him. One of the girls should have picked me up off the floor and dusted me off. That's what I keep them around for, after all." I snort.

Reggie says, "They were all pretty wasted too. Except Nemesis."

"That's what I get for falling in with troublemakers. How are other partiers supposed to have my back?" I frown. "Then again, it's never been a problem in the past. I just would have screwed that wolf who hit on me. I've never had someone actually take care of my dumb ass without the enormous benefit of my wickedly hot body."

"That's Max for you." Reggie shrugs.

"Nice guys are so like that," I snarl.

Nice guys are notorious for making me feel like shit. They're so perfect and lovely, it makes me feel like I'm even more of a screwup. Plus, then I have to apologize and thank them for things when I never asked them to be there or do anything for me in the first place. I end up being a bitch to them and feeling bad because they're the *nice guy*. It's a tragic cycle."

"Right . . ." Reggie says, eyeing me like I'm a freak. Which, to be fair, I am.

"I should get down there and check in with the girls," I mutter, standing up.

"Sure thing. I'll see you later!" Reggie says perkily before standing up and walking away.

I can just shake my head. What is up with these cheerful people? Don't they know if I'm unhappy, they should all be unhappy as well? No one is allowed to have a good day if I'm not having one! Yes, because the world revolves around me.

I go downstairs and find all of the girls lounging in the living room. There are very few werewolves about, which leads me to believe they've run them off from their own home. It's something only us girls can accomplish. With Aergia asleep leaning against a large potted plant, Lyssa and Enyo having a mock duel with their Twizzlers, Nemesis painting her nails, and Dysnomia throwing popcorn and shouting at the TV, I can't blame the wolves.

"Ana!" Nemesis says when she catches sight of me. "We need to go over your costume for the event tonight!"

I wish I'd left the room when I had a chance.

"Um, costume? I thought I just had to look hot and hold a sign. That first one is a given, the second one is up to someone else. Obviously," I say, standing over her where she's perched on a plushy couch.

"That's only part of your job. I was talking to Ares, and we thought if the girls are the ones passing out the ambrosia, that more customers would buy. So we're going to have you, Apate, Enyo, and Lyssa dressing up, selling ambrosia at a table, and acting as the ring girls," Nemesis chats calmly away, as if this idea is the best ever.

"Hold up there, Chief. If you came up with this brilliant idea, don't you want to actually see it through? By being one of the girls to sell?" I point out to her.

Nemesis gives me a very condescending smile. "Aren't you adorable. Since I'm the brains of the operation, I don't have to be the face of it too. Well, or the tits and ass, as this case seems to call for."

"Dysnomia came up and told Apate and me that we were the only ones voted to be ring girls," I say in confusion. "If you only need two, I'm sure Enyo and Lyssa are up to the job."

Nemesis raises a dark brow at me. "It was decided that four of you would be needed when we came up with the ambrosia idea. Two of you will be at the ambrosia table at all times. The other two will serve as ring girls or taking trays to sell ambrosia out in the crowd."

"This is going to suck."

"That's the spirit!" She grins at me.

"I didn't mean suck in a good way." I frown at her.

Nemesis shrugs. "So hard to tell with you pervy girls like Peitho and Dysnomia."

I roll my eyes. "What's the outfit? If I have to be careful about what bra or panties I wear with it, then I'm vetoing!"

"You can't veto the outfit. You get what's coming to you when you drink like a sailor and don't take part in our house meetings," Nemesis tells me with a sadistic little smile, obviously intent on showing me who's boss.

"Give me the damn uniform, and I'll see if I want to bother fighting about it," I tell her through clenched teeth.

Nemesis stands regally, towering over me. "Come on."

I follow her farther into the living room until we appear to be in a small, clean laundry room. I look around but don't see any glittery slip of cloth. That's when I see the four hangers. With bits of clothing folded on them.

"All right. Looks like a T-shirt. That can't be too bad," I say with narrowed eyes, seeing a black shirt with the pub name, Fountain of Youth, scrolled in red glittery letters.

"We modified them a bit," Nemesis begins. "Yours is on the second hanger. They were cut to show off all of your unique assets."

"Who is the 'we' in that statement?" I ask her.

Nemesis hesitates, which is never a good thing. "Ares and a few of his wolves helped—"

"Then why the fuck can't some of his wolf whores prance around instead of us? You know that Ares has notoriously slutty taste in clothes. He started that craze with wetting the toga slightly so it was transparent!" I point out.

Nemesis's face clouds a bit. "Hmm, I don't remember that fashion statement. Anyway, the point of all ring girls being immortal is, he wants to keep a good eye on the ambrosia supply. He trusts us not to skim or overdose."

"Really? He trusts us not to steal ambrosia from him? Is he truly as dumb as he looks?" I burst out.

"Ana, just try on the costume. We have to go get ready at the pub soon, and I want you dressed before we leave," Nemesis says to me in her scary, no-nonsense voice. "You might as well go change and bring the other girls their clothes as well."

I grumble, pretending to be a rebel, as I pull the hangers down.

* * *

Turns out, if considerable effort is involved, a T-shirt can be worse than a bra. It's how I think of it when I find myself in a shirt that's been cropped to less than half of its original size with the front completely cut down the middle. Once the two halves of the shirt are tied together, my boobs have been pushed to my chin while simultaneously spilling out. I suppose the fact that I was allowed to wear plain old jeans kind of makes up for it. A little.

"Shit. I'm not going to be able to sit," Apate complains from next to me, both of us looking in the mirror.

While I have my chest on display, Apate was given tiny shorts to prance around in. Shorts so small only a thong would do or her panties would be showing from the back. And the front. I can only imagine what Enyo and Lyssa are wearing.

"Don't bend over, or I'm sure someone will take you up on the invitation," I suggest to her.

Apate just shakes her head. Together, we walk down the stairs, where everyone else is gathered to walk over to the pub. The wolves give us smirks or looks of interest. Hard to blame them when the goods are so clearly on display.

"Ah, here are the rest of the girls who will help make sure our business is booming!" Ares says loudly, looking right at Apate and me, motioning us forward.

I try not to roll my eyes, which is when I catch sight of Enyo and Lyssa. Enyo has on jeans with her shirt turned into some sort of tube top, the back having been ripped apart and tied back together even tighter. Lyssa has on a black mini skirt, and a tiny halter is the result of her shirt's transformation. Good goddess, they don't even seem pissed.

"How did you two get roped into this?" Apate mutters at them.

Enyo looks confused. "We were happy to help Brother with business. Especially after those bitches at the council were disrespectful. We heard he might lose customers, but we'll make sure that doesn't happen."

"Damn straight we will." Lyssa nods emphatically.

"Great," Apate says dryly. "They've picked up a cause."

Following Ares, we walk over to the pub. When we get there it's pretty dead, but that's to be expected, since we're here hours before the fight is scheduled to start, to set it up. Nemesis gets us to work quickly enough, setting up tables and measuring out preselected servings of ambrosia for the anticipated crowd. Under her watchful eye, we don't manage to sip any ourselves, which was the only thing that would have made this bearable.

Hours later, the place is hopping. Ares holds the fights in the pub basement, which is mainly one large room with a small bathroom and office/storage space. The open room is finished, clean, and pretty bare. A makeshift ring has been set up as well as chairs, a bar, and our table for the sale of ambrosia.

Around the ring is a crowd of supernaturals waiting for the fight to start. As far as I can tell, there's a lot of shifters but other supes as well. I thought I even saw a harpy ambling around. It seems like Ares gets a pretty healthy amount of customers at these events.

Apate brings out the first tray of ambrosia and we start selling. They're in small shot glasses, only half full. In them is weak, watered down ambrosia wine. I could have ten of the cups and probably not even get a buzz. We're only allowed to sell two per customer, so their hands are marked as soon as they buy them. We do this in the hopes that there will be no overdoses.

"I think this is going well. I don't know what they were all worried about," Apate says to me.

Enyo nods. "I'm not surprised. My brother excels at everything he does."

Apate and I roll our eyes at one another. Just as the fighters enter the room and everyone starts cheering and acting insane, I see Max sneak in. It's the first time I've seen him all day, since he's been working here at the pub. I make my way through the crowd until I'm next to him.

"Hey, I heard that you helped me out last night when I had a bit too much to drink. I wanted to thank you for looking out for me," I tell him when he turns to me.

Max looks surprised and says after a pause, "Yeah, not a problem. Not that I want you to get drunk like that again, or often. You might consider slowing down a bit."

"Relax, I don't have ambrosia a lot, since I'm here in the mortal world. We usually only manage to get some for holidays, so it's not like an everyday thing. It was nice of you to get me back home. Plus not take advantage."

His eyes widen. "You think I would have?"

"Of course not. I'm just saying other guys in your position probably would have. So it speaks a lot about your character that you were such a . . . gentleman," I say awkwardly.

The first thing that pops in my mind now is: *what if he's gay?* Apparently, only gay men are nice and don't take advantage of drunk girls in my mind. Yeah, my thought process is way screwed up.

Max looks at me like I'm a weirdo. "I would rather help you out than leave you to God knows who's mercy."

"Thanks," I try again.

"Sure," he says.

"Yeah, I'm sure you didn't want any rumors starting up. So sorry about that too," I continue.

Max looks at me uncomprehendingly. "What rumors?"

I wave my hand at him dismissively. "Silly nonsense about you and me hooking up. Apparently, the wolves back at the house thought you being nice to me meant you previously got or were hopefully going to get it in. Then again, let's face it, wolves aren't the brightest bulbs in the pack."

"Thinking we're involved?" he says after a moment. "Yeah, ridiculous."

"Exactly what I thought! Since we're clear about everything, it shouldn't be too long before everything simmers down. If wolves weren't such idiotic gossips . . ." I say.

He smiles, though it doesn't reach his liquid brown eyes. "Yeah, idiotic wolves."

We stand there looking at one another like we're strangers. I'm not quite sure how we got in this awkward place when we had been doing so well in a friend-type manner. I knew I should have asked Nemesis to watch my drunken ass last night before I got plastered. Zeus knows what I did or said to the poor boy as he assisted me.

"Hey, you! Yeah, ring girl. I got this 'drink of the gods,' and I swear it's just red wine. I've had it before, and it didn't taste anything like this. Are you trying to screw me over?" some big wolf says, all of a sudden getting in my face.

I react without thinking, raising one of my small hands up and pushing him with ease. When he's a few feet away, blinking in surprise, I say, "Give me your cup."

The man is silent as he hands me his half-full shot glass of ruby red liquid. I stick my pinky in the cup and lick a drop of the liquid off of my finger. I can't help but cringe. It is indeed mortal red wine. Cheap, weak, mortal wine.

"There must be some kind of mix up. Follow me, and I'll remedy it immediately," I tell the man.

Max frowns at me. "Want me to come?"

I just shake my head at him with a small smile. "I've got it under control, and you've already helped me so much."

I lead the big, rowdy wolf back to the ambrosia table. Lyssa and Apate are currently working it as Enyo sells within the crowd with a full tray. People move aside as the wolf and I make our way in front of the table.

"Girls, we have a problem. This man got mortal wine when he bought from us," I tell them.

Lyssa raises a brow. "How do we know that he didn't drink the ambrosia and fill his up with wine in the hopes of getting a refund or another drink?"

I look at her in surprise. "Sometimes I forget you're actually clever."

Lyssa shrugs. "I don't like getting played."

"Try the ambrosia. Enyo, you try one of the cups, and Apate, you drink from a bottle," I instruct them both.

Apate looks too pleased with herself as she raises the bottle to her lips. As the liquid fills her mouth, though, her expression changes to that of disgust, right before she opens her mouth and spews the wine back out. It spurts all around her, though luckily away from me.

"This is what mortals are used to? It tastes like shit!" Apate exclaims.

Lyssa, mouth in a tight bud of distaste, says, "Have to agree with you, for once."

"Great, so we've been selling regular old red wine this entire time? Nemesis is going to kill us!" I say.

Apate shrugs. "It's not like we could have known. The bitch told us we weren't allowed to try it!"

Lyssa looks at her in surprise.

"What?" Apate asks, looking down her front for anything amiss.

"It's like I suddenly understand what you're saying after centuries of only hearing 'blah, blah, sex, blah, blah.' It took a while, but I think you're finally growing on me," Lyssa tells her kindly.

Apate just glowers back. "I wish I could say the same."

"Hey, guys, fill me back up! These are selling like condoms to nymphs!" Enyo says with a grin, putting her empty tray down on the table.

We all look at her.

"What?" Enyo asks.

Lyssa carefully says, "There's been a slight problem. I'm not going to blame anyone, but we seem to have been selling mortal wine instead of ambrosia. I will say that the wolf who dropped off the last bottle seemed to be a little shaky on their feet . . ."

Enyo's violet eyes become bright with fury. "You mean, we've been helping ruin Ares's reputation by distributing this . . . this red, thin imposter!" she says, motioning at the wine currently in the small cups.

"I'm sure Ares will understand—" Apate tries.

Enyo barely seems to hear her, continuing to talk quietly to herself, "They've pitted blood against blood, sibling against sibling! How dare they make me betray my one true brother? I shall *kill* whoever is responsible. I will see how they enjoy their pathetic lifeblood running. I'm sure it'll be thinner than this sad excuse for ambrosia!"

"Ummm, I'm not sure that will be helpful in this situation. Maybe we should let Nemesis know and have her deal with things," I suggest.

Apate and Lyssa nod their heads frantically.

"She's always good at dealing with boring little mix-ups like this!" Apate agrees.

Enyo narrows her eyes on us. "Call her, then. If she doesn't find who's responsible and make them pay, I shall begin my own search. As it is, I now have the unfortunate job of telling my brother about his horrible mistake."

I look after her, watching the solemn expression on her face. I turn to see Lyssa walking worriedly away to find Nemesis. I can't help but turn to Apate and say, "Sweet goddess, it's just fucking ambrosia! Most of these dumbasses don't know the difference anyway."

Apate shrugs. "Yeah, well, they're insane. At least our unique brand of insanity is *fun*."

Three hours later, we're finally back at the dorm—I mean pack living apartments. Nemesis and Ares did what they could to save face by telling everyone there was a bad batch of ambrosia and it wasn't the pack's fault. Of course, refunds were handed out, but things did get a bit heated.

"I don't understand, who could have done this? Do you think it was connected to the other crime leaders telling me not to sell it anymore?" Ares asks once we're all sitting in the common room.

Nemesis gets up and looks at the bottles lying on the table. "They appear to all be legitimate. I think they carried the actual product at one point, though I'm not sure if that's what was sold to you or not."

"Wait! Can you hold that one up again?" I ask her, seeing a flash of white near the bottom of the bottle.

I get up and walk over to her, taking the bottle. There, on the bottom, is a plain white sticker with rather messy script saying, "You've been had by The Foxes. Happy whining!"

I read it aloud to the others.

"Damn thieves. No wonder I didn't notice anything amiss in the pub. If there's anything foxes do best, it's getting in and out of a place without detection. There's a fox shifter couple here who run a little burglar group. They mostly stick to antiques and art," Ares explains.

Dysnomia groans. "You never want to mess with a fox. I mean, even their 'I got you!' message was clever! Whining indeed."

"Foxes. I could use a new pelt," Enyo says viciously, pulling a knife from her pocket and flicking it open with frightening familiarity.

All of the wolves cock their heads to the side and look at her like well-trained dogs. To be fair, they're all probably used to living in this modern world, where problems aren't solved with the price of a life. It's almost adorable, the look of confusion. They should really spend some time in Olympus. They'd see the real barbarians then!

"It's a very . . . nice sentiment, Enyo, but I think this time we'll take a less direct approach," Nemesis says, eyeing the blade with narrowed eyes.

Enyo mutters a bit, but puts the knife away, to just about everyone's relief.

"What were you thinking?" Ares asks, keeping one eye still locked on his sister dearest.

Nemesis answers quickly, "I think we should let them have this one jab. If they try anything else, we'll hit them hard. With our tenuous place in the community, it would probably not do to come up guns ablaze. We don't know if the foxes were acting on their own or with the help of others, so we should try to keep this problem localized, if we can. It would be best not to have any more enemies."

"That sounds reasonable," Turner says with some surprise.

Apate glares at him. "Dude, just because we're fun doesn't mean we can't be logical."

Turner just blinks at her, while Marsha puts a possessive arm around him.

"Don't worry, Godzilla, I don't go back for seconds. Besides, I like my men willing and eager." Apate winks at Marsha.

Nemesis shoots her a look and clears her throat to regain the room's attention. "For now, I think we should all be on guard but not actively do anything about it."

"Agreed," Ares says grimly.

CHAPTER 7

―――∞―――

MAX

S O, THINGS COULD BE GOING better. As it is, everyone seems to have gone a bit crazy. I guess that's what happens when the foxes target you. They can get in anywhere and do anything they want without us even noticing! Yeah, it's a scary thought.

I mean, what if they had replaced the ambrosia with poison? Ana would be dead right now. Actually, she wouldn't be dead since I don't think true immortals can die, but it might have made her sick. Plus, it definitely could have killed or harmed the mortal immortals who had it. I guess I'm more concerned with Ana since I actually know and like her. As a friend. Strictly as a friend.

Even though when she was a drunken mess she looked at me so sweetly and said, "Max, you're like a modern-day hero. My hero." After that, I knew I had to watch her stumble around the pub and make sure she was okay. Then that pushy wolf who's friends with a pack member hit on her. He was practically pushing her toward the exit. I put a stop to that right and quick. Though maybe it was a bit rash.

When I took her home, actually carrying her across the street to the apartments, it was worth it. For one thing, she clung to me tightly with her head pressed against my neck. No woman has ever done that before.

Luckily, not that many people were back when I took her home. Both of her roommates were still at the pub drinking. I set her down on her bed and tried to let go, but she gripped me even tighter and made protesting sounds, so I sat next to her. After rubbing her back a bit, she relaxed and let me go. When I kissed her forehead, she murmured, "My hero."

Obviously, she didn't know what the hell she was saying, let alone remember it. The only thing is, *I* remember it, and I'm having a hard time telling myself that it didn't mean anything. It meant something to me, even if it was hardly anything, and I doubt she even knew it was me.

Ana made it pretty clear yesterday that she definitely doesn't see me that way. She happened to call the mere idea that we could be together "nonsense." That doesn't evoke any confidence that she could have feelings for me.

After all of that, we've been assigned by Ares to go to his distributor to pick up a new batch of ambrosia. Ana was assigned to come because she'll know for sure if it's the correct product. So here I am in a large SUV with her, Reggie, and Olly. Unfortunately, Reggie's even driving, which is frightening in itself.

"Maxxx," Ana whines from the seat next to me.

My head snaps in her direction. "Huh?"

Ana rolls her big golden eyes at me. "I've said your name like three times now. Way to pay attention."

"Sorry, I was just thinking," I say quickly.

"Well, don't hurt yourself. I was telling you that I know Reggie from the other day, and that I actually met Olly a while ago, when we were both at the international shifter convention!" Ana tells me excitedly.

My attention shifts to the blond wolf sitting in front of me. Sure, I can only see the back of his head, but I already know what the full visual is. Pretty much the face and body that would rival anyone back at Olympus. From the look on Ana's face, she isn't immune to it.

"Yeah, we were in the same group for a lot of our activities," Olly agrees. "I'm surprised you remember me."

Ana grins at him from the backseat. "It would be hard to forget you when you made those boring meetings bearable."

Olly laughs. "You guys won't believe the trouble she started . . ."

On and on it goes. Their witty banter that I thought only Ana and I had. I suppose I should have realized it's not just *me* she can be witty with. It wasn't actual flirting. It was just passing the time in what she probably sees as an amazingly boring situation. Now she's got something better.

"We're here," Reggie says, and I look up to see her watching me brood from the rearview mirror.

"Great." I get out of the car and check my anger so my door doesn't slam.

I hate how irrational feelings are.

"Where are we? This is a gas station," Ana says, wrinkling her nose at the smell.

Reggie explains, "We know a guy in the underground who runs this place. He's usually not here but shows up once in a while. I guess he's a real immortal, like you guys are. Ares knows him really well and usually makes the errand on his own. Since things are weird back at the pub, he didn't come this time."

We all walk into the shop and look around, since none of us have been here before. Behind a thick layer of bulletproof glass sits a man, face hidden behind a newspaper. Hmm, an illegal seller of supernatural goods yet interested in current events.

"We're prepay only," the man says in a deep voice before letting the newspaper slip down.

Ana lets out a little gasp and says, "Kydo? What are you doing here, you old trickster!"

The man's black eyes focus on her, and he lets his face fold into a fierce-looking grin. "Ana, what kind of trouble are you getting into? Wait, I think Deimos and Phobos mentioned you girls were going to be coming into town."

"What are all three of you doing here too?" Ana asks.

"When Ares moved to town, we decided to set up our base operation here. I'm the only one in the shop now, but I'll be sure to tell them that you're here. I bet they'll stop by to say hi to you all," Kydo continues, then looks curiously at Olly, Reggie, and me. "Normally he stops by on his own . . ."

Ana gives a little chuckle. "Right, sorry for leaving you hanging. This is Reggie, Olly, and Max. They're all part of the gang. Guys, this is Kydoiomos. He's all about the din of battle, confusion, etc. Pretty decent once you get to know him."

Kydoiomos gives a little snort at that comment. "You always have been a flatterer."

"Yeah, whatever. Girls with faces this pretty shouldn't have to *flatter*. You have the goods?" Ana asks him.

Kydo nods to her. "Yep, two cases of it. You guys really went through the last two quickly. It's in the back. I'll show you."

"Super duper. I'm sure Ares will tell you and the lads all about the last two cases," Ana says, looking back at me with a joking wink.

Reggie elbows me in the ribs at that, practically doubling me over. I don't think I'll ever get used to wolf shifters and their immense size. Especially when it comes to the females. Wild dogs are some of the smallest shifter species. Therefore, Reggie is pretty much a head taller than me. Doesn't do much for the male ego.

"Here we go," Kydoiomos says, looming over all of us, motioning at two boxes in front of him.

Ana suddenly becomes serious as she commands, "Open it."

Kydoiomos raises his brows at her. "Distrustful of *me*, Ana?"

She gives him a startlingly blank face. "Of everyone, darling Kydo. I wouldn't want you to think you're special. Now open the box and prove yourself to be as reliable as you seem to think you are."

He shakes his head. "I never want to know what the eight of you have been through. You girls are tougher than all of us combined."

Ana says nothing, just waiting for him to pull out a bottle. When he does, he dutifully hands it to her. Without any flourishes, she makes quick work of the cork. Hovering the bottle above her mouth, she lets the smallest bit of liquid in. Then she smiles beautifully. It's almost painful to look at her gorgeous face and know I'll never get her to smile at me like that. Let alone have her for myself.

"Exquisite quality," Ana congratulates Kydo.

"I guess I'll have to take that as your apology," he says sarcastically. "Need help getting the boxes out?"

Ana laughs lightly, looking legitimately amused. "Since I'm just a little old lady, I'll let the big bad wolves save me from looking like a fool."

Kydoiomos actually seems chagrined. "I didn't mean that you couldn't get it—"

"I know, darling. I know what you meant. The other girls are the only ones who seem to remember that even though I look like I can barely hold up my own body, I'm as strong as any of you. Well, maybe not Artemis, but she's just a freaky butch brute."

"Ain't that the truth? Still hasn't gotten over it?" Kydoiomos grins.

Ana sniffs. "I hardly think it's my fault for confusing her for a guy. She was in her full battle getup. Back then, it was enough padding to make anyone look like they had a dick."

Kydo says, "Ana, she didn't have her helmet on at the time."

"Artemis was turned away from me! I only saw his back! I mean *her* back."

He laughs. "I can see why it's still an issue. I'll have to take your word for it, since we both know her face is clearly feminine. Anyway, it was good to see you. Give everyone my love, and don't be a stranger."

"I certainly won't be, now that I know what being your friend can get me," she says, tipping her head at the boxes Reggie and Olly are now easily holding.

I sit in the backseat with Ana as the others load the back of the SUV up. "He seems pretty nice."

Ana smiles easily at me, the left side of her mouth going up. "Yeah, he's been around us for a while now. Actually, he kind of has an on and off relationship with Dysnomia! He's friends with Enyo's nephews, Ares's sons."

"That's interesting. I guess Dysnomia and him are off now?" I ask, amazingly relieved by her words.

"Yeah, they have been for a few centuries now. They were more of a fling anyway. He loves confusion, and she's pure chaos, so they really get things fired up when they're together," Ana tells me.

I can feel my eyes widen. "I can just imagine."

"I bet you can!" She laughs.

"What are you two laughing about?" Olly says, twisting in the seat he recently dropped into.

Ana just smiles. "Eh, nothing. An inside joke."

Olly's face falls slightly. "I see."

I fight to keep a big smile off of my face, and suddenly the car ride seems much nicer.

When Reggie pulls into the pub parking lot, Ana speaks up, "Max and I can bring the ambrosia in, if you want. I'm feeling hungry anyway. Greasy bar food sounds like just the thing! How about you, Max?"

I feel my stomach tighten, but despite it, say, "Yeah, I'm starving."

"Super, let's get this in, then," Ana chirps, ignoring the surprised faces of both Reggie and Olly, jumping out of the car.

When I follow her she's already got a crate in her arms, holding it easily as she motions at the other one. "Be a love and get that one for me? I actually wanna be able to see."

True, she could probably stack the two and have no problems with the weight, but the second crate would be taller than her head. I hide a little smile and grab the other crate, letting her shut the door behind me as she balances her box in one hand. It's nice to know that she realizes that even though I'm smaller than most men she knows, I'm still strong too.

Ana kicks open the back door and drops her box none too carefully in the middle of the storage room. I place mine down much more gently next to it. Before either of us has a chance to do anything, Darrel walks in.

"Oh good, you guys are back. Did you make sure everything's in order?" he asks Ana.

"Yep." She nods.

He just keeps staring at her.

"Dude, we came back with product, didn't we? Make the deduction." Ana rolls her eyes at him.

I have to stop myself from grinning when he glares at her.

"Just making sure." He grunts before turning away from us, probably to let Ares know.

"I really hate stupid people," she says with narrowed eyes.

I finally let the grin loose and say, "Darrel isn't really stupid per se. He's just really annoying."

"I've found that most authority figures are." She turns to me, left side of her mouth slowly rising in a little grin. "Now it's time for you to feed me! I'm definitely looking forward to fries. What about you?"

That's how I find myself, about twenty minutes later, sitting at a table piled high with all sorts of fatty foods, watching as Ana dominates the lot of it. She's masterfully worked her way through a platter of onion rings, fries, mozzarella sticks, and an order of ribs. Meanwhile, I've watched in amazement, eating a burger. Once I tried to take an onion ring, and she jabbed at my hand with her fork, gave me a threatening look, and said, "Nuh-uh, I don't share. Should have gotten your own!"

"You guys ready for the check?" our waitress, a large female werewolf, asks while eyeing Ana with reluctant respect.

Ana promptly says, "No way, we still need some sweets. I'll take any kind of brownie dessert with a scoop of ice cream, chocolate syrup, and nuts! Extra whipped cream on top."

I feel my eyes widen.

"What? Didn't think I could eat? For your information, immortals don't *have* to eat like you guys do, but we like it. Besides, it's not like I can gain weight, so it's not a big deal. My stomach is full of a delightful acid that turns all of this yummy food to nothing!" Ana tells me proudly.

I can't help but smile, even though I can feel it's my goofy wild dog smile. "No judgment coming from this corner. You forget I've lived with the wolves and their larger-than-life eating habits."

She leans in to me to whisper, "They're so huge! It's very alarming. I feel like a five-year-old around them. Plus, any wolf guy would have to, like, bend down on a knee to kiss me!"

I gulp. "Right—alarming!"

"Exactly, not to mention totally awkward! I think I'll leave the wolves to Apate and Dys. They don't seem to be my cup of tea. Since they're huge, dumb, and not all that cute," Ana complains.

Not all that cute?

"I mean, I guess some of them are okay-looking, but they're so damn arrogant! I hate people who are so self-important. They can fuck themselves if they think they're so wonderful," Ana says with no small amount of disgust.

I can't help but snort at that. "I would have to agree. Wolves do appear to be the most confident of the shifters."

"The most confident, yet unfounded." She winks at me. "Anyway, I need your help."

Great, here it comes. The asking of male advice like I'm one of her girlfriends. Or having me help her with something that she's been assigned to do by Nemesis but she doesn't want to do. She'll bat her pretty little eyes at me, ask pretty please, and knowing me . . . I'll probably do it.

"What do you need?" I ask with resignation.

She frowns. "You needn't look so down. If you agree, I'll even share my brownie with you. I need your help with brainstorming ideas for how to get more customers in here."

I blink in surprise. "More customers in the pub?"

"Yes, silly, way to keep up! We need to get them back, which may not be easy after selling them fake ambrosia. The community is probably pissed about it, so we have to do something major to get them back. The sooner we do that the sooner we can get out of your hair," Ana explains to me as if I'm being stupid.

I don't know why, but the prospect of her leaving soon makes my throat tighten.

"Sure, I can help with that. Go through some advertisement ideas?" I suggest.

"That's great! I thought it would be good to ask you, since you know how this place is run and such," Ana says.

"Definitely. We can go over it now if you want," I suggest.

She frowns. "How about back at the house? Then we can write stuff down and really brainstorm. Here, you've earned some of my brownie dessert now!"

Back at the house, I try to ignore the way the wolves are eyeing me. Mostly because Ana is currently holding my hand and leading me up to her room. Sure, she's taking me there to talk business, but they don't know that. Especially after they think my taking her back here the other night meant more than it did.

"Don't worry, the roomies are out, so we won't have to worry about them interrupting," she says, opening the door and ushering me inside.

"Great," I say hoarsely, trying not to think about the fact that we're in a room with two beds, all alone.

Ana plops down on a bed, making my casual thoughts even harder to ignore. When she pulls a notebook off of the side table and a pen out of her bra, I know it's time to get down to business. I sit on the edge of the bed near her and try to think of ways to make people come to the pub. I attempt it despite the fact that I can't think with her so close to me. At least, not about that.

"Okay, first idea," she says, making a little note, then looking up at me.

"Um, well, we already have a fight night and karaoke night," I say.

"True. What about a girls' night? With half-price drinks or anything like that?" she asks.

I shake my head slowly. "No, I don't think we have anything like that."

"What? Why ever not? All of the bars around our homes do that. It's great. I always get free drinks anyway, but it really fills the bars up with people. We should definitely add it to the list," she says, and scribbles it down.

"That's a really good idea," I agree, a little surprised.

"What else you got?" she asks me.

I shrug. "Um, I don't really know. I never went to bars that much before getting involved in this pub thing."

"Right. Do you guys have a dance floor?" she asks.

"Yeah, we have one that we use on karaoke nights," I explain.

"Super, maybe we can have a dance night. Like disco and stuff. I know a lot of people like to dance. Even I like to dance!" She grins.

I frown. "I don't really like to dance. It's hard when your partners are about a foot taller than you."

"You're taller than me. We wouldn't have that problem," Ana points out.

I feel a shiver go down my spine. "Nope, we definitely wouldn't."

Ana suddenly lets a large, beautiful smile brighten her face. "We should dance now! I'll just put on some music . . ."

A few buttons pressed on the side table and a hoppin' beat is popping.

I gulp. "I don't think that's such a good idea . . ."

"Max, dance with me!" She says it as a command, but her eyes are questioning.

It's her eyes that make me stand up and let her lead me into the middle of the room. I'm not really sure what to do, but all of a sudden her hips are against mine, grinding intimately as she flings her arms in the air. I let my hips be guided into a rhythm. When I don't know what to do with my hands, she takes them and places them on her hips. I hold them lightly, feeling my blood start to boil.

Ana shimmies around me, turning around and letting the swell of her ass rub against me firmly. If I knew more people who danced like her, I might have enjoyed dancing more. She lets her slim arms go up my chest to wrap around my neck, facing me.

"My, oh my, Max, just what kind of muscles do you have hiding under all of these clothes?" she asks me in a teasing voice, arms feeling my shoulders.

I try to keep myself from flexing. "The normal kind?"

She chuckles huskily. "Not one to take a compliment. I don't know if I find it endearing or annoying. Want to know why?"

"Why?" I ask.

"It means that you probably have no idea that I'm hitting on you," she whispers in my ear.

I feel myself stiffen in more ways than one. "Hitting on me?"

"I see I'm going to have to be clearer," she says, and I can hear the smile in her voice.

With that, Ana's small hands reach up, cupping my face. I find myself being guided, persuaded to bend down closer to her face, as if I'm trapped in a dream-like haze. I know it must be a dream when she moves a little forward, and suddenly our lips are glued together. Quite frantically.

She presses her body fully against mine, lips planted against mine tightly, moving seductively. I easily slip my tongue between her lips, exploring the depth of her mouth and groaning at the sweetness. Her tongue twines and swirls with mine as she pulls me more urgently to her. Before I know it we're short of breath, kissing one another again and again, each more rough and needy than the last.

Ana's tongue thrusts against mine as her hips follow the beat, rubbing my hard cock through the layers of our clothes. I can't help but groan and rock into her, feeling harder by the second, and uncomfortably frenzied. Before I know it she's used her body to push me back down on the bed, quickly falling down on me, legs straddling my waist. All of this is done without removing her hungry mouth from mine or lessening the pressure of our locked pelvises.

With startlingly practiced motions, she makes quick work of the buttons on my shirt. Then she rips her mouth from mine, and whips the two halves of my shirt aside with a flourish. Her eyes then dip down to stare. For an uncomfortably long time.

I'm not vain, and I'm not the sort of person who worries constantly about what I look like. Still, having her look down at my bare chest, no longer touching or rubbing against me, has me quite worried. I know I'm not the most muscular guy around, but I'm not totally lacking either. So is she used to huge guys with bulging muscles? Does my slimmer body disgust her? God, my abs are still defined! Maybe it's the piercing . . .

"Yummm. I'm gonna lick your six-pack until you tremble. You can use those big, strong arms as you hover over me. Most importantly, I'm going to let you use your biggest muscle to reach deep inside my body," Ana says, eyes flicking up at me as she licks her lips seductively. "Doesn't that sounds good, Max?"

I gulp. "Oh, yeah."

Ana lets out an almost purr-like noise. "Delicious. I just don't know why you bother to wear clothes when you have a body like this. I like to see you're not so straight and narrow."

With that last little comment she finally touches me. Ana lets her hand trace gently up from my waistband to my left nipple. They're fairly normal male nipples, small, flat, and a rosy brown. Though there's the little side note that a silver hoop is going through each of them.

"I always have liked body jewelry," Ana confides. "Sadly, my body rejects them. When I try to get anything pierced, my body pushes the foreign object out and heals itself."

I can't help but chuckle a bit breathlessly. "Hopefully it won't push my 'foreign object' out."

Ana smiles at me, looking almost captivated. "I knew you'd be fun in bed, but not this much fun!"

I perk up at that. "I have my limits."

"I certainly hope to reach them with you," Ana says, her voice a dark promise.

With that, her hands once again begin wandering along my chest. They trace my abs, making them jump and harden. Her nails sharpen and grow into rather delicate-looking talons. Part of me begins to worry about that, but she carefully traces them along my body, leaving only a raised red line in their wake.

It begins to become torture not to move, to let her explore me. Especially when she leans down to circle my belly button with her tongue, then dip it inside, making my stomach clench. One hand sneaks up my chest as she continues to tongue my stomach.

A talon oh-so carefully runs around my left nipple, the sharpness stinging slightly. It makes me shiver and my balls grow heavier with need. Which is nothing compared to when she hooks a talon through the silver hoop and gently but firmly tugs. It elicits a sharp hiss from me.

"Dysnomia will be so disappointed. If she thought you liked pain . . ." Ana comments.

I shake my head. "Don't like much pain."

Ana looks down at me with an unreadable expression. "We're ideally suited, then. I like some games, but I don't want to walk away bleeding."

"Exactly. I don't want to have to pay the price for pleasure with later pain." I nod.

"Lovely, we have our rules in place, then. Perhaps it's time for you to take off your pants and let me get the full picture?" Ana suggests.

I struggle against the suggestion, trying to ignore how her hand is still playing with my nipple, seemingly absentmindedly. "Me get naked while you're still fully clothed?"

Ana rears her torso up off of me, making me want to take the words back. She looks down at herself in surprise, legs still on either side of my waist. Then she chuckles a little. "I see you're right, Max baby. I'm terribly overdressed for this activity. Why don't you fix that?"

I gulp. "Fix it?"

"Undress me, lover," she instructs, removing her legs from around me to lay down on the bed, smiling softly.

Ana has on a plain black T-shirt and a poofy red skirt. I'd thought that she looked a little revealing in it before, way too little covering to go on a drug run. Now, it looks like way too much. But where to begin? She lifts her hands over her head, clearly giving me a hint.

I sit up and loom over her, feeling a bit uncomfortable yet excited all the same. I'm usually around more dominant women, so that's the personality type I'm most used to in the bedroom too. While Ana is very dominant, she seems to share the control when it comes to this aspect of her life. Which I like. A lot.

I grasp the edge of her shirt in both hands and gently pull it up as she lifts her body so the back rises as well. I slowly pull the fabric higher, and I savor the bits of flesh revealed by the second. Her stomach is gently curved and smooth. It's not sickly flat, nor muscular, or pudgy. It's very feminine.

When I reach her chest, I have to force the shirt to leave her breasts, as the fabric clings to them tightly. I feel myself lose brain cells when she's finally revealed to me. A black satin bra with red lace is uncovered. Her breasts are large, round, and perky, perfectly displayed in her bra. The cleavage suddenly in my face has my mouth watering and me wishing we were farther along in our game. I lift the shirt off her face and arms quickly after that.

"There's a zipper on the side," Ana tells me silkily when I turn down to her unreasonably short skirt.

Couldn't I just lift it a bit out of the way? I look to her face and see that no, I can't just do that. For one thing, she isn't rushing things right now. For another, I'm looking forward to seeing her fully nude and stretched out beneath me. I'm not giving that up.

I find the little zipper at her side and carefully pull it down. Then I slide the bit of cloth away as she lifts her hips to make it easier. Sadly, a tiny black square is covering her when I get the damn skirt out of the way.

"There, isn't that better? The only thing that could make this perfect is if you were in a similar state of dress," she says easily, looking down at my jeans pointedly.

I stand up without ado, unbutton my pants, pull them down, and fling them off in about five seconds. "All done."

Ana pouts. "You were supposed to let me do that!"

I look down at my nearly embarrassingly tented boxers. "I don't think you need to work me into a bigger state of passion."

"What a way with words you have! Unfortunately, *work* you is exactly what I had intended to do." Ana grins down at where my cock is just barely staying covered.

I groan at the images her words send spiraling in my mind. "No one likes a tease."

"Good, because I fully intend on delivering," Ana says, sitting up to reach behind her.

I watch curiously, then let my mouth fall slack. She's undone her bra and pulled it off with no flourish or sensuality. Just matter of fact, and her breasts are matter of factly the best I've ever seen. Round with light pink nipples budded and staring right at me. They're pointed slightly up, high and proud.

Before I can do anything about this newest development, she's reaching down for the last article of clothing she has on. Ana wiggles from her tiny scrap of underwear, leaving her as bare as the day she was born. Short, dark red curls are nestled in a neat triangle over her womanhood. As I watch, she spreads her legs wide, giving me a clear and unashamed view. I can see her opening is glistening. For me. So wet and ready.

"What are you waiting for, Cowboy? Time to giddy up," Ana says, wiggling her brows at me in a more playful than seductive manner.

I definitely don't have to hear the invitation twice. I drop my boxers and scramble up on the bed swiftly, until I'm hovering over her, nearly face-to-face. She smiles up at me, arching her back so her breasts rub against my chest, making both of us moan. Then she begins kissing and nibbling on my neck.

"You sure?" I ask, more of a formality at this point.

"Aren't you?" she counters, sucking on my neck.

I groan as she begins rubbing herself on my cock. "Very sure."

"Just don't forget to glove up. I don't need a little one running around. *So* not ready for that," Ana tells me. "Here, it's one of my special monogrammed ones."

After reaching on the side table, she hands me a bit of foil. I open the package, slide out the condom, and roll it over my cock. All the while trying to imagine the most unsexy of things, as she lets her arms trail along my body and her mouth explore everything close enough to touch.

I reach down between us to open her up wider, then guide myself into her. Ana starts breathing more quickly as I push myself deeper and deeper inside of her. She's so tight, yet wet and ready to be stretched. When I'm fully imbedded in her, I wait a moment for her body to get used to the feeling. That, and to get used to it myself.

I don't think I've ever been this turned on. I mean, all we are is lying together and touching in this one area, but I've never been closer to letting it all go. She's just so damn warm and tight. Plus, she's pulsing her muscles around me, making me groan and want to explode. Literally. If I ever had any doubt that she's a goddess, I wouldn't any longer. Clearly, she's got a one-way ticket to Heaven. Definitely the closest I'll ever get.

Ana reaches up to gently kiss me. I don't think I've ever been in a more intimate position, her face almost level with my own, eyes able to clearly meet mine. Our kisses become more deep and intense, as if they have a life of their own.

Slowly, I pull myself out of her and surge back in until we build up a rhythm. Her legs wrap tightly around my waist, and she meets me thrust for thrust, pulling me deeper into oblivion each time. We become more frenzied, and I push myself more roughly within her. I know she feels the same, as she pulls me to her and tilts her body for better access, using her legs to push me at a faster pace.

Before I know it, her muscles begin spasming around me, and she starts moaning my name huskily. I hold back my own orgasm, watching her face as her eyes go to half-mast and she seems to only see me. Though it's like I'm the best thing she's ever seen. She grinds against me more insistently, and I know she's been pulled into another orgasm.

The second wind of spasms send me falling into my own bit of paradise. I don't think I've ever come so hard, so fast in all of my years. I can feel myself pour every last drop of what I am into her, and wish it'll never stop. For a moment it's like my soul is touching hers, and it's the most amazing sensation in the world. I want them to rub together for eternity. Then, too quickly, it's over.

I lie on top of her for a long moment, worn out and deeply satiated.

"So much better than I thought, and I knew it was gonna be pretty damn amazing," Ana murmurs into my neck.

I lift my head to look at her. "You did, did you?"

"Of course. Anyone who wears those ugly ass loafers has to be secure in their masculinity," she replies cheekily.

I laugh, making our bodies rub against each other once again. "I have to agree on one thing. It *was* pretty amazing."

Ana smiles up at me, that wonderful kind of smile that is almost too bright, too happy. No one should be able to look like that. Least of all at me. With that too-beautiful face. Let alone that fucking incredible body.

"We should probably talk about this," I say, then wish I could take the words back.

She looks at me curiously, obviously having no idea what I'm talking about. All too soon, it becomes crystal clear. Ana wanted a bit of fun, and I was there. I was there to take the edge off, and I was the safe choice. I don't know what made me think she was actually interested. Ana said nothing of liking me. She said she liked what we did. Big difference.

"Sure, talk away," she invites.

I look down at her, conflicted. "It's nothing. I was just going to say I should probably leave before your roommates get back. We don't want any more rumors about us."

Ana's face becomes blank. "Yeah, we wouldn't want that."

"Thanks for the good time," I offer awkwardly as I stand up and start pulling on my clothes.

She looks at me oddly and says, "Didn't you know, Max? That's what I'm best at."

CHAPTER 8

H E DID *WHAT?*" DYSNOMIA AND Apate ask simultaneously, looking shocked.

I glare at both of them from where I'm lying on my bed, the two of them on either side of me. "He thanked me."

"To clarify, what did he say, exactly?" Apate frowns.

"He said he should go before rumors started, then thanked me for the good time." I sigh, repeating the rather humiliating information once again.

Dysnomia shakes her head. "That's just cold. I didn't think the little guy was very suave, but to thank you? Really? He needs to look up some romance books or take part in guy gossip. It's just not something that's done."

"Unless you're getting paid for it," I huff.

"At least he thanked you and didn't say 'Man, I deserved that!' " Apate tries.

Dysnomia and I just glare at her.

"Yeah, I'll admit, that was a little weak. I say we punish him right and proper," Apate says.

I frown. "I'd really rather forget about the entire thing. Nothing like that has ever happened before, and I'm having this utterly strange sensation. Like I've done something wrong."

"Oh my goddess, you're feeling regret!" Dysnomia says with widened eyes.

"What? That's impossible. It's so close to shame that it just shouldn't be able to reach me, a lovely free-spirited creature!" I say.

"Right, but that's what you just described, and, frankly, I can't blame you. I've regretted lots of things. I've regretted that guys aren't better in bed, that I have such sex appeal that distracts from my brains, and I once regretted leaving a battlefield to go to court," Dysnomia lists off.

Apate and I just trade a look, not willing to talk about this one.

"Yeah, it's totally natural to regret spending time with a guy who then acted like an ass. It's called a waste of time," Apate says with solidarity.

"I mean, it's not exactly shame. I have no shame for screwing him. I came, I saw, I conquered." I shrug.

Dysnomia smiles. "Now there's the cold-hearted bitch I know and love!"

"Most importantly, what the fuck are you doing lying in bed at seven? We should be out and about. Especially after this little episode. I know just the thing to make you feel better!" Apate says with a clap of her hands.

"Oh no, the last time she did that, I ended up waking in the middle of the Underworld Prison with a female cellmate who had reverted to her more masculine side. She wanted to call me Mickie cause I was gonna be her quickie!" I say with a hostile glare at her.

Apate shrugs. "Who knew that they made a law against immortals interfering with high mortal government?"

"Read the fucking *Guide for Immortals Visiting Earth*! It has all of the laws right there for your viewing pleasure," I growl.

"Like you've read it before. I really don't think flashing the silly House of Parliament—or whatever it is—is that big a deal." Apate sniffs. "Besides, once you slashed her with your claws and sent her writhing in a poison-induced pain, you got sent to solitary. I bet it was the first time you'd gotten a bit of alone time in centuries!"

Dysnomia gives a dainty cough. "You said something about making Ana feel *better*, right?"

Apate huffs. "Yes, exactly. My plan is that we go out to a hockey game."

"Blood on the ice!" I shriek on instinct.

Dysnomia turns to her laptop, and after a few merry clicks, she sighs. "There are no games anywhere near here, you idiot."

"I won't lie, that was anticlimactic."

"Like your sex life?" Dysnomia asks me.

I hiss at her. "Bitch. I said I *came*, saw, and conquered."

"Eh, at least you came. Goddess, I can't imagine the bitching I'd be putting up with right now if he didn't at least have that going for him . . ."

"So, great idea, Apate. No hockey." I turn to her, ignoring Dys.

Apate frowns. "Don't blame me. It's not as if I control such things."

"Aha! I was looking up popular things to do around here. Turns out there's a bingo hall just down the street. Anyone down to beat some old ladies to the coupon prizes?" Dys asks with glee.

I give her a small smile. "You do know how I enjoy taking candy from a baby, or in this case, a mortal."

"Perfect. Throw some clothes on, and let's get our asses in gear. This place is sure to be hopping." Apate grins.

It takes us barely ten minutes to throw on decent clothes. In my case, that means shorts, my official Immortal Representative T-shirt, a hat, and sunglasses. Sure, the eight of us might have had to order our own official immortal representative gear, but it still counts. We also came up with the mottos and styles. In this case, being a tiny midriff-baring T-shirt saying Immortal Representative: *My powers indicate one of us is thinking about sex.* On the back in big, bold script it says *It's me!!!* Yeah, so this design was Peitho's, but we all got to do one.

"I miss her." Apate sighs.

"I'm really glad she went with that design instead of the 'good boys go to heaven, bad boys cum to us' idea. It's so much classier," Dysnomia says.

"Bingo Hall." Apate opens the door for us.

Luckily, we don't run into any of the other girls besides Aergia, who is sleeping on the stairs. One would have thought she's learned her lesson after the shifter convention. The wolves are lazing about with hoards of food, shouting, and scratching themselves with reckless abandon. Then, we sneak out the back door.

Apate lets out a cackle. "We are freeeee!"

"Whoa there," a female voice says as Reggie walks up to us. "Whatcha doing?"

We all exchange a look. "Nothing."

She eyes us. "Right."

"Fine, fine, we're about to go play a game of chance that could result in the ruination of many lives!" Apate blasts out.

Dysnomia and I just eye her in shock.

I look back to Reggie with a nonchalant shrug. "She's a known liar. We're going to play a little game of numbers, if you must know."

"Sounds . . . fun?" Reggie asks.

"Fine, fine, it's bingo! Good goddess, you should work as an interrogator at the Underworld Jail!" I huff.

Reggie's eyes widen. "Um, thanks. I think."

Dysnomia eyes her up and down. "You seem all right, for a mutt. Wanna come?"

My eyes widen. I was pretty sure this was meant to be a girls' trip. Like, just us girls.

Dys gives me an exasperated look. "You know, Reggie, you could tell us all of the pack gossip."

Oh. Well, that makes more sense. Still, I don't want to hear all the gossip about Max. Been there, done that—literally. Now I'm over it. Screwing up once is enough for me. He's off my radar. I'm sure the next time I see him I'll have no reaction to his presence.

Reggie shrugs. "Sure, if I stick around here Ares will probably make me work another shift. It's busy now that we have the ambrosia back in stock."

"The bingo hall is supposedly down the street. Mind steering us in the right direction?" Apate asks.

Reggie nods. "Sure, it's in walking distance. Ares goes there a lot. Must be an immortal thing."

The three us ignore that little comment and follow her down the street a few blocks until we reach a rather nondescript building. Getting inside, we pay a cover charge then an option of two card styles. We can go old school with a big sheet of paper containing sixteen cards, or get an electronic board that holds even more. I go for the paper. I just love stamping off the numbers!

"We have to sit in the back, so we can see what everyone else is doing," Apate says wisely.

"Plus, you know, so we don't leave our backs wide open for an attack. Let's face it, we're not exactly superstars around here," Dysnomia mutters, while two old biddies give us dark looks. "Even with the mortals."

"Forget them. They're just hardcore. Hate having more competition," Reggie says, giving them an answering smirk. "With our reflexes, when Ares forces us to come here with him, someone from our group always wins."

"Only to be expected." Apate sniffs her superiority.

I shrug. "Superior is superior."

"B-05," an older woman says, standing at the front of the room and reading from a plastic ball.

"I've been duped," I mutter.

Dysnomia glares at me before turning to Reggie. "How long have you been with the gang?"

Reggie shrugs. "Pretty much since it started. We had to go through a task to prove our worthiness, and I passed."

That distracts me from my pursuit of numbers. "What was the task?"

She smiles absently. "I stole Felicity's gang's pet tortoise."

"I'm going to go out on a limb and say that didn't make you guys any friends over there," Apate says with a little shake of her head. I hear her mutter, "A *tortoise*?"

"Okay, yeah, that kind of started the feud. Apparently, the thing is like two hundred years old and has been with her since it hatched. I'm inclined to believe it, since the sucker's huge," Reggie says.

"Wait, do you guys still have it?" Dysnomia asks.

Reggie's eyes bug out. "Hold up there, I definitely was not supposed to tell any of you about this!"

My eyes narrow. "Was this tortoise's name Freddy, by any chance?"

Reggie's face pales. "Max told you, didn't he? I'm going to kill him."

"Max told me he didn't know who Freddy was," I say, teeth clenched with anger.

"Uh-oh." Reggie sighs.

"Are you telling me that he's known about Freddy?" I ask.

She shrugs at me a bit helplessly. "He's the one who helped me get Freddy back to the house. He's one of the only people who has a car around here. The tortoise definitely wasn't fitting on the back of my bike."

I bite off a curse.

"This fucker has no idea who he messed with," Apate says, watching my eyes start bleeding black, little fangs lengthening. With a flick of her hand, I know that she's made it so the mortals around us will instinctively not look this way, and if they do, not quite remember what they happened to see.

"Whoa there, girl, what's your problem?" Reggie asks, eyeing my fangs.

I grip the table with annoyance. "You don't want to know."

"Right, that's why I asked," she says with a roll of her eyes, stopping when I let out a low hiss.

"He lied to me when I asked him about this *Freddy*. So yes, I'm a bit annoyed," I finally bite out, voice coming out with a more pronounced accent. The accent I've tried so hard to leave behind. One of an ancient immortal language that never quite made it to the mortal world. My words slur and become more guttural. Almost sounding like a combination of French and German.

"Plus, she kind of fucked him earlier today. While you expect random guys to lie about you in the hopes of getting laid, he seemed kind of trustworthy. It's only all right if you're expecting it," Apate says wisely.

I groan.

"You slept with Max!" Reggie squeals with excitement.

"It didn't go so well, so don't make that noise again if you plan on keeping the use of your mouth," Dysnomia advises her.

"What do you mean, it didn't go well? They have sexual chemistry to last for centuries," Reggie says stridently.

I can't help but let out a low hiss once again. Honestly, this girl is much too outspoken for this sort of information.

"I'm sure if you give it another go, it'll be fantastic," Reggie says.

So am I, but I don't say that much out loud.

"He's a really great guy. You could definitely do worse," she continues.

"He thanked me!" I finally blast out.

She looks at me silently with a perplexed expression on her face. "I'm not sure what you're talking about."

I sigh. "Max thanked me for the good time after saying he should leave so no one would see him in my room and start rumors. It left a warm, fuzzy afterglow to bask in."

"Oh." Reggie sighs. "Sometimes guys are such asses."

"Preaching to the choir." Dys nods.

"I just don't get it. He's such an amazing guy. Granted, he's not very smooth. Maybe he's just stupid and not actually rude?" Reggie asks. "Dumb boy syndrome?"

"I'm not sure what would be worse. Having a guy who means to insult you or having one who does it because he's so inconsiderate," Apate says with a sneer.

I shrug. "It was a one-night stand. Actually, it was just an afternoon delight. At this point, it doesn't matter because it's over and done with. What does matter is this whole Freddy business. You know it's why Felicity won't budge about anything."

Reggie opens her mouth to argue about Max, but closes it when I give her a sharp look.

"Wolves never can take a joke," Apate says with exasperation.

Dysnomia nods. "Plus, they hold grudges like no other. It's their stupid animal pride."

"Why would Ares even have you do something like that as an initiation task?" I ask in confusion.

Reggie shrugs. "I don't know why. Just a funny joke, I would assume. Mortals seem to have lots of fun stealing opposing sides' mascots. I imagine that's where he got the idea. I definitely was ace in accomplishing it. They never knew what hit them until they got the ransom note."

I close my eyes briefly. "Ransom note?"

She gulps. "We didn't want her to think he just ran away."

"It was a fucking tortoise! They don't just run away like cats and dogs, you know. They're pretty noticeable, especially a nice big one," Apate says. "Besides, they don't exactly gallop."

"Okay, fine, I admit that it wasn't the most thought-out of plans." Reggie grimaces.

"Yeah, yeah, what did the note say?" Dysnomia waves away her indignity.

Reggie shrugs uncomfortably. "I don't quite remember, but I believe it was something about giving us a sum of money or we'd make turtle stew."

"Oh, sweet goddess. If this is the only thing that cold bitch Felicity had in the world, she probably tripped balls. What did she do when she got the letter?" I ask, already dreading the answer.

"Well, erm, I believe she came to the pub and threatened Ares. She demanded Freddy back or she'd make his life a living hell. He got rather pissed off with the whole 'a mere werewolf threatening the God of War' thing. Needless to say, she didn't get the tortoise back, and things haven't gone well ever since," Reggie says.

"At least we know how to fix this. We just need to find a two-hundred-year-old tortoise and hand it over. Do you happen to know what species it was?" Apate asks her.

Dys says, "I really can't believe he had you make turtle soup of it. I mean, tortoises are just not the same as turtles. Hence the different name."

The large wolf girl once again looks uncomfortable, eyes shifting about the room as if for an escape. "Well, erm, that's sort of the thing. Ares kind of got attached to Freddy."

Apate lets out a slow breath. "Are you telling us that the tortoise is still alive?"

Reggie shrugs helplessly. "He didn't have the heart to kill him."

"Not the heart—are we still talking about Ares here?" Dysnomia asks in disbelief. "Whatever, at least now we don't have to go searching for another tortoise. We'll just return that one, and hopefully things will get back to normal. We'll make nice with Felicity, and she'll stop getting the others to pull full-out war on Ares."

"Ares won't give Freddy up."

I close my eyes with annoyance. Only Ares. "Look, he doesn't have much choice at this point. Once we tell Nemesis what he's been up to, she's going to set this to rights. That means the tortoise is going back to the bitch. Hopefully, once she realizes her beloved Freddy is still alive, she'll find it in her heart to lay off Ares. Then we can get the hell out of here."

"Ares commanded us not to tell any of you about this. If he finds out, he's going to be pissed, and he is not going to give up the tortoise. Telling him may not be in anyone's best interest," Reggie says evenly.

"Maybe you shouldn't have stolen the tortoise! *That* wasn't in anyone's best interest," Apate snaps at her.

"Are you saying that Ares would rather continue with this mock war with everyone in the community than give up one silly tortoise? Why would he even care?" I ask in confusion.

Reggie sighs. "Ares really likes that Freddy has his own built-in armor. He said that he's a born warrior."

"The shell is a defense, because they have no offense," Dys says.

"I never said he was a biologist."

"If we tell Nemesis, she'll make sure that he gives Freddy up, and pronto. Once we fix things with Felicity, I doubt he'll have any more problems around here," Apate says wisely. "Then I say we take a little vacation to our Lake Michigan beach house."

I nod. "I do like the house of nymphs who live next door. They really know how to throw a party."

"You *can't* tell Nemesis, or anyone else, about this. If you do, Ares is just going to get mega pissed. Then he'll refuse to give Freddy back, and he'll probably refuse to let you help at all. As you can tell, he's barely cooperative as it is," Reggie says urgently.

Apate, Dys, and I all look at each other and shrug.

"That's not really up to us, sugar. Nemesis is our fearless leader, and these kind of things are totally up to her. We believe in a full disclosure dictatorship here. Unless, of course, we decide to vote on something. Rules as they come, if you will," Apate tells her.

Reggie looks at me pleadingly.

I roll my eyes. "I'm not taking sides, just presenting the information."

"Impartial doesn't begin to cover us," Dysnomia agrees.

"We're the definition of cool, calm, and collected," Apate adds.

The woman at the front of the room says, "O-75."

I dot my board and cry out, "Bingo!"

"How did you even keep track?" Apate asks with wide eyes.

I give an evil little grin.

"Oh, yeah, the bitch is back," Dysnomia says with no small amount of satisfaction.

* * *

"Nemesis, what are you doing?" I ask when I spot her dark head hunched over.

She seems to jump in surprise and look up guiltily. "Huh, what's up?"

It's then that I see she's playing a video game with one of the other pack members. Some little wolf female. They seem to be doing a quest together. I'll never quite understand how someone like Nemesis can love video games so much. It just seems so impractical.

"Can Apate, Dysnomia, and I have a quick word with you?" I ask, motioning upstairs.

Nemesis looks annoyed, even as she nods her head regally. "Collect the gems I got from beheading the troll. I'll be back directly."

I nod at my head to Reggie so she knows not to come with us. She looks like she wants to argue, but even she can see that's not exactly the best idea. After living with one another for thousands of years, we've learned to be quite secretive and not trust "outsiders." It's not paranoia, it's prudence.

"What is it?" Nemesis asks with blatant irritation when we're safely in her room.

I flick my hand around the room and loose some of my power, looking like it sparks out of my fingertips like fire. Instantly, the room is sealed from any eavesdroppers and completely soundproof. This secures it from people outside the door and immortal eavesdroppers alike.

Nemesis perks up. "That important, then? Usually you're all so trivial."

"Nemi, that isn't really the point, but thanks for the constructive criticism. We've got information on the feud between Felicity and Ares. I don't like to brag, but this is some good shit too. Totally boner worthy," I say with a satisfied smile. It's high time she's learned we're not just the screwups of the group.

Apate rolls her eyes. "She means you're going to piss yourself when you hear what we have to spill!"

"What they're both trying to say is, we're totally going to spank your ass," Dysnomia says.

Nemesis just looks further annoyed with each word we say. "Are any of you actually going to say what it is, or am I going to have to work some magic?"

Apate huffs. "No need to get pissy."

"Reggie, that little werewolf girl who's super clumsy? She went out with us tonight and told us why Felicity and Ares are arguing. To be more precise, why Felicity hates Ares. Turns out that he had Reggie steal Felicity's two-hundred-year-old pet tortoise as an initiation task. There was also a ransom note that said she had to pay an amount of money or they'd make turtle soup out of him," I tell Nemesis, waiting to bask in the glory of her admiration.

"He killed her tortoise?" she asks in bewilderment.

Apate coughs. "Er, that's not exactly true. He seems to have adopted Freddy as a pet. He's currently living in the shed in the backyard."

"What you're telling me is that all seven of us, some of the most powerful beings in the mortal world, were called in to help Ares. Not only has he been acting like an immature child, but the fight that's the cause of all of our problems is that he stole a werewolf's tortoise? Which he's now decided to keep? Really? *Really?*" Nemesis asks in a quietly seething voice.

Apate, Dys, and I exchange looks. We thought she would have been much more pleased about the whole issue. I mean, not only did we dig around for this information, but we came right to her about it! When she couldn't even sense the thievery right under her nose.

"He swore them to secrecy?" Apate tries.

Nemesis lets out a long breath. "As if that should matter to this gossiping pack of immature mimmortals. I just don't know what we're going to do with Ares. The Olympians are going to need to get him in check."

"Right, but we were kind of wondering what's going to happen in the here and now. Are you going to have Freddy returned, or are you going to let Ares keep his new plaything?" Dysnomia asks.

"Of course the tortoise will be returned to her. It will end this entire mess," she says as if the three of us have recently gone insane. It's been a long time coming.

"Yeah, we had some time to think that one out too. We know that, in theory, it seems like the perfect solution. However, Ares will get very pissy and uncontrollable if we undermine him and take away something that he wants. It may not solve anything with Felicity, since she could still seek revenge for the incident to begin with. Also, it may make him seem untrustworthy to the others in the community, since he stole something from one of them and lied about what he did with said possession," I say.

Nemesis argues, "There's also a chance that it could solve all of our problems."

"Worth the risk?" Apate asks.

"One moment, and I'll get a taste of the situation," Nemesis says after a moment, eyes bleeding black from her pupils as she closes them for concentration.

Nemesis is the Goddess of Retribution for evil deeds and extraordinary good fortune. That means she's like a modern-day Robin Hood. She takes away from the grossly lucky and gives to the unlucky. It doesn't always make fans of some. Either way, she's all about balance.

"She will seek retribution for his deeds. I don't know what that will be or to what extent, but even if he gives back the creature, she won't let the matter go," Nemesis says after a moment, opening her eyes to blink rapidly, as if clearing away her vision, the whites of her eyes showing once more.

"Why didn't you sense that he'd betrayed Felicity when we were all meeting?" Apate asks.

Nemesis sighs. "Ares has wronged many people. It can confuse the senses. Also, Felicity has betrayed Ares in a comparable amount to how he has wronged her. They are seemingly balanced in that way."

That would confuse her senses. They only focus for a lot or a little. No middle ground.

"What do you think is best?" Apate finally asks.

Nemesis sighs, and I can tell she really doesn't like what she's about to say. "I think right now, we should keep the Freddy issue to ourselves. We already know that Felicity is upset with Ares and how she's decided to deal with it. Adding this unknown variable could make it a little or a lot worse, but I've seen that it will not appease her. If you could please not tell any of the other girls?"

"Of course, Nemi. We would for sure be lost without you," Dysnomia says with a sarcastic little salute.

Nemesis just looks up at the sky, as if asking Hera for patience. "Try not to get in trouble while I go save the virtual earth. Let me know if you hear anything else. Also, don't let on to Ares that you know about his dirty little secret. Best to keep him as off guard as possible."

Apate nods. "Seriously, though, a tortoise?"

We sigh collectively at the stupidity.

CHAPTER 9

S ERIOUSLY? YOU'RE JUST GOING TO sit around here all
day while we work?" Apate asks me with some annoyance.
"You realize if I didn't have to be here I'd be out so fast
you'd get whiplash?"

"There's nothing else for me to do," I whine.

"Anything is better than this," Dysnomia says with scorn.
"I'd even rather be training with Lyssa, Enyo, and Ares than
babysit the mimmortals. Hell, I'd settle for taking a nap with
Aergia or hunting lucky ducks with Nemi."

Olly, Jordy, Skip, and Darrel are sitting in the booth across
from us. We're currently set up with cups and a bottle of wine,
ready to sell the ambrosia for the day. Strictly speaking, it's Apate
and Dys who are supposed to be in charge of it, but I definitely
didn't want to be stuck back at the clubhouse without them.

"I mean, we're stuck with the mutts and their tragic wet dog
funk," Apate says, wrinkling her nose dramatically.

I can physically feel the weight of the four male werewolves
staring at us.

"Once again, nothing better to do." I sigh.

Dysnomia nods sympathetically. "Plus boy problems."

"Shut up, you hag! I have no boy problems. I'd have to care
and be committed to have any problems with any of them." I sniff.

"Of course. Then again, men in general are a problem." Dys
sighs. "I hear you ran into my ex, the tragic love story of my life.
You didn't even tell me! That's so a violation of the girl code."

I roll my eyes. "You and Kydoiomos haven't seen each other for over two centuries now. I didn't think it was a big deal at this point."

"Two centuries doesn't erase the memories, my dear friend."

"Then try harder," Apate suggests. "There are lots of things I can't remember! Two centuries might not erase them, but there are a fuckload of fun substances that will!"

"Men are the worst. Especially shifters." I groan.

Darrel finally turns to us, giving us his undivided attention. "You three know we can hear everything you say, right?"

I turn to look him slowly up and down, licking my lips, and say in my native tongue, "My mouth was created for your cock."

Darrel gives me a confused look, while Apate and Dys start laughing.

I wink at him and push at the inside of my cheek with my tongue, giving him an idea.

Darrel looks around uncomfortably and says, "I don't speak that language."

I sigh. "Guess that's a no, then."

"Can't win 'em all." Apate shrugs.

"True, but here I thought he was checking out my amazingly bangable body and double D's," I say, cupping my breasts to make them shimmy at Darrel.

The girls laugh.

"Bitch, those are double C's, at best," Dys jokes.

"Oooh, looks like your lil doggy caught the tail end of that," Apate says, eyes looking over to where Max is leaving the kitchen, face carefully turned away from us.

As I continue to stare at him, he looks over at me and makes eye contact. He doesn't look happy in the least. In fact, it's almost like I see hurt in his little puppy dog eyes. Not that that's very likely. He's the one who threw me away like last week's chew toy.

"I still can't believe you slept with a wild dog. Let him . . . bury the bone, if you will." Apate giggles.

Dysnomia whistles. "Sure looks like the puppy isn't over you."

I shrug. "Max had his chance. That's all the boy wanted anyway."

"It's what all of 'em want. Bastards." Dysnomia sighs. "We're allowed to use them for sex and lie to them before or after. Since when did they think it's okay to turn the tables on us? Completely unforgivable."

"Right, as if I'd moon after the guy. Clearly he doesn't know men like him are a dime a dozen. Just another one around the corner begging to worship me without the added bonus of acting like a total ass afterward," I say, getting irritated the more I think about it.

"Damn right! Love 'em an' leave 'em before they have a chance to leave you!" Dys agrees.

"He doesn't own you! You can flirt with anyone!" Apate agrees.

I look over at Olly. "Too right you are! And right now 'young and dumb' seems like the perfect flavor of the day."

All of us turn back to the three wolves, Max slipping out the front door.

"On to bigger and better things," Apate says, all of us still speaking our native tongue.

"Go big or go home," I agree.

Dys giggles. "Guys always get so offended when I say that . . ."

The men start to shuffle under our returned attention.

"What's up with this place? It seems like Tuesdays would be slow, but it's packed in here," I point out, looking around at all of the people who seem to have come out of nowhere.

Darrel shrugs. "Maybe they heard we have ambrosia back in stock."

"With this crowd? Doubtful," Apate says low enough that only Dys and I hear her.

I have to agree with her. Most of the people look like they're on their lunch break or are college students slumming it. Pretty much not the supes who want to spend some extra cash for an exotic drink while out on the town. Plus . . . it's a Tuesday!

"Ooh, what about those guys? They look like easy marks!" Dysnomia says excitedly.

Glancing up at a group of three guys, I'm forced to agree. They're most likely shifters of some sort with medium body types. One has dark hair and eyes. The second is blond and carrying a briefcase. The last guy is a little smaller, with glasses and an unsure look about him.

They stumble about as a group until their eyes find themselves glued to us.

"Hey, is this a 'seat yourself' kind of place?" the guy with dark hair asks, obviously trying to break the ice.

"Yeah, you can say that," Apate says with a grin, playing the good girl like a pro.

"When did you guys open up? I haven't seen this place before," he continues.

I shrug, then look over to the guys. Olly speaks up with, "We opened up over a year ago."

The three look surprised.

"Wow, I can't believe we haven't been here before. We all work really close by and are always looking for a decent place to eat lunch," the dark-haired guy says, speaking for all of them like he's rather used to it.

"We're definitely the restaurant you've been looking for, then! We have a great lunch menu full of exotic foods. We have elk, antelope, zebra, and all sorts of other proteins for your more varied needs," Dysnomia says encouragingly.

"Wow, is that even legal?" the shorter guy asks, adjusting his glasses.

I give him a little wink. "We do what we have to for our clients."

There's an awkward silence as they try to interpret those words.

"We also have this drink in stock that's the only one of its kind. This is the only place it's sold for states," Apate tells them in a hushed tone. They all lean closer with interest.

"Is it that drink with the worm in the bottle?" the blond asks with distaste.

Apate and I exchange a puzzled look. Oh, to be young.

"No, it's a very lovely drink called ambrosia. We have it right here and are selling it by the half cup. You're allowed only two cups each, since it's very strong," Apate explains, even though we all know it's been watered down quite a bit for the little mimmortals.

The blond's eyes crinkle. "Just how strong can it be?"

I shrug. "More than you're used to with any other drink."

The smaller guys says, "Look, guys, we have to go to work right after this. I don't think we should be doing any wonder shots right beforehand. Let's just get some wings or something, and maybe a beer."

The dark-haired leader waves his friends' words away. "Now they have me interested. Besides, a half cup of anything won't make me unable to work."

The three of us decide not to correct him. A sale is a sale.

"So you'll want one cup?" Dysnomia asks.

"Sure, any of you guys want one?" he asks the others. The blond speaks up, but the other one keeps silent.

They both grumble about the price, and even I'll admit it's a bit steep. They still manage to both hand out the cash. The smaller guy looks on with disapproval, and I feel like he's the token reasonable friend who gets pushed into the background.

"What's ambrosia? Some kind of tequila?" he asks.

I can't help but smirk at that as Dysnomia lines up the cups.

"It's more of a wine. Sweet and thick," I say.

"Right, and it packs a punch?" he asks with sarcasm.

"You don't really notice it until about five minutes later and you're flying high as a kite, or so I hear." I smirk.

"A really strong, really expensive wine." He shakes his head.

"It's commonly called the drink of the gods. It was directly imported too, so I can guarantee it's good stock."

He laughs. "Right from Heaven? That's quite a slogan."

I can't help but frown at that. "No, from the gods and goddesses. As in Olympus."

"Greek mythology? Here I thought this was a new drink!" he jokes.

I look at Dysnomia with confusion. "What did you guys say you were?"

He jerks his thumb at the blond guy and says, "He's an accountant, and the other guy is a lawyer. I'm in marketing."

"Yes, but what *are* you?"

He just blinks at me. "Um, Canadian?"

I shake my head. "Shifter? Merman? Dragon? Phoenix? Any of those ring any bells?"

A brow lifts at me. "Lady, how many of those magic drinks have you had today? You're not making any sense at all."

"Oh, this isn't good at all. Are you saying you three are . . . mortals?" Apate asks as if it's some great affliction.

"Is this a joke?" he asks. The other two look unsure as well. Olly stands up and walks over, soon followed by Darrel.

"Are you three being serious? You don't know what they're talking about?" Darrel asks, all business in capacity as second-in-command to Ares.

"Who are you guys? Whatever—no, of course we don't know what they're talking about. Is this one of those themes bars?" the dark-haired man asks.

Olly shakes his head. "Sure. So none of you have seen this pub here before?"

They shrug, and finally, the smaller guy says, "No, we've just always kind of gone past it. Today we just noticed it on the way to work and decided it would be a good place to stop for lunch. There's nothing wrong with that."

"Yeah, only, we've been set up for over a year and they're just noticing the pub after working nearby for that long? There's for sure something going on. Maybe a glitch with the . . . system?" Olly asks Darrel.

Darrel gives a sharp shake of his head that basically means "shut up." He turns to the humans and says, "We're going to close up shop. Sorry, but you'll have to try out our lunch specials some other time."

"Wait, we already paid for two drinks!" he protests.

Dysnomia quickly hands the dark-haired and blond guys their cash back.

"Everyone, we're having problems with the computer system and are going to have to shut down for the rest of the day! Please collect carry out boxes, a complimentary coupon, then make your way out!" Darrel says, starting to organize the other diners.

The three men leave huffily, the smaller guy looking around with something akin to curiosity. I quickly tap into his mind. It's not something we try to do that often, since it's sort of frowned on in most company. Still, I quickly fuzz over his memories here so he'll recall coming to the pub, but not the details of our conversations. I do the same to the other two to make things easier on everyone. As if we need more problems.

"You took care of them?" Dysnomia asks.

"Yeah, they're good to go." I nod.

"Good of you. No wonder this place was so busy. It was crawling with mortals all this time," Apate says with a curl of her lip.

Dysnomia groans. "We sold a few cups of ambrosia to mortals. This is going to get us in major shit if anything happens to them. Darrel! Find any mortals with a black X on their hands and have them stay. We'll control them, but we need to keep watch and make sure that the ambrosia doesn't harm them."

Darrel gives a quick nod. "I'll send them your way."

By the time all of the customers have left—including the supernatural clientele— we're watching over six mortals. Luckily, they all only have one X, which means they're not dealing with double the dose of poison. I mean, it's pretty strong for supernaturals. It's definitely too much for mortals. You can tell they're hopping.

Dysnomia makes quick work of their minds. She makes sure that they'll stay sitting and complacent, which is good since people tripping on ambrosia are known to hallucinate. Luckily, after her handiwork they're all in a good little trance. The only thing for them is to wait until it's out of their systems, which could take up to eight hours.

"Are they all right?" Olly asks, eyeing them with concern.

Apate shrugs. "Yeah, they're under our spell! So far they're okay, but we'll keep an eye on them to make sure they don't go south. Which can happen pretty fast."

"Did you call Ares?" I ask.

Olly says, "Darrel is telling the other staff to leave for the day, that it's food poisoning. Then he's going to call Ares and have him meet us over here. So far we're keeping it on the down low."

"What happened? I thought mortals weren't supposed to be able to notice the place?" Apate asks.

"Either the witches' spell failed or they removed it," Olly says grimly. "No matter which, Ares isn't going to be happy. They're the only witch coven for hours around."

"Felicity sure does wield power with the others." Dys whistles.

Olly winces. "I wouldn't say that around Ares if I were you."

Darrel comes out of the kitchen and heads straight for us. "Thanks for handling the mortals. Ares said he'll be right over with the rest of you goddesses and a few other people. We're all supposed to wait for him."

"Wouldn't miss it for the world." Apate makes herself comfortable on a barstool.

Darrel turns to Dysnomia and me. "Is there any way you can make the mortals take directions from Skip or Jordy? I'd like them to watch the humans in the basement while the rest of us are meeting."

"Sure, let me do a quick rewiring. Just don't let them abuse the power, all right? I'm setting them to listen to Skip," Dysnomia says, then closes her eyes to focus.

Olly eyes us warily. "I'm not sure how I feel about magic like this."

"It's our goddess-given right, so I suppose it doesn't really matter how you feel about it," I tell him.

"Oh, shush, Ana, let the boy have his confidence! Olly, in case you wanted to know, we're not really supposed to use our bigger powers on you guys. One of Ares's rules. It seems to be a common one where we go. A whole 'don't hurt other guests or allies' type of thing," Apate tells him.

"Apate! Did you really have to tell him that? We could have had so much fun," I whine.

Dysnomia opens her eyes, then jumps into the conversation. "With everything else going on, do you really think rocking the boat is the best thing to do?"

"What have they done to my pub!" Ares cries, rushing in dramatically.

"Who dared tamper with my brother's beloved house of food? I will *kill* them and make a maraca of their teeth and knee caps!" Enyo says savagely. She spots Apate, Dysnomia, and me. "Did I tell you Lyssa and I are going to start a band? It will be our first instrument!"

"Oh, man," Dysnomia mutters.

"That there's crazy on two legs." Apate nods.

Lyssa walks in next and says, "Ugh, it stinks of mortal in here now. Mortal and mutt. Someone . . . spray something in here. I may gag."

"Most of the world is made of mortals," Aergia mutters, trailing a blanket behind her, then lying down on the bar top.

"Something else I one day hope to change about Earth." Lyssa nods firmly, as if Aergia has reminded her of an important task on her to-do list.

"Let's all focus on the problem at hand, please. Are you all sure that the witches' spell has been broken? It could have simply been a few mortals with minimal mimmortal blood in their genetics," Nemesis says calmly.

I shake my head. "Three random guys who were in no way related? That's a negative. Plus, we have six others in the basement who are fully human, as Dysnomia knows from digging around in their noggins. They've had some ambrosia, so we're keeping them for observation."

Nemesis nods. "Good of you to be careful."

I can't help but freeze and turn my head when I catch a scent that I've gotten to know better than I thought I would. I hadn't noticed Max enter the fray, what with the others' dramatic entrance. But there he is in the back of the room, looking calm and ready for anything. What an ass.

"Get a grip, girl," Dysnomia says, knocking into my shoulder. I try to relax and will my claws to shrink back up.

"The real question is, if those low-class magicians meant to do this, or if it was an accident. I suppose I could forgive them if it were the latter. If it's the former, it means war!" Ares says.

"I hate to break it to you, but we're already at war with the supernatural community at large over here. I don't think you want to welcome new members to that list with open arms," Apate tells him dryly. Ares ignores her, as he's rather used to doing.

"Tell me where they congregate and I'll go to them. I will find out if it was an accident or not," Enyo promises.

"Thanks, but killing people at this point probably wouldn't be helpful," Apate shoots her down.

Enyo glares at her until Lyssa pats her head soothingly. Creepy girls.

Nemesis holds up a hand for silence. "What we're going to do is not overreact or panic until we have all of the information. First, how are the mortals afflicted by ambrosia doing?"

"So far, they are well. They're all seeing mild hallucinations, but I've made sure that they cannot do anything to injure themselves or others. They're currently being watched by Skip and Jordy," Dysnomia reports.

"Make sure that all precautions are taken so that they see their way through this. Ares, you know that if you've been found to supply humans with ambrosia, you will be held to the immortal law of no distribution of harmful substances to mortals. Keeping these humans alive should be your priority, not revenge," Nemesis says in her empty voice, yet still comes off as scolding.

He pouts lightly. "I do have two of my men watching over them."

She simply raises a brow at him, then talks to the few other shifters. "They should be watched for at least twelve hours, to make sure that they will face no adverse effects. Make sure this happens. If they do seem to be becoming ill, find one of us immortals. We are better equipped to take care of them in such a situation. Do not take them to a hospital under any circumstances."

"Do as she says," Ares says when they subtly turn to him.

"Now to deal with the spell's malfunction. If it was done deliberately, there's nothing we can do about it. If it was an accident, they are incompetent, and we will need to find someone else able to sustain the spell," Nemesis says.

"They're the only coven for miles around!" Ares blasts.

She looks at him calmly. "Throwing a tantrum isn't going to change that. You'll either have to be prepared to deal with mortal clients or get a witch from farther away. The choice is yours."

He semi-silently seethes. Which means he mutters angrily to himself.

"We for sure can't have mortals trampling about. I mean, we'd have to hide the fighting and ambrosia. Plus, you know a drunk mimmortal is pretty much an open book. Or when there's a fight. Like they'll be good at hiding their powers!" Apate says with a sad shake of her head. "I just don't think so."

Ares nods his head at that. "The shifters do tend to be a rowdy bunch."

"Probably always shifting shape, then pissing in the corners," Apate adds with distaste. The shifters glower in her direction but are smart enough not to comment.

Ares sighs. "Fine, close up the pub for the rest of the day. I'll make some calls and see if I can find anyone to fix this mess. Until then, we'll remain closed. That doesn't mean I want you all to slack off, though! There are still things for you to do . . . around . . . places."

The shifters smirk, knowing they'll be getting a vacation.

"Darrel, you're in charge of closing up shop. Apate, Ana, Dysnomia, if you could continue your duties by watching the humans?" Ares says to us.

I open my mouth. "Actually, I'm not working today—"

Nemesis gives me a dark look. "You will continue here with Dysnomia and Apate. I'm sure, between the three of you, there won't be any problems. I expect you'll have to stay here through the evening. Call if you need blankets or anything brought over."

"Oh, great. A sleepover," Dysnomia mutters.

Nemi cuts her a sharp glance.

"Right, well, as fun as helping close this place down sounds . . .

we have very important mortals waiting for us in the basement. Catch you players on the flip side," Apate says with a fake little wave.

The three of us are downstairs before any of them have a chance to say a thing. Little worker bees for our respected leaders. The humans have been put in one of the side rooms in the basement. It's pretty comfortable, with chairs, a television, couches, and everything one would need for hardcore relaxing. The six hopped-up, drooling mortals are lounging about.

"Hey, Skip, we got this now," Dysnomia tells the werewolf, waving him away regally.

He jumps, not having realized we'd entered. He turns to Jordy, who is similarly surprised, then looks around the room at the mortals. Quickly, and without question, they pack up the cards they'd been playing and leave. It's good to have such wonderful help. Then again, they've probably learned not to question Ares much. He can get so crabby.

"Don't worry, I took the power you had over the mortals back," Dysnomia mutters at the door they've already left.

We survey the humans, watching them for any ill effects from the drug. Luckily, most of them are larger men who should quickly metabolize the ambrosia. There's one thin woman and a younger male who may have more trouble processing it through their systems, though. We will have to keep a closer eye on them.

"Don't worry, everything is going to be okay," Apate tells them soothingly, and I think everyone in the room can hear the lie in her words.

CHAPTER 10

MAX

"Y OU NEED TO COME TO the pub as soon as possible!" Ana says into the phone, sounding panicked. "Find Nemesis and Ares and come right away."

She hangs up before I have the chance to respond.

It's the first time she's willingly spoken to me since the incident in her room. Something dire must have happened for her to call me in a mad search for Nemesis and Ares. My heart starts to thud with worry for her and our pack.

"Ares, Nemesis, we need to go back to the pub," I interrupt their conversation to tell them.

For the past few hours they've been on the phone calling various magic users to see if they could fix the spell. So far, they haven't had much luck. The coven we've hired in the past isn't accepting our calls, and no one seems to want to go against the community by helping us.

"What's wrong?" Nemesis's eyes light on me.

"That was Ana on the phone. She said that we need to get to the pub as soon as possible," I explain, hoping that my urgency comes across.

Nemesis frowns. "That's all she said? Whom did she ask for?"

"You and Ares. We need to get there now. She sounded really worried on the phone," I persist.

Nemesis quickly stands, pulling Ares with her. "We need to get to the pub *now*. What if something happened to the humans? They will never forgive us if a human overdoses."

"The community?" I can't help but ask, more concerned with the human lives than our stupid political blunders.

"No, not the community," Ares says grimly. "The Olympians."

We rush to the pub, and it's chillingly quiet when we open the front door. We make our way quickly to the stairs, taking them two at a time to make it to the basement in record time. In one of the side rooms, five humans are sitting on couches with glazed eyes. Apate is with them, watching them closely for any signs of illness.

"Where's Ana?" I ask in confusion. "She just called."

Apate gives us a look, and I know without a doubt that whatever she's about to say won't be good news. "Ana and Dysnomia took him to the other room. We didn't want to upset the others."

Apate motions across the hall to the storage room.

Nemesis pushes me out of the way, quickly opening the storage room door to hopefully help the human. "Goddess, what happened?" she whispers coldly.

Ares and I elbow our way into the room with her. There's a small man, young and slim, lying on the cement floor. Blood seeps from his mouth, ears, and eyes and gathers in a pool of red around him. Ana is crouched over his body, straddling his waist. Her eyes have bled black, blood dripping form her mouth and her wrist.

"We tried to save him. We did everything we could. He was just so weak. So young and small . . . barely even legal," Dysnomia says in a broken voice, bringing our attention to where she's standing with a large knife, a fresh wound on her arm.

"What did you do?" Nemesis asks.

"He started to seize and bleed out. I attempted to take some of the toxins from his blood, and give him some of ours. It had already reached his brain and heart. It was too late," Ana explains, hissing around her bloodied fangs.

"This is it. They're going to send me back for this." Ares runs a hand across his beard. "The Olympians will never understand that this was a mistake, that we didn't even intend to give any mortals ambrosia."

Nemesis shudders. "We'll have to explain that the spell was deactivated, causing this unfortunate mistake. It wasn't purposely or callously done."

"They don't care about the intent. What they care about is the result. God, why couldn't you two take care of this for me? Why couldn't you do something right for once? I trusted you to take care of the humans, and you couldn't do that one simple task? Now I'm the one who'll bear punishment for your incompetence!" Ares thunders at Ana and Dysnomia.

"What are you talking about?" I seem to have lost control of my mouth. "They're here helping us after you continuously made enemies of everyone in our community. They were here looking after the humans, while you were across the street making *phone calls*. Ana just had to deal with a human dying in her arms over an accident that she would have no involvement in, if not for you. Now you want to blame *her*!"

Ares takes a threatening step toward me, raising his arms. "How dare you—"

Nemesis steps in front of me, "Ares, what is done is done. Trying to blame others isn't going to change the outcome. We need to deal with this."

Ares lowers his arms, taking a calming breath. "You're right. I'll contact someone to come take care of the body. Is Apate okay with the other humans?"

"I'll stay with her and help make sure that the others are okay," Nemesis confirms.

My phone rings loudly, making everyone turn toward me. I answer quickly. "What's going on?" I ask Darrel.

"The witches called. They'll be here in an hour," Darrel explains.

I look over at Ares and Nemesis, knowing from their expressions that they've heard what Darrel said. "We'll be back at the house in a moment."

"If they hadn't deactivated the spell, none of this would have happened," Ares rages. "They should have at least warned us that humans would no longer be deterred from the pub. They brought death to our door."

Nemesis says coldly, "We will handle the witches. Go back to the house and prepare, Ares. I'll be there after I check on Apate. I'll send Enyo and Lyssa to collect the body. We will get this taken care of, one way or another."

The two of them sweep out of the room, clearly on a mission. Dysnomia gives me a hazy look before stumbling after them. Ana stays on the ground, eyes downcast. I've never seen her look so small and breakable before. She's never seemed less immortal than at this moment.

"Come on, Ana. We need to get you cleaned up." I walk toward her.

She looks up at me blankly. "You shouldn't have said those things to Ares. You shouldn't provoke his anger."

I feel my own anger ignite, remembering his words. "He should never have tried to blame you for what happened. You did everything you could, and should never have been put in this situation to begin with."

Ana is silent for a moment before whispering, "You think so? I should have realized he was ill sooner . . . I could have done more . . ."

I ignore her words and scoop her up into my arms. She's stiff against me for a tense moment, before she relaxes and falls against my chest. Her arms circle my body, her nose burying into my neck, where she scents me and gives a little sigh of comfort. I know that Ana has led a difficult life, and that death isn't something new to her. Unnecessary and accidental death should never be something someone becomes accustomed to.

It's like déjà vu as I carry her in my arms back to the house. She waves her arms around, using magic to traffic and making others on the street not give us a second glance. I hold her tightly, worried at her blood loss and the emotional trauma of the situation. At the house, I quickly take her to the room she's been sharing with the other girls, hoping to get her cleaned up and presentable.

"Do I need to bandage your arm?" I ask her, rooting around her side of the room for a change of clothes.

I find piles of clothes haphazardly thrown around. I grab an outfit that's wrinkled but appears to be clean. When I look back at where I've set her down, it's to find her eyes half closed and her arms wrapped around herself.

"No, it's already closed," she mutters.

"We need to wash the blood off of you," I say hesitantly.

I reach out to her, and she lets me grasp her hand, leading her to the bathroom. I turn on the water, playing with the temperature until it's hot but not scalding. Before I can ask if she needs my help, she's torn her shirt off, pants and undergarments quickly discarded.

She steps into the shower, calmly placing herself directly below the spray of water. Ana closes her eyes and just stands there, body language defeated. Without giving it a thought, I strip out of my clothes and follow her into the shower. I put my arms around her, purely offering comfort. She leans against me, allowing me to hold her despite everything else going on.

I lather my hands with shampoo, massaging the suds into her hair. The ends are sticky with blood, and it takes me a while to untangle them. I tip her head back and rinse the hair before lathering it again, until the water runs clear.

I take her body wash and gently rub her back and shoulders clean. I trail my hands down her arms and back up, massaging as I wash her skin. Ana's eyes close, and she becomes less and less stiff the longer I touch her. I try to ignore her wet, soft skin, even as my eyes devour the sight. She's so damn beautiful, I have to remind myself of the circumstances that brought us here.

Ana brushes against me when she moves to rinse off, and I'm instantly embarrassed of my arousal. She arches her back to rub herself firmly against me, but I grip her hips and hold her away from my body.

"It's not about that, Ana, it's about making sure you're taken care of," I say hoarsely.

"But you want me," Ana replies in obvious confusion. "Don't you?"

"I never don't want you, but this isn't the time. I've been meaning to talk to you, to explain my behavior the other day. I know that it seemed like I was using you or rejecting you, but that wasn't what I meant. I was trying to take myself out of the situation before you pushed me out the door," I say.

It's probably not the right time to bring it up, but I can't keep letting her think that I didn't want her, or didn't enjoy every moment we had together. Just because the truth is embarrassing doesn't mean she isn't owed an explanation. If I could go back in time, I would have never left her bed.

Ana turns toward me in surprise. "Why would I push you out the door? I know it was just a hook up, and that's fine, but I also thought that we were becoming friends."

I look away for a moment, not sure how many of my insecurities I should shed light on. "I know I'm not the typical guy you hang out with. Guys like Olly are more your type. I know that you're out of my league, and I didn't want to overstay my welcome. What happened between us was perfect, and I didn't want it ruined by seeing you regret it."

"I don't live by regrets. When I want something, I go after it. I'm too old to play games like that. Don't sell yourself short. I wouldn't have been with you if I didn't want to," Ana says softly.

"I'm sorry. I'm so incredibly sorry for telling you thank you and suggesting I didn't want anyone to think I was with you. I'm sorry for making you feel unwanted or like you aren't special. That's the last thing in the world I want. I wish I could always make you feel wanted and like the most special woman in the world, because you are. You're so amazing, and I'm sorry for making you feel like anything less than the most important and spectacular person. You don't deserve anything less than the best," I murmur to her, holding her close.

Ana holds me tightly. "Thank you for saying that, even after what you saw today. I know how it must have looked, me over the body with blood all over. I was only trying to help him."

"What do you mean?" I ask.

"I tried to save him, despite my gifts, I really tried . . ."

I grip her chin, forcing her to make eye contact with me. "I know that you tried. I know that your gifts don't define you. You did the right thing today, and even though his life wasn't able to be saved, that wasn't your fault. You did everything you could have for him. Don't let anyone try to tell you otherwise."

"I know things have been tense between us, but thank you for taking care of me. Thank you for caring about me," Ana whispers against my neck, holding me close.

"I'm glad that I was there for you. I know we haven't known each other long, but I feel like there's a connection between us. It might just be friendship, but I feel like we could be close if we wanted to. I would like that," I confess.

I feel Ana kiss where my shoulder meets my neck. "I would like that too. I can always use more true friends, the ones I can count on."

"You can count on me."

I let myself hold her under the water until the heat seeps away and it becomes cool. Then I pull her out and dutifully dry her off. She dresses herself in the clothes I grabbed for her without comment, pulling her long hair back as I dry myself off.

"Will you be okay here while I go get a change of clothes?" I ask her.

Ana gives me a subdued smile. "I'm okay, Max, really. It was an unfortunate situation, and I won't pretend that it didn't affect me. When an innocent person dies in my arms, it will always affect me. That doesn't mean I'll break down. I'll be okay."

I smile back at her, unbelievably proud of her strength. I don't know if I would be handling things so well if it had been me in her place. I grip her hand and give it a comforting squeeze before resigning myself to going. I wrap the towel around my waist and go to the door, peeking out to see if anyone is nearby.

As I'm shutting the door behind me, Enyo comes rushing down the hall.

"Is Ana in there? Tell her to hurry up and get downstairs. The witches are coming!"

CHAPTER 11

REALLY? FIVE WAYWARD WITCHES CAUSED this mess?" Lyssa whispers loudly from the seat next to me. Max, on my other side, gives my hand a comforting squeeze. I'm not sure what I think about this new development yet. All I know is that I needed someone, and he was there. He gave me exactly what I needed without demanding anything in return or making me ask. His presence is comforting, his support intoxicating.

Ares, Darrel, and assorted pack members have gathered in addition to Nemesis and the rest of the girls. Apate is still at the pub with the humans and a medic, just in case something happens. Nemesis examined them and didn't anticipate any concerns. Now it's just waiting for the drug to pass.

"Not exactly 'wayward,' sweetheart," a tall, dark-haired witch says with a sarcastic smile.

Ares quickly points to them and says, "That's Jax. The others are Candy, Tess, Brent, and Dex."

"Pleased to meet you," the somber Tess says.

"Did Ares tell you about the spell malfunctioning?" Nemesis asks, her eyes taking them in with no mercy.

Tess's lips quirk, her dark blue eyes flashing. "Not exactly. We knew that there would be some . . . problems today."

"Meaning?" Ares asks dryly.

"We purposely disabled the spell."

"What were you thinking?" Darrel asks.

Tess shakes her head, white-blonde hair flying everywhere.

"I know it must come as a surprise to you. The fact is that you've made some very powerful enemies here in town. Ones who happen to be our allies. I'm sure you can appreciate the political pinch we were put in. It's not that we like to make moves against paying customers, but we also don't want to step on any of the toes that you've managed to tromp on."

"You may not have realized this, but Ares is a rather large power player," I point out.

Tess nods in agreement. "He is indeed the most powerful being I've ever met. That doesn't change the fact that he doesn't have the best contacts here in town, which is the issue. I can't stand beside him instead of others, who could do more damage to our careers."

"All of you came here just to explain that?" Enyo asks aggressively, though she shuts up when Nemesis jabs her ruthlessly with her elbow.

Tess explains, "We are willing to reactivate the spell."

"Really? Then go for it," Ares says.

She shakes her head. "It's not quite that easy. I would like to show that we've made some sort of consistent resistance against you. Stopping the spell unexpectedly was a good start. Charging you an inflated fee to 'fix it' would be . . . better."

"I see," Ares says darkly. "What is the inflated price you'd charge for reestablishing the spell?"

Tess calmly pulls out a piece of paper and scribbles the price. The paper is then handed to Ares. When he glances down, his eyes widen considerably. Which kind of means something, since Olympians have poor understanding of money.

"We paid less than a quarter of this to get the spell in place to begin with!" Ares thunders, the house subtly shaking from his anger.

"We'll figure it out," I tell him soothingly.

Ares just glares at everyone like they're all at fault. In his twisted mind, maybe they are.

Tess shrugs. "We can't risk doing the spell for any less. We'll give you a day to pull your funds together, if needed. It's all we can offer at this point."

"Unacceptable," Ares hisses, eyes flashing a warning of full red. I have to give her credit for seeming as calm as possible.

"It's the only offer you'll receive from us. The word has also been spread in the magic community that you've been labeled Untouchable," Tess says.

"What the fuck does that mean? Like he has herpes or something?" Dys asks in confusion.

Nemesis levels her with a swift kick to the shin. How mature.

"Under supernatural law, we're unable to refuse anyone service. Prices are still at our discretion. Those who are Untouchable get the worst service and highest prices. We will make it as hard for you as possible to navigate through our community," Tess explains.

"So you're saying that if he doesn't pay this price and have you reactivate the spell, the chances of him getting some other coven to do it is pretty much zilch?" Darrel asks, eyes wide with shock.

"It was a rather dangerous stunt you pulled," Nemesis says chillingly.

"What do you mean?" Tess asks.

"In stopping the spell, you made it possible for mortals to enter the pub. We were also selling ambrosia. Since it was assumed that everyone there was a supernatural creature of some sort, mortals were served," Nemesis says.

Tess's face clouds over, but she finally says, "This is no fault of ours. You shouldn't be selling ambrosia as it is. It goes against a direct council vote. The fault lies solely on all of you."

"One of the mortals died. Do you care about that?" I can't help but ask bitterly, seeing red at her blasé attitude.

Max gently grips my thigh, offering his strength.

"You allowed one of the mortals to overdose?" Tess asks in shock. "You should have prevented it!"

"Mortals react differently to ambrosia than mortal immortals. This is why we got the spell in the first place, to protect the humans! Removing the spell was one thing, but failing to inform us caused this," Ares thunders. "Your negligence cost this young man his life!"

This time, Nemesis just nods.

"We didn't sell poison to him to begin with!" Jax says hotly. "You'll bet the council will hear about this. Then you'll have no leg to stand on. You might as well leave town now."

"You're right, the council will hear about this. I'll be telling them that due to your actions, a life was lost," Nemesis warns them.

"We won't be paying the new price for your unreliable magic, and we certainly won't take the blame for this situation. You'll be leaving this town long before we do," Ares tells them.

"You realize this is your only option, right?" the smart-mouth Jax says.

Ares looks at him with a scathing glare.

"The decision was made," Nemesis says coldly. She doesn't appreciate the witches baiting an obviously unstable immortal any more than the rest of us.

"It's your problem anyway. As far as I see it, you forced our hands. We were only trying to keep peace with all of you by this offer. Now, you're on your own." Jax sneers.

"Leave, or I won't just take your lives for your impertinence," Ares tells them with a deadly calm.

Tess's eyes are dark with understanding, but Jax still looks cocky.

I turn to Jax and say, "Sweetie, he's telling you he'll torture your precious little body before ripping off your head. Or punish your family as well. Nope, your magic won't help you. We've found cutting out witches' tongues and chopping off your fingers makes it hard to cast spells. Oh, I wouldn't raise your hand up at me like that. I have magic too, you know. Obviously you don't know much of it, or you'd sure as fuck be out of this room by now."

Jax keeps his finger firmly pointed at me, then starts muttering under his breath.

I cloak myself in a protective layer of power. When the spell hits me, I feel barely a tap. Clearly he's both young and unskilled. Jax is merely a witch; the lowest guild of spellcaster compared to sorcerers and wizards. He looks confused when nothing happens.

"Does the witch wanna play?" I mutter with a little grin, aggression quickly filling me after everything that's happened today.

I stand abruptly and jump onto the table. I run swiftly across it so I'm only a graceful blur to the naked mimmortal eye. I kneel before the silly witch, with his finger outstretched as if to harm *me*. How naïve those of the mortal world have become. I grasp the finger and, with a flick of the wrist, bend it back until I hear that beautiful, telling pop.

His eyes widen and start to water with pain.

I pull my hand out to gently stroke his hair. "You silly, stupid boy. Go home and read about every supernatural creature there is, since they are all stronger than you, and you don't want to be caught off guard again, do you?"

He does nothing, so I grip his head by the hair and shake his head no.

"Ana . . ." Nemesis begins.

I feel my fangs lengthen threateningly as I look back at her. "He slighted *me*. His life is *mine*."

"I do not question this." Nemesis sighs, knowing I am right and my nature won't let me walk away without punishment.

"Mercy!" Tess asks desperately.

I turn to her, smiling until my fangs bite into my lower lip. "As he would have shown me? That spell was meant for pain, as we both know. If I had been mortal or he more skilled, I would be crippled."

Tess hangs her head, having no contradiction to that.

"Is a broken finger a lesson learned? A life given freely?" I ask her, running a long, sharpened claw lovingly down his cheek.

I'm sure if he knew that my fangs and claws are very, very poisonous he would tremble twice as violently. As it is, I'm good at evading flesh unless it's my intended target. If the silly twit thinks I'll kill him for that halfhearted spell, he deserves anything I give him.

"I didn't mean to!" he cries.

I tsk. "Don't lie to me. It's so unappealing. We both know you meant to do it, and would be pleased right now if your spell had succeeded. Surely now you know better than to trifle with beings stronger than yourself. Don't challenge danger if you have no hope for protection. It's just unwise. It shows disrespect to you and me both."

I look to Ares.

He nods regally. "It would be a clean kill. He made the first move against you. These mortals must learn that we are their superiors in every way. Fear is sometimes a healthy thing."

He certainly seems in better spirits now that there's a life on the line.

I look deeply into Tess's eyes. "I will spare his life. In return, I would like you to keep Ares's name off of the Untouchable list. Also, if I so much as catch a whiff that you mean me harm? I will fucking *kill* you."

Jax nods frantically when I release his neck.

I turn to Tess, who says, "It is a worthy trade."

Jax makes as if to stand and leave.

I flick my head to the side and mutter, "My spirit is not satisfied with a finger." With that said, I quickly stand on the table so we're the same height. With an iron grip, I grasp his shoulders and drag him closer to me. Like a snake springing to attack, I coil and launch myself at him with no mercy. I slide my fangs deeply into the meat of his neck, feeling him stiffen and gasp with pain as a drop of venom flows into his system. I allow his life blood, full of his essence, to fill my mouth before pulling back and spitting it out.

Jax gasps and stumbles away from me when I let him go, gripping his bloodied neck with fear in his eyes. His coven mates press close to him protectively, eyeing me warily.

"Something to remember me by." I smile.

"Will it always hurt?" he asks, voice husky with pain.

I shake my head. "No, it will fade, and it will not kill you. I will, however, be able to reactivate the venom there if you displease me. A little incentive not to come back for revenge."

"Reactivate?" Jax asks in surprise.

I shrug, and focus on the poison. He gives a shout of surprise. "I control the amount of pain."

"I think it's time for you all to go now," Nemesis suggests. "I'm sure you'll be hearing from us or the council shortly."

Tess watches us with cold, calculating eyes, the last to leave the room. None of us get up to make sure they make their way from the house all right.

"Was all of that necessary?" Darrel asks.

"He slighted one of my own. That deserves punishment. You all need to learn that I have been very, very lenient with all of you. Other immortals will not be. That right there? It was mercy. Times are not like they used to be, but we still must receive payment for certain acts," Ares says coldly. "I personally would have done worse."

Nemesis nods. "It was rather tame. Good job, Ana. You forget that she is the Daimon of Ruthlessness. The spirits inside of us hunger for what they desire. We've learned to control them to a degree, but to do nothing? Impossible."

"What are we going to do about the pub?" Darrel jumps in.

"I'll make some phone calls." Ares sniffs importantly. "I think it might be time to meet with the council."

CHAPTER 12

I TIPTOE AROUND THE DARKENED HOUSE, thankful that my immortal genes allow me to see everything clearly. I can't help but smile to myself, thinking of how the day turned out. Even through the stress, Max stayed by my side.

Ares and Nemesis were able to set up a meeting with the council a few days from now. They gave them the brief version of what happened with the witches, and even if they aren't on our side, it certainly didn't sound like they were on the coven's either. We might be able to get through this after all.

Nemesis tracked down the human's family and informed them of the loss. He was a young college kid who passed much too soon. We set up an anonymous fund and used magic to get them to accept it. It'll never make up for the loss, but at least it might help in their time of need.

Now, in the wee hours of the morning, I can't bring myself to sleep. I creep along the hallway until I find the tantalizing scent I've been searching for. Soundlessly, I ease the door open, looking inside with interest.

It's a tasteful room decorated in muted blues and grays. It's mainly a simple bed, side table, dresser, and desk. Fairly nondescript and masculine. I expected his room to be a bit more decorated, what with his preppy style. Sure, the bedspread is striped blue and gray with a few decorative pillows on top, but that's it.

I close the door behind me, walking quietly to the side of his bed. I pull my nightgown off until I'm completely bare, knowing that he finds me rather attractive in this state. I can't stop myself from stroking his relaxed, sleepy, content face until his eyes begin to blink open.

Max's mouth falls open. "Dreaming?" His voice is husky from sleep.

"You said it wasn't a good time earlier. I thought this might be a better one." I grin.

He smiles at me, that magnificent smile that turns my insides to jelly. That self-satisfied man smile mixed with disbelieving little boy. It's enough to make a girl power-drunk! I shouldn't be able to make anyone happy enough to smile at me like that. Not someone as old, jaded, and, well, evil as me. That's the smile of innocence and joy. It should never, ever be directed at me. But, there it is.

"Is that a yes?" I ask.

"Not just yes, but *hell yes.*"

Max laughingly growls as he grips me around the waist and pulls me onto the bed. I jokingly shriek and kick out so he has to grip me even more firmly. He maneuvers us until I'm under his body, my arms pinned above my head and his legs straddling me.

I close my eyes briefly as he leans forward to nuzzle and kiss my neck.

"Did you miss me?" I tease.

"I was dreaming about you." Max chuckles against my ear, his lips tugging and sucking on my earlobe.

I clear my throat against the rush of sensation. It's always felt like my ears have a direct line down to my clit. I'm not entirely sure why. Every little suck and nip feels like he's touching an entirely different part of my body, in the best possible way. I lean into his touch without entirely realizing it.

"Like that?" he asks, bringing up a hand to rub my other ear. I feel myself get wetter and more needy to have him inside me.

"Do *not,*" I gasp.

Max suddenly let's go of my ear in order to look me in the eyes. "My mistake, then."

I can't help but pout at that. He lets go of my wrists so he can lift a finger to flick my lip. I suck his finger into my mouth and swirl my tongue around it. He quickly removes it and taps my nose with it.

"Now, now, don't be naughty." He grins.

I pout more. "Can't I have any fun?" I sigh.

"If I can't have fun, then you can't either," Max tells me.

I brush my hair back. "Well, I suppose I do kinda, sorta like that thing you were doing. A little bit."

"A little bit?" He raises a brow at me.

"Okay, a lot a bit." I roll my eyes.

Max just smiles at me. I lay back and wrap my legs around him, then pull. He ends up lying on top of me, body flush against mine. I love the feel of him completely on top of me, his weight pinning me down. I arch my hips up and grind against his hardening dick, never happier to find a man who sleeps in the nude. He closes his eyes at the sudden sensation.

I grin at him when he opens them. "I want you. Inside me. Now."

He groans at my words and sits up, making me frown at the loss of his body. "No," Max tells me.

"No?" I ask.

He smiles at me, his nipple rings glistening in the light. "It's been so long since I've seen my new best friends! How are you two doing?" he asks my breasts, cupping each of them with a hand. He leans forward as if listening to them, then looks up to me and says sternly, "They say they've missed me."

I can't help but giggle. "I'm sure they have."

"What's that?" he says, leaning down once more, his thumbs gently rubbing against my nipples. "They say that we should visit one another more often. We'll need to have more play dates. For their sake, of course."

"Of course." I grin, reaching up to trace his muscles and gently pinch his nipples, playing his the little hoops in them.

Max hisses out a breath. "None of that."

"No?" I pout once again.

"No," Max says, then bucks his hips against me, rubbing his dick against me without entering. "None of that *yet.*"

"You're such a tease," I complain, even as it makes my blood race with excitement.

Max sits back up, straddling me. He moves back slightly and brings his hands down to lightly stroke my stomach. He reaches down farther, lightly stroking and exploring me. I moan as he makes small circular motions around my clit. About time! I need more. More now.

"Are you wet for me, love?" he asks with a smile, his eyes seeming to devour me.

I make a little noise, and he looks down into my eyes. Seeming to know exactly what I need, he bends down until his mouth brushes against mine. He rubs his lips against my own, his tongue opening my lips to tangle and dance with mine. All of the sensations drive me into a frenzy for more.

"Max," I say as a command against his lips.

I put my legs around him, preparing myself for the intrusion. He gently bucks his hips against mine until his hard length rubs against my opening . . . then away. I gasp at the sensation and disappointment. Then he does it again.

That little tease!

I arch my hips up, trying to urge him forward. He grips either side of me to hold me down firmly. I moan at the sensation of being so conquered in the most intimate way. He bucks his hips forward to rub against my clit, then away again. So close, yet so far. I feel myself become a mass of needy, wanting sensation. He moves his hips above me, rubbing and finally entering me suddenly and completely. Amazingly full. I gasp at the awareness of having him inside me at last.

"Was that what you wanted?" he asks in a strained voice, carefully unmoving.

"Oh, yes!" I respond enthusiastically, without thought.

Max chuckles lightly, moving out of me just to drive home once more. I wrap my legs more firmly around him, moving with his body as he works in and out at a fast and steady pace. I can feel myself grow tight around him, so close to being there.

He stops his perfect rhythm and grabs my legs. He moves

back from the bed, pulling me with him by my legs. The repositioning leaves him standing at the end of the bed and me lying with my hips at the edge and my legs still wrapped firmly around his hips. He drives into me deeply and rushes in again and again so fast, and harder than before. It sends me spiraling into oblivion and a sensation so sweet it must be wrong.

Max groans as I come, saying, "So tight. So wet."

"For you," I agree.

Max pushes me back farther on the bed when he feels me stop spasming around him. I look up at him, eager for more. He jerks my legs apart firmly, still careful not to hurt me. Max gives a swift and thorough lick to my center, making me gasp. He really isn't taking any prisoners this time. He licks my clit at a steady rhythm as he fingers me at the same time. Just as I feel another orgasm coming on, I jerk back from him.

"No," I tell him this time.

He looks up at me in confusion. "No?"

"I'm supposed to come with you inside me."

Max's face suddenly stills, then opens into a slow and sweet smile. He covers my body with his own and wraps his arms around me. I feel so completely enveloped in him. So amazingly protected and cared for. He looks down at me tenderly and gently rubs his mouth against mine. I gasp and arch into him to kiss him more completely, matching his tenderness. Max deepens the kiss slowly, tightening his arms around me as his tongue plunges into my mouth to tangle with mine. I put my arms around him to hold him as close to me as possible.

As he kisses me more passionately yet, he reaches down to stroke along my side, touching every sensitive inch of me and making me come apart. I pull against his back, urging him closer as I arch into him with a rush of feeling. When I can't take it anymore, he enters me once again, his dick hard and throbbing. He enters me slowly and steadily, looking at me the entire time, making me gasp at the sensations and intimacy of it all. I lean up so I can kiss him deeply as I feel myself get close once more.

I quickly fall in love with the sensation of his tongue in my mouth while his dick is in my body. I tilt my hips and match his slow and steady rhythm. I feel myself clutching him inside of me, driving me crazy. He moves to kiss along my neck and up to my ear, gently biting. I feel my claws lengthen, and without meaning to, I sink them in his back as I try to pull him closer, even though we're already as close as two people can get.

"Going . . . to . . . come," he says shakily against my mouth.

"Oh yes," I gasp back, feeling myself so close as well.

He groans against my mouth, surging forward into me just as I tighten and spasm around him once more. I arch up into him until we're both sighing with release. He collapses against my chest, lying on top of me for a few moments as both of us catch our breath.

"Sorry," he says, lifting his chest off of me and starting to move to the side.

I wrap my legs and arms around him tightly, keeping him in place. "For what?"

"I can't exactly be light." He laughs.

I snuggle into him happily, relishing the weight of him. "You're fine where you are. In fact, you're great where you are."

He laughs but relaxes on top of me. "I am, huh?"

Max seems to like it when I tell him these little things. "You are."

We're silent for a few minutes, relaxing in the perfection of the moment.

"We should probably talk about what just happened. Don't you think?" Max asks me finally.

I frown. "Talk about what?"

"We just did that thing that we said we probably shouldn't do again, in the near future at least. Don't you think we should talk about that so the same thing doesn't happen as last time?" he asks.

"I seriously doubt you're stupid enough to say the same thing twice. Especially since I decided to rock your world." I snort.

He raises an eyebrow at me.

I sigh. "Fine, you rocked my world too."

"I just think talking about it wouldn't hurt," he continues.

I look up into his eyes. I know he means best, but seriously, talk things out? That almost always ends poorly. I mean, what does he want me to say? It was awesome, but I'm not sure what he's looking for here. Praise?

"It was even better than the first time," I tell him.

"It usually is," he agrees.

I nod. "True. It rarely gets worse."

"So . . . we're still friends?" Max asks.

"Intimate friends," I agree.

Max frowns a little, then rolls off of me, making me instantly miss the weight of him. "Is there anything else you want to say? Nothing has changed or anything?"

"Um, no? Things were great. Nothing that feels that amazing can be a mistake . . . right?"

"Nope. Of course not," Max agrees, putting an arm around me and giving me a wild dog smile.

I move into his arms, resting my head on his chest. "It never is."

He looks at me with those big, sweet eyes, and I realize I don't really know him at all. It feels as if we're so connected and understand each other on a level I can't even comprehend. A totally different way than I'm connected with my girls, but surprisingly just as strong. Nothing so random can be real. Nothing so fast and consuming can last. I don't even know him, and he definitely doesn't know me.

We won't last. I can feel that with every fiber of my being. Not in a sad way, but I know he's not for me. I feel so abstractly certain of this, deep in my bones. It's a fact, and you can't get emotional about facts. We are not meant for each other, and we won't be together for long, even if I let this flirtation continue.

I'm too old and too wise for this.

Thoughts keep rolling in my head, again and again. I'm not sure why, since I've never really been the one to think things out for an extensive amount of time. I just feel off, different. He shouldn't be able to invade my mind like this. I don't want him there. Just as my thoughts turn angry, Max interrupts them. He wraps his arms around me and holds me tight to his chest.

"We're okay," he tells me.

I don't know what he's talking about, and I doubt he does either, but it actually helps. Which is surprising, since I don't even know what's wrong. I'm not sure when I started having so many messy emotions and doubts, but I don't like them. At all.

"Max?" I ask him softly.

"Yes?"

"Don't hurt me." A quiet confession. Barely acknowledgeable in the light of day.

Max holds me closer. "Never. Never ever."

Chapter 13

S ERIOUSLY? YOU FORGAVE HIM?" DYSNOMIA asks. Dys, Apate, and I are lounging in front of the pub. Even though it's closed down, we have information to hand out about the grand reopening in a week. At least, we all hope a week is enough time. Ares is already going a little stir crazy.

"Don't you know we have rules for a reason? You aren't following them at all!" Apate adds.

I sigh. "The rules haven't exactly led me down the right path in the past. Just saying, if things aren't working, why stick with them? Besides, Lawless, are you really preaching rules to me?"

Dysnomia bristles. "That was Apate! I, of course, totally respect your decision to be a rebel and do your own thing. On the other hand, I don't want to have to hear you bitch about this at a later date. Seriously. If this all blows up in your face, I want nothing to do with it. There's only so much we can help you if you aren't willing to help yourself."

"I don't know why you guys are making such a big deal out of this! It's really not that major," I protest.

"Riiiiight. You've only decided to be exclusive with the wild dog for the remainder of your time here. Not a big deal at all. I'm still not sure how the little bastard pulled it off." Dysnomia shakes her head. "There are just some things you can't come back from. Look at Peitho."

"Oh, Zeus! She is not a cautionary tale, you crazy bitch. Peitho is happy," I exclaim.

"Sure she is. At least, she thinks she is. Now that Peitho is soon to join the cultish lifestyle of wife and mother." Dysnomia sighs.

"Now it's a cult? Really? I wonder how Peitho would like it if I told her that's what you think?" I say threateningly, pulling out my phone from its conveniently placed hiding spot—my bra.

"Don't tell her I said that!" Dysnomia shouts, making a dive at me to tackle the phone away.

I sidestep, and she lands heavily on the ground.

"Then don't be a bitch. She's happy."

Dys sighs and props herself up on her elbows. "I know she is. It doesn't mean we all need to follow in her footsteps."

"Max and I agreeing not to see other people while I'm here visiting is smart. It's hardly comparable to Peitho being pregnant and getting married. It means that I have a go-to person for ass. It makes things simpler, not more complicated!" I say.

"Uh-huh, as if you're just after easy ass. I don't want to alarm you, but getting ass isn't exactly *hard* for you. It's not really *work* to find someone willing to sleep with you," Apate says mockingly.

I huff, then mumble, "Well, I guess I kinda, sorta . . . like him a bit. Just a little. Nothing serious."

"This sounds less and less serious the more you explain about it," Apate says sarcastically.

"You just like him a little?" Dysnomia asks.

"Yeah, just a little," I confirm.

"Even if that were true, which I highly doubt, that's still more than you've liked anyone in, oh . . . centuries! Besides, we're totally not buying it that you're practically impartial. We know you have a soft spot for the little mutt. Though I don't understand it, quite frankly. Have you looked in the mirror? Suddenly been hit with a case of low self-esteem? You know you could do so much better," Dysnomia says. "At the very least, someone who's truly immortal."

I stare at her for a moment. "That's unfair, and you know it."

"He isn't worthy!" Dysnomia says sharply.

Apate steps between us. "Dysnomia, you know that it isn't

your place to say or even think that. Besides, it's untrue. Don't ruin this little adventure of Ana's just because you can't deal with your own issues. Yeah, I went there, and you know I'm right. Do you really not want Ana to have a chance of happiness—granted, not lasting happiness—just because you're jealous?"

The three of us are silent after that outburst.

I'm not really sure what to say. I've been close with Dysnomia for the last few centuries, but before that, she spent more time with Nemesis. Before that, she was mostly with Lyssa and Enyo in battle. Which pretty much shows the natural progression of violence and unhappiness. Back then was when Kydo and Dys had their big falling out. The two of them have fooled around since, but never been the same.

I guess she still isn't quite over it. At all. I don't know the entire story. She doesn't talk about it much, and we weren't a group back then. It was so long ago, we hadn't yet learned to lean on one another. We were so young and innocent. We were invincible. All good things come to an end.

"You're right. I was out of line," she admits softly. "Nothing I say matters anyway. I want you to do what you want to. No one else knows how you feel."

I nod. "I was trying to pretend that this wasn't a big deal to myself, I guess. But it is. If I'm not going to be serious then I shouldn't do it. It's not fair to the other people involved. Decisions are hard, though."

"There are many paths in life you can choose to walk. Some of them may be better than others. For humans, it's a scary thought. For immortals, it's scarier. We have the ability to walk them all and make all mistakes possible. Again and again. When was the last time you took a chance? Take a chance on him. You could end up happier than you have ever been," Apate suggests.

"I'm not unhappy," I protest.

"If you're suddenly okay with the mediocre life you've been living, then we have so much more to talk about than your fake relationship status," Apate counters with a raised eyebrow and half-smile.

"Point taken. I deserve more than that. Extraordinary!" I grin.

Dysnomia smiles at us a bit weakly. "You sure do. We all deserve something extraordinary. Love isn't the be-all and end-all. We can have anything we want. Anything at all. Just have to decide what that is!"

"Maybe you'll be the next one to ascend," Apate speculates.

"What do you mean?"

"Peitho was able to ascend when she found the love of her life. Maybe Max will be able to help you ascend, then we'll be one step closer to the end goal," Apate says.

"Then I take back anything negative I ever said about the two of you being in a relationship. You're totally meant to be and should work as hard as possible at ascending," Dys states. "It will only help us in the long run!"

"Thanks for caring about my happiness," I tell her dryly.

Could they be right? Could Max be the person who will help me bind my powers to Earth? Sure, I'm eager for more power and to finally break away from Olympus, but I didn't give the rest of it much thought until now. Am I ready to be in a serious relationship? Am I ready to be completely vulnerable and put my heart on the line?

"You'll have to let me know how it goes. I'm pretty sure it'll take me a while to find Mr. Right, assuming I'm ever able to. Sorry, it might slow down our progress with taking over Earth," Dys says glumly.

"Clearly, it happens when you least expect it!" Apate reassures her.

"Until then, what will we do to keep us busy while everyone else drops like flies and leaves us behind?" Dys asks.

Apate claps in excitement. "We could all start having babies! We can create an immortal army!"

A petite woman walking toward the house looks up at us with raised brows. "You'd have cute kids."

My mouth drops.

"Yeah, but, unfortunately, they haven't found a way to combine all three of our DNA together. It would be the perfect kid. Fingers crossed that in a few years, they'll have it in the works!" Dys tells her.

Apate gives me an evil grin. "You've met Max's sister, Sophie, right?"

I look at the woman in shock. "Nice to meet you! We're not really having babies."

She nods. "Just don't let Max put it off forever. He's not getting any younger, and I'm ready to be an aunt. Plus, if you have a few of his babies, I'm pretty sure it would be way harder for you to leave him when he inevitably says something stupid."

Dys and Apate fall over themselves laughing.

"I'll keep that in mind!" I sputter as she walks away. I turn to Apate with narrowed eyes. "You knew she was walking by, I'm guessing."

Apate starts wiping tears from her eyes. "I'm not sure whose face was more priceless. Yours, Sophie's, or Dys's!"

"You guys suck."

"What's family for?" Apate grins.

"Look alive, girls! The eagle has landed!" Dys says.

Apate and I give her a look. "Did you shart in your pants, again?" Apate asks.

Dys glares at her. "I thought we agreed to never talk about that. Ever. And for the record, I was really drunk. It's not as if that was real life."

"But you being drunk *is* real life."

"Hey, are you three immortals?" A group consisting of about fifteen people ranging in age and looks approaches, the middle-aged woman who spoke obviously their designated spokesperson.

Apate motions dismissively at the flyers detailing the reopening of the pub.

"I'll take that as a yes," the woman says. "I'm Farrah, and I represent the local supernatural clients in this area."

A few from the group nod in agreement, others twitch, and the rest look around uncomfortably. I give a subtle sniff to confirm that all of them are supernatural. They are, but, surprisingly, not all of the same species. If my nose is right, and it's rarely wrong, there are different kinds of shifters, a siren or two, nymph, and a witch hidden in there. Only one thing could have brought them all together.

"Let me guess . . . by clients, you mean you're interested in some services that Ares usually provides you?" I ask.

Farrah looks at me in surprise. "No, we've never really gone to Ares for our needs. The people whom we normally go to are on strike, though. I believe they said someone named Felicity had something to do with it. We make it a habit to stay out of pack politics, and we don't appreciate when we're dragged into them."

I sigh. "I see where this is going. Dys and Apate, you're going to have to take one for the team. I'm guessing the guys are here for handies or blowies. I'll have to go get Ares so he can take care of you and the rest of the ladies, if that's okay with you?"

"Whoa, I can be the one to go get Ares for you!" Dys argues.

The three of us turn to one another with glares.

"Wait!" Farrah gets in the middle of us. "What kind of services did you think we're looking for?"

"Um. Well . . . erm. What kind are you looking for?" I ask after a moment.

She sighs. "We're talking about drugs, not prostitution."

"Oh, thank goddess! Not that drugs are good, mind you. They're very bad for you and a horrible habit to start," Apate tells them sternly. "I, personally, have never done them. My strong religious beliefs help me say no to temptation."

Dys and I take a moment to roll our eyes at one another over that.

"Why would your drug dealer stop supplying you? That kind of ruins their business, doesn't it?" I ask.

"They haven't stopped selling to everyone. Just people who live in Ares's territory, pay for his protection, or have come here to the pub on a regular basis. We all fall under one of those categories," Farrah explains.

"That sucks for you guys." Apate sends them a sympathetic glance.

Farrah's eyes narrow. "Yeah, we aren't too happy about it. We're being punished for supporting your pack. We want retribution."

"No, let's get real. You want your fix."

"That too," one of the guys speaks up to say.

There's a general murmur amongst them. Looks like all of them want their drug of choice, whatever that may be.

"I'm not sure what you expect us to do about it. We don't have drugs. We don't sell them or supply them or have them in general," Dysnomia tells them in a rather dismissive tone.

"We either want you to find some for us or make it up to us with ambrosia," Farrah says, the others behind her nodding as a united front.

"Let's back it up a bit. How do you expect us to find you drugs? I'm assuming that not all of you are using or on the same thing. You can't expect us to just give you ambrosia instead of that. It might get you by, but it's not something you should be on long-term. It's also our product, and we aren't going to hand it out for free just because you all asked us to," I say, putting my foot down.

Farrah shrugs. "We aren't leaving here without something. It's your fault that we're in this mess to begin with. So it's up to your pack to fix it."

"What's going on, guys?" Olly asks, coming up behind us.

I frown at him. "We're going to need Ares. Tell him to meet us down in the basement. Apate, go clear things up down there. We better settle this and settle it quickly."

These people are right to think that ambrosia would be the answer if they can't get their usual fix. Some of them might be recreational users, but others are going to go through withdrawal if they don't get their buzz on within a certain amount of time. Ambrosia can help with that. It makes detoxing better. To an addict, it can be especially addictive, though. In reality, it isn't that addictive a drug to immortals or mimmortals. Under normal circumstances, anyway.

"Follow me," I tell the group.

"Is Ares on his way?" I ask Olly when he pops up again, after I've gotten everyone settled calmly, for the time being, at least.

"Yeah, he might be a minute. I interrupted his bath. He wasn't all that happy," Olly explains.

"He is such a divo sometimes," Apate says and rolls her eyes.

"Did you just call me a divo?" Ares asks, walking in with damp hair. He ignores the mimmortals, giving them a moment to get used to his aura of power and roguish good looks.

Apate shrugs. "Did not."

"Really? Because I could have sworn that I heard you call me a divo. Not that I even know what that means," Ares continues, shaking his damp hair.

"It's the male form of diva. If someone were to call you one, which I did not, then they would be calling you a diva. Which you couldn't really blame one for doing, since everyone knows that you are."

"I have never heard anything so absurd," Ares says.

"I know!" Olly agrees. "To come up with a male form of—"

"I mean, I'm obviously not a divo!" Ares says, ignoring Olly. "That would be Apollo. Or maybe even Zeus. I'm much too rugged to be a divo."

Dysnomia laughs. "I know that you and Peitho have gone for a manicure together before, so you might want to rethink your argument."

"That is not being a divo. That is simply taking care of yourself and your body," Ares protests.

The mimmortals look like they're about to lose control at that.

"Um, Ares, the reason that we called you here is because Felicity has bullied the local drug dealers into refusing to sell to regulars here at the pub, those who buy protection from you and the pack, or who live in your territory," I explain.

Ares looks at the people gathered around, then turns to me and shrugs a little. "So? Times are tough for all of us. We might as well suffer like a pack."

"That's the thing. We shouldn't all suffer because we aren't all a pack. Some of us have bought your protection through necessity, or happen to live on land that falls under your pack's territory. We don't take part in wolf politics. We just want to buy our drugs and carry on our lives like usual," Farrah argues.

"Should have thought of that before you picked a fight with the neighboring wolf pack," Ares tells her.

Farrah frowns. "We didn't; you did."

Ares nods. "I see your confusion."

"Because we don't have any conflicts with anyone and therefore shouldn't be suffering?"

"I understand why you would think that." He smiles.

"I don't think we're on the same page here." Farrah frowns. "We either want you to be able to supply our drugs, or we want you to give us ambrosia. It's the only fair thing to do. It's your pack's fault that we can't just go buy our goods like usual. It's up to you to take care of us."

"It's nice of you to offer your business to us, but we just aren't into the whole drug-selling thing. Thanks again for the offer!" Ares smiles brightly.

Farrah shakes her head. "If we can't buy our drugs from our normal dealers and you refuse to sell them or supply them to us, then I think you should make it up to us by giving us ambrosia. It's not fair that we aren't able to buy from our dealers just because you're having a fight with Felicity's gang and we've been dragged into it."

"You should have thought of that before taking our side. Now you all have to deal with the consequences. Maybe you can take up caffeine or exercising instead," Ares suggests.

"That's really not the same thing," Farrah protests.

"Well, if you're all really upset about this, you can always feel free to speak with Felicity about it. After all, she is the reason you aren't able to buy your drugs. She's the one who won't let your dealers sell them to you. I've stayed out of such matters. In fact, this really has nothing to do with me. If you want to complain to someone, either complain to your dealers or Felicity," Ares suggests.

"You know as well as I do that going to Felicity won't do any good," Farrah says.

"Neither is coming here. I don't know what you expect me to do about it. I can't make them sell you all drugs," Ares says.

I cough. "You probably could try, at least."

"Either that or we expect ambrosia as compensation," one of them insists again.

"You won't be getting that. Let's just say ambrosia is probably much more expensive than whatever any of you are buying. We aren't just going to hand it out to you so you can go home without hurt feelings," Ares says.

"Why don't you give us a day to try to figure things out so you're able to go about your business as usual, buying from whom you normally do and everything," I suggest to them.

Farrah turns to the others, talking and thinking it out for a minute. I can feel Ares and Dysnomia get bored and contemplate using their magic to move things along. I shake my head at them.

"You have one day. We'll be back tomorrow at this time, and you better have figured out a solution by then."

Ares gives them a dismissive look. "Or what?"

Farrah shrugs. "You don't want to piss us off. There are a lot more of us than are just gathered here, from all different levels of power."

"So?" he asks.

Farrah just gives a little smile, her pale blue eyes flashing. "You'll find out."

Apate, Ares, Dys, and I watch all of the druggies go back upstairs to leave. Once they're out of the room, I turn to Ares and say, "I don't think the wolf was bluffing. Some people in their group probably are more powerful than you'd assume. There are a few things out there that you don't want to mess with. A supernatural's drugs is one of them."

Dysnomia nods. "It's a quick way to make some real enemies. We don't need any more than we already have."

"What do you suggest I do?" Ares huffs.

"I suggest that you put on your big boy panties and make an arrangement with some dealers!" Apate tells him.

"Fine. I'll get one of my minions to make up a list of them for me. Though why this has fallen upon my shoulders, I'll never understand. Why can't it be like the good old days when a man could move somewhere, start a gang, begin running the town, and own a restaurant/drug house in peace and quiet! These silly mimmortals have grown above their station, thinking they can challenge me instead of just agreeing I am supreme. Too bad we have all those pesky rules about how much power we can use," Ares complains.

"If you want to show off your power, you can. Back in Olympus. Go push around people who are your size, figuratively speaking," Apate suggests.

The three of us look at him hopefully.

Ares huffs some more. "It's a bit boring back there. It's kind of nice here in the mortal world. Where no one knows you and your whole life story. Olympus can be such a small town. A bit cliquey, you know?"

I roll my eyes. "Nope, never would have guessed."

CHAPTER 14

W HY ARE YOU DRESSED LIKE that?" I ask Max, raising my eyebrows.

He looks down at himself in surprise, then back up at me. "I'm not sure how to answer that."

I feel Apate, Reggie, and Olly stifle laughter from behind me.

"You look ridiculous. Is that really how you think drug users or dealers dress?" I ask him.

Max puffs up his chest, looking even more insane. He has on a tight black shirt, long gold chain, sunglasses, a backwards baseball cap, and jeans that are too big so they're falling off his ass. His boxers are black as well, instead of his normal pastels. What he thinks he's doing is beyond me.

"You're asking *me* what *I'm* wearing? What about you? We're going to see drug dealers. You look more like you're going to a pimp looking for a job!" Max counters.

I have to stiffen my mouth so I don't smile.

"You've got a chain on," I say, as if that proves my entire point. Then again, when it comes down to it, it kind of does.

"It's stylish. Jewelry isn't just for women, you know," Max tells me.

Dysnomia snorts. "I don't think she's commenting on it because of a gender thing."

Ares walks into the foyer with Darrel, and both of them stop to give Max a not so subtle once-over. "Go change," Ares dismisses him.

"What do you mean?" he asks in exasperation.

Ares tilts his head at him. "Good point. It would probably be best if you just stay here and wait for our return. Can you make me one of those ice cream sandwiches you're so good at making?"

"A cookiewich? Wait! No, I'm going to this meeting with you!" Max says. "I can be really persuasive when I want to be."

"Clearly that must mean we've never seen him really want to be." Darrel laughs.

Max frowns, glaring at Ares and Darrel laughing at him.

Olly joins in. "Sure the chain is ridiculous, but I think it's the hat that puts him over the edge. It just doesn't look right. At all. You look like a kid trying to fit in with the cool crowd or something. And failing."

I frown. It's one thing for me to tease him, but for the rest of the guys to? That's just unacceptable. That completely emasculates him and makes it mean of me to tease him instead of cute and snappy, like we usually are! They're ruining our entire dynamic. Time to put the ball back in his court.

I put a twitch in my step as I sashay up to him and trail a finger down his chest. "Now, Max, do you really want to go with us to the 'bad side of town' or would you rather make us a tasty snack and conserve your energy for later?"

"Conserve my energy . . . ?" he repeats.

I give a firm nod. "Mmmhmm, conserve your energy. You're kind of going to need it. Oh, and you might not want to change. This little outfit has kind of grown on me. I'm just a good girl looking for a bad boy to corrupt me. Of course, I hope I don't get corrupted too much. I'd hate to have to get a spanking."

Max's mouth drops open. "Bad boy . . ."

I grab a hold of the chain around his neck and yank his head down. I give him a short, intense kiss, biting his lip when I pull away. "No need to be shy, Max. No one can blame you for succumbing to me. Everyone knows that I get what I want. Go get yourself ready, and I'll be back in two hours, tops."

I turn Max around and push him away, ignoring that cute, dazed look on his face.

"Ready to go, or what?" I ask the others, pleased to see their surprised faces.

If my girls are surprised that I'm not trying to hide my little interlude with Max, they really shouldn't be. For one thing, there's nothing worth hiding. I've never been ashamed of my needs or who I share them with. Shamelessness isn't a state of being. It's a way of life.

"Subtle much?" Apate raises a brow.

"What's the point of being subtle? You'll just hear it all later tonight, anyway." I give her a saucy wink.

Ares bursts out laughing and gives me a smack on the ass. "Oh, damn, I've missed you, Shameless. You're like the perfect combination of Peitho and Enyo. A really sexy killer. Never tell them I said that, of course."

"I'll be too busy trying to forget you said it! Comparing me to those two? For real?" I smack him away.

Olly shakes his head, looking amused. "Some things you can just never guess. Come on, let's go to the meeting before they think we're standing them up. It's enough that I got all of them to agree to meet in one place to begin with. There's a lot of rivalry between them, as I'm sure you can imagine."

"They have a system of seniority and ranking to decide who's allowed to sell what. That way there's less competition between them and they can work together more," Darrel explains.

"That's . . . very organized," Apate says.

"Criminals are very organized now, or hadn't you realized yet?" I say.

"Where's Dys?" Apate asks, looking around.

"She opted out of this one. Trying to fix things, organize them, and come to a compromise is kind of getting to her. You know, Lawless doesn't handle these sorts of things well," I point out.

"Does that mean . . ."

"Oh, yeah." I nod.

"Ready to go?" Nemesis asks, walking out in full glory. Her hair is pulled back in an unsexy bun. She's wearing tight jeans, heavy-duty boots, and a black halter top. The halter top is mainly due to the large feathered wings sprouting from her back. Normally, she keeps them hidden under a thin layer of skin, showing only as an intricate tattoo.

"A bit worked up, huh?"

Nemesis casts her a dark look. "Is there something wrong with my natural state?"

"Nope, none at all." I zip my lips.

Clearly all of this conflict and backstabbing is getting to her primal nature as well. Can't say that I blame her. If I had her particular powers, I'd be scoping out everyone and righting a few wrongs. Or just causing a few wrongs in the hope of balance. She has more control than that, though. Nemesis has a system so she doesn't create more chaos from her deeds.

Nemesis pulls out a pair of thin black glasses and puts them on. "Well?"

"You wear glasses now?" Ares asks in surprise.

Nemesis gives him a condescending look. "They're for flying. It also helps block the wind from my eyes. All of the benefits of a helmet without the helmet hair."

"I'll drive!" Ares offers as we leave the compound.

With that Nemesis quickly scampers out of sight, none of us even seeing her catch flight. Just like our fearless leader to leave Apate and me behind in the midst of life-threatening danger. I'm not sure if I've seen Ares drive since his first car. Which was a good several decades ago. And was a hell of a lot slower.

"I thought we'd take my car," Darrel says quickly. "Yours isn't big enough for all of us."

"Fine," Ares huffs. "I get gun shot, of course."

Reggie giggles. "He means shotgun. None of us have the heart to tell him the correct phrase. Plus, it would just take away from future fun," she whispers.

"Where are we going?" I ask after a moment of driving.

"Number one's office," Darrel says.

"They get offices now? I wonder if there's a benefit package," Apate contemplates.

"How many of them are there?" Reggie asks.

"Four, from what I understand," Darrel says. "Their leader is a siren. Then there's a nymph, troll, and elf. Kind of a misfit group, if you ask me."

"No creatures of significant power, at least," Ares says.

I frown at him. "Just because they don't have great offensive magic doesn't mean you should count them out of hand. All of their skills are mainly toward the defensive and persuasive. Which is worse in our case than pure offensive would be."

"Yes, yes, the skippy woodland creatures shouldn't be underestimated." He rolls his eyes.

"Don't say I didn't tell you so." I shrug.

Sure, he might screw everything up, but at the same time, I don't think the Olympians expect a miracle from us. They know that this whole mission is riding on how cooperative Ares wants to be. They won't be pleased with us if we fail, but they'll also understand there's only so much we can do.

We pull up to a rather nice building. It's all tall and shiny, with marble floors and engraved names. The kind of building you might go to if you wanted to talk finance, see a therapist, or visit a publisher. Not the kind of place you would go to hoping to score your regular fix. Then again, this is the type of place I'd want to go to for such a thing.

"Third floor." Darrel leads us into the building in typical pack fashion, and right into the elevator.

"I hate elevator music," Nemesis comments as the doors close.

All of us turn to her. "Where did you come from?"

"The sky?" she counters.

"Immortals." Reggie sighs as we shrug it off and move on.

At the third floor, Darrel leads us to the receptionist's desk, who is busy typing away on her computer. "Can I help you?"

"We have a meeting with Celine," Darrel says.

Ares looks around, shifting from foot to foot in a no-good antsy manner.

"Name, please?"

"Ares," Darrel says.

"Right this way, please." She stands up and leads us through a hallway to what I'm guessing is either an office or a conference room.

There are already four people inside. One is a pretty dark-haired woman with brown eyes. The other is tan with brown hair and green eyes. One of the men is huge and sturdy with short brown hair. The other man is slender with light curly hair. All in all, not at all what Max would have been expecting.

The woman sitting at the head of the table with the dark hair and brown eyes stands up and offers a practiced smile. "Hello, I'm Celine. You must be Ares."

That's when I know this meeting isn't going to go well. She shakes Darrel's hand.

"I'm Ares, actually," the man in question says firmly, stepping forward and practically knocking Darrel into the wall. He might be a wolf and therefore larger than the average human, but he still has nothing on the size and muscle mass of the God of War. That's just to be expected.

Celine blinks but doesn't break face. She calmly offers Ares her hand and says, "It's a pleasure to finally meet you. As you can imagine, we've heard much about you and your group of werewolves."

"I'm sure you have," Ares answers, finishing off the handshake and sitting down with a thump. In her seat. At the head of the table.

I can see Celine think about it and then decide that you really have to choose your battles wisely. She takes the seat after the three people from her party, across the table. Ares motions for us to sit at his left. I sit next to him so that I can kick his shins if necessary. In battle, he might be correct. In negotiation, he's forever wrong.

"What can we do to help you?" Celine asks after a moment of silence.

"We've been informed that you won't sell to patrons of our bar or gang. We'd like you to continue to supply them with what they need," Ares says.

Celine smiles. "We hold the right to sell, or not sell, to whomever we choose. We understand that this sometimes displeases individuals, but it's business, after all. I'm sure you can understand that."

"What I understand is, you and your associates aren't being fair. You're discriminating against the people who support me and my business. I don't appreciate that, and I would like to know why you've decided to no longer sell to them. If possible, we can come up with a solution so that my patrons get their product, you get your money, and I don't have to deal with drug addicts suffering just because they've had a meal or two at my pub," Ares says.

"I can appreciate what you're saying, but I don't think that that's going to be possible at this time." Celine smiles artificially.

Ares frowns. "Why did you stop selling to them?"

Celine's smile finally starts to fade a little bit. "Why we decide to sell to some of our select clients isn't something that we feel like discussing with you right now. We have the right to decide whom we want to make our product available to. We decided that we no longer wanted to retain them as clients, it's as simple as that."

"Did that bitch put you up to this?" Ares storms.

Celine raises a perfectly shaped eyebrow. "I'm sure I don't know what you're talking about."

"Look, lady, I'm sure you're not as dumb as you're obviously trying to pretend. So let's cut to the chase. How much is it going to cost me to get you to sell in my territory again?" Ares sighs.

He's never been that good at negotiating.

I cough. "I think what Ares is trying to say, is that we'd be willing to pay an incentive to keep you selling to our patrons."

"There is no amount. Money is not an issue in this case," Celine says blandly.

Apate looks around and lets out a low whistle. "True, money clearly isn't an issue in general. Looks like the drug-selling business is going pretty damn well. Guess the economy isn't that down. Looks to be a good future in it too. You have to be what, three hundred years old? From the looks of it, anyway. Obviously you're doing something right here."

Celine stiffens at the little dig. "We do well for ourselves."

The other woman gives a disdainful cough. "Though what that has to do with this situation, I have no idea."

Apate nods. "Yeah, I'm sure you don't. See, we're always looking for new business opportunities. We get pretty bored, having lived for quite some time, you know. Longer than all of you combined, actually. Ares is always looking for things to spice things up. Getting in the drug market might be just the sort of thing he needs to keep him busy for the next century or so."

The four of them stiffen.

"Who are you, to suggest business ventures to a god?" Celine looks down her nose at Apate.

She smiles that innocent smile. "I'm the Daimon of Deceit, of course. Ares and I? We go way back. That little piece of ass over there? She's Shamelessness, Ruthlessness, and Unforgiveness. You might know my girl Nemesis too. No? Well, here's a helpful tip: don't get on her bad side."

"You hope to intimidate and threaten us? That's not the way to build business relationships," the slender man says silkily.

"You already burned the bridge, love. Can't come back from pissing off a God of War. Didn't you know that? I know it's been a while since any of us have been earthbound, but my goddess. Seems like you would know better than to directly defy a legend." Apate smiles carelessly.

The four of them start to shift uncomfortably.

"There are rules that must be followed. You have rules while you're visiting the mortal world. We are not in true danger," the green-eyed woman says uncertainly.

Ares finally smiles. "Rules?"

Apate, Ares, Nemesis, and I all look at each other and laugh lightly.

"They can try to govern a god, but which of them do you think will actually come down from Olympus to make sure he follows the rules? Better yet, how do you like the odds of anyone coming down here to stop Ares, if they were able to, before he can do any real damage? If I were you, I wouldn't like those odds at all." I giggle.

"You've made your point. What is it you want?" Celine finally asks.

"We want you to continue to sell to the people in my territory," Ares says.

Celine sighs. "We will make you a compromise. We will continue to sell to them, but they must travel outside of your territory, to the surrounding ones. We will sell to them there, not directly on your land. They still get their product, but we can tell . . . others who are not pleased with you that we're not selling on your territory."

Ares frowns. Nemesis lays a hand on his arm and says softly, too softly for the mimmortals to hear, "I think this is the best outcome you could ask for. I know you're not pleased with a compromise, but there's only so much you can ask for without creating more enemies. Well, more obvious enemies."

He nods. "You're right. That doesn't mean I have to pretend to be happy about it."

"What do you say? It is a good offer. Everyone wins," Celine says after what seems like a moment of silence to everyone else in the room.

Ares looks up with hard eyes. "It is unfair to punish my people like this. You and I have no argument. Felicity should not have brought all of you into our slight disagreement. That being said, I do not agree with you refusing to sell on my land. However, I'm willing to agree to your offer if you're willing to sell product at a discounted price to the people from my territory, who are being forced to go out of their way to buy from you."

Celine cocks her head at him. "There is no other option for them to buy from. I am the only one selling product for counties."

"That doesn't change the fact that you're making it harder for them to buy. If I really wanted to, I could import product for them. Hell, I could start selling it myself. Or bring in outside competition for you. Surely you're not under the impression that I don't know such people? Or that they'd be anything other than happy to have more clients and make more money? Possibly extending outside of my own territory? You give me ambition," Ares praises her.

The four of them look at one another.

"Felicity is probably refusing to let her sell in her territory if she continues to sell in yours. This is business for her," Nemesis tells Ares softly.

"This is business for me too. It's Felicity who's put her in this situation. Not me," Ares points out.

"Yes, and who started that conflict?" Nemesis says.

Ares pouts. "I really don't think I'm to blame for that, either! It was just a small prank. I thought mortals were supposed to be famous for their little tricks and joking. Apparently, they take some things too seriously."

"Most people take their pets seriously. Look at you with Enyo and Lyssa." I laugh.

Ares sends me an affectionate look. "Yes, I see what you mean."

"We will give them a ten-percent discount," Celine finally offers.

"Fifteen," Ares counters.

"He really is ruthless," Apate whispers, to which he smiles.

Celine scowls. "Fifteen percent. You have a deal. Our associates will be waiting to hear from them. Please inform your buyers to contact them by phone and see where their new location just outside of your territory is. They will be keeping their normal business hours."

"I will let them know as soon as possible. It was nice to finally meet you." Ares gives his charming smile, the one that he often wears when he's spattered in blood after a particularly invigorating battle.

We stand and file out of the conference room, our business clearly at an end. The four of them stay seated behind us, probably needing to contact their dealers to let them know about the new arrangement. The receptionist stands as we make our way back to her desk.

"I'll show you out," she says brightly, having been told to make sure our asses leave the building.

"Kind of you," I murmur with a little wink.

Ares starts to whistle a little tune as we're led to the elevator, the receptionist pushing the down button for us. After a moment the light goes off and the door opens. She watches us all pile in, her face disappearing as the doors close. Ares's whistling becomes more insistent.

"I think that went very well, all things considered," he says brightly.

"Our druggies will get their supply, so that's a good thing. Especially considering we don't know any mortal drug dealers. At least, I don't," I point out.

"Me either," Ares adds.

Darrel gives him an amazed look. "You mean, you were bluffing in there? They could have easily called your bluff and we'd be left with a bunch of angry detoxing supernaturals!"

"Yes, but the point is that they didn't," Ares says with a smile.

"I can't believe you took such a risk."

Ares raises his brows. "You can't? Silly Darrel, that's what separates us. I'm a leader. I take risks. I negotiate. And I win. You follow me. See how that works?"

Darrel just shakes his head, at a loss for words.

"Granted, he won't mention how many times that kind of logic has gotten him in deep shit. It's amazing that people think with age comes great wisdom. I'm pretty sure none of us have actually learned from our mistakes." Apate laughs.

"Hell no. We would have had to make mistakes in order to learn from them. I don't know about you ladies, but I simply don't make mistakes." Ares sniffs.

Apate and I exchange an amused glance.

"Mistakes are for people too weak to accept the consequences of their actions," Nemesis says coldly.

"Now, guys, mistakes are only . . . human," Darrel finishes lamely.

Reggie gives a laugh that sounds more like a howl. "I think that's kind of their point."

Nemesis smiles. "At least we were able to resolve one conflict. The sooner things are taken care of, the sooner we can go back home."

Apate tilts her head thoughtfully at me. "Yes, I forgot we'll only be here for a couple weeks or so, at most."

Reggie looks surprised. "You're only staying here for a couple more weeks?"

I frown at her. "Yes, of course. Were you expecting us to stay longer?"

Reggie clears her throat, looking uncomfortable. "It just seemed like you guys were all really getting along with us. It will be kind of weird not having you here anymore."

"We were sent here to help resolve the conflict between Ares and the other organized supernaturals in the area. Once we're done, we must move on. We're immortal representatives for the rest of us in Olympus. That means we have other duties. We can't just stay out here for the foreseeable future. Even if we don't have an assignment directly after this one, we have homes that we can go to. People we can see," I say, thinking of Peitho.

"Yes, of course. I just forgot for a moment that you'd be leaving us. All of us," Reggie continues with some significance.

I lift a brow. "I can assure you that we won't be leaving you before everything is resolved, if that's what you're worried about. We'll make sure the community has fully accepted your pack before we leave."

Olly shakes his head a little, looking exasperated. "I don't think Reggie's too worried about that. We can handle ourselves here."

"Then what?" I finally snap.

Apate laughs and punches my shoulder. "Ana, think with your girly brain for a moment. Why would they be worried about you up and leaving? Ares isn't exactly the man they have in mind for whom you'd most affect by your absence. You get what I'm saying? Goddess knows I could spell it out for you. In many languages. You know, if you need me to."

I frown. Oh. They mean Max.

I shrug after a moment, looking up at Olly and Reggie. "Very few things last forever."

CHAPTER 15

~∞~

MAX

I REALLY DON'T UNDERSTAND WHAT WAS wrong with the outfit. Granted, I'm pretty glad I changed back into my normal plaid shirts and a polo before walking over to the pub with Olly to let the junkies know about the compromise. I'm not really sure why we're helping them. True, I have no idea what any of them are buying, but I don't think we should go out of our way to help them buy drugs.

"So, Ares actually agreed?" I ask, surprised.

Olly shrugs. "He didn't have a ton of options at that point. Besides, he definitely worked that compromise around so he got almost everything he wanted out of the deal. In fact, if he thinks back on it, I bet he imagines that the entire compromise was his idea and he managed to trick the others into bending to his will. Or something like that."

"Isn't that how he thinks of every argument?" I ask.

There's a small group of people waiting for us in the basement. They're lounging on chairs, reading, talking, or playing video games. They generally look like pretty normal people. In fact . . . I can't see a gold chain among any of them. Dammit, she was right again.

"Do you have any news for us?" a pretty blonde asks with some authority.

"Hey, Farrah. Yeah, we just got back from meeting with your suppliers. Ares was able to work something out with them," Olly assures her.

"Yes, and . . . ?"

Olly continues, "Bear in mind that they were able to agree on a compromise. So while you all might not be completely pleased, this is the best they were able to do. Which is better than nothing, right?"

"That remains to be seen," Farrah replies.

"Your suppliers have agreed to inform their employees on the outskirts of our territory to sell to you all, as long as it's not directly in our territory. So if you go a short distance away, you can meet with your dealers like normal. You'll also get a fifteen-percent discount off of what you buy, since you'll have to travel a little farther," Olly explains.

Farrah blinks. "You call this a compromise?"

"Well . . ." Olly begins, holding his arms up in a placating way.

She smiles broadly. "This is victory! Do you know how small your little territory is? We could go just a few blocks over and be in neutral territory, just like that. With the fifteen-percent discount, we're really the ones coming out ahead here."

The others start to murmur excitedly, probably planning on how much they should buy in bulk now with their discount, before everyone becomes allies again. Well, at least they aren't upset about not having any door-to-door deliveries anymore or whatever.

"I'm glad it worked out." Olly smiles his handsome, make-every-girl-in-sight-swoon smile.

"Uh-huh." Farrah nods, barely glancing his way as her eyes land on me. She looks down at my loafers and smiles. "I don't think I've met you before. You're not a wolf, are you?"

"What, did my height give it away?" I joke.

She smiles, laughing lightly. "That, or your scent."

Bad form to mention smelling me in public, but whatever. "You're right. I'm not a wolf, I'm a wild dog shifter. One of two wild dogs in Ares's pack. It keeps things interesting."

"I bet." She winks. "How's it been hanging with the wolves? I hope they're not giving the rest of us a bad name."

I shift from foot to foot, slightly uncomfortable. "Nope, it's been working out pretty well. I like it a lot, actually. No plans on leaving them anytime soon, that's for sure."

Farrah cocks her head to the side, leaning closer. "Really? I'm surprised to hear that. I just assumed you were with them until you could find a pack of your own kind."

"If I wanted to do that, I'd be back in Australia."

She laughs again. "Would you like to get a drink? Celebrate our victory? You could tell me more about the Australian packs. I've never been there, myself."

I lean away a bit. "Thanks for the offer, but Ares is expecting us. We'd better get going. We just wanted to let you know how the meeting went. Oh, and they said to call your normal suppliers to find out where they've been relocated. I hope it all works out for you. Let us know if it doesn't."

"Can I have a number to reach—if things don't work out with our suppliers, that is," Felicity asks flirtatiously.

"Go ahead and call the pub. They'll let us know," I tell her with a little smile before turning away, Olly right with me.

"What on earth are you doing?" Olly asks me under his breath.

I look up to him in surprise. "I'm going back to the house, duh. I bet the immortals are out of their stupid meeting by now. As if we don't all know they're in there playing ping pong and gossiping about the ones in Olympus."

"Not that, Max. What were you doing back there with Farrah?"

"Turning her down? I think she was kind of asking me out." I frown as he stops me from walking once we're at the top of the stairs.

"Exactly. Why would you do that?" he asks.

I shrug. "Not that it's any of your business, but Ana and I are kind of seeing each other. We agreed not to see anyone else while she's here. Besides, I'd rather go hang out with her than have a drink with some stranger anyway."

"What's wrong with Farrah? She's cute, has a rocking body, is a shifter like you, and she lives around here. She's a part of the community. That's just the sort of woman you need in your life," Olly tells me.

I frown. "Yeah, but she's not Ana."

"That's kind of the point, Max."

"I'm not sure what you're getting at," I tell him.

"Maybe it would be good if you stop taking this thing with Ana so seriously. It's just a little flirtation. Like Farrah wanted to start with you. It's not going to go anywhere. Not like things could go somewhere with someone like Farrah. I'm just trying to look out for your best interests here, Max. I think you're ready for something more serious than just a little fling," Olly tells me, sounding so serious.

"What makes you think I can't have that with Ana? We're taking things slow right now, but things could eventually become more if we wanted them to," I say.

Olly shakes his head. "Not with a girl like that. She's a wanderer. You barely know anything about her besides she's a troublemaker who splits her time up traveling the mortal world and wreaking havoc in the immortal one. The only reason she's been here so long lately is because she's the immortals' representative on Earth."

"I know she's their representative, but she likes being here in the mortal world. I know I don't know her the best, but that doesn't mean I couldn't get to know her or like what I learn."

"What if you don't have the chance to learn more about each other? I don't think she plans on staying here much more than she needs to. Once Ares and Felicity make up, I think Ana and the rest of the girls are going to be on their way, like usual. I don't think the fight is going to last all that long," Olly says cautiously.

I hadn't really thought about that, to be honest. "No," I say absently, "the fight between them probably won't last much longer. It's running on fumes as it is."

"Then they'll be gone. There'll be no reason for them to stay, and they might get another assignment that will take them out of the area. I'm not trying to be mean. I just want you to look out for yourself. These girls are not the settle down and marry type. I've seen them all before. They're rowdy and crazy and the best sort of fling there is. But they're almost impossible to hold onto," Olly says.

"Yet you've met one that is. Settled down, that is," I point out.

He nods slowly. "Yes, Peitho, the Goddess of Seduction. If any of them were to settle down, that would have been the last one for me to guess. But she is. She even has a kid on the way. Almost impossible to imagine, if I'm being completely honest. You couldn't find a more carefree and wild girl. Back then, at least."

"So it is possible. Maybe Ana and I could try the long-distance thing while we're still getting to know each other. We could talk to each other and visit one another as often as we can or want to," I suggest.

"Do you really think a long-distance relationship could sustain a girl like that?" Olly asks speculatively.

I think of her moaning beneath me, always eager for me. I frown more deeply. "No, I don't imagine that would work out very well after all. Maybe we could date a bit more casually. We wouldn't have to be exclusive. We could see other people while we get to know each other more."

Olly raises a brow. "Would you actually date anyone else? Better yet, would you be fine with knowing she's out there 'seeing' other people, while you care too much about her already to be interested in seeing anyone else?"

I glare at him. "Aren't you supposed to be on my side?"

"I just want you to think about this a little more. If you wanted your relationship to go anywhere, what options are there? Better yet, do you even want it to go anywhere? Or does she?" Olly asks. "Maybe you should just enjoy your fun while you're lucky enough to have it."

With that little bit of advice, he nods his head at me and walks off. He just doesn't understand. I don't flirt or date, and women aren't always asking me out. I don't want them to. I would rather have something a bit more meaningful than a moment of completeness to pretend as if we aren't empty and alone.

I can't help but sigh to myself. Sure, she's the first female I've been even remotely interested in for quite some time. I mean, I've had a few crushes here and there. They rarely went anywhere. I quickly realized it wasn't right and didn't prolong the torture, or they realized it first. Or I waited too long to make a move and someone else did. Which is fine. Clearly they weren't meant for me.

That being said, I suppose there's really nothing for me to do. I can't make her stay with me, I can't go with her uninvited, I don't know where this is going, and I really don't want to end it before I figure it out. That only leaves me with one option. Calm the fuck down and go with the flow. No point in worrying about something before I need to. It's not as if she's about to leave right away. I still have time before I have to panic or make any decisions. With that thought comes a surge of determination. I'm going to enjoy my time with her while I still have it.

As I cross the street, I notice almost every other pack member walking the other direction, toward the pub. In fact, they have almost every immortal with them. I look around for her curvy little body, but I don't see her with them.

"You're going the wrong way," Reggie tells me with a laugh.

"What's going on?" I ask.

"We're celebrating, duh. We totally got one over on the dealers today. We're going to have drinks and dance! Maybe even some bingo!" Ares says.

Apate punches up into the air. "*Yes*, bingo!"

I smile as I watch them walk away for a minute before going up to the house and hoping Ana's still back here instead of off doing who knows what.

"Ana? Are you here?" I ask once I get to the house. "I just saw everyone leave for the pub!"

I don't hear anything. Maybe she really did go out. I mean, why would she have stayed home all by herself? There are tons of other, more exciting things for a creature like her to do. None of them including other men, of course.

I stop to lightly sniff the air, smiling when I catch her scent. I become a bit restless. Louder, I yell as I enter the living room, "Ana, I can smell your scent. I know you're here!"

"One minute, Max! I'll be right down. I know, I know, I'm supposed to be here for you and the others. Constantly on call in case there's a crisis. I hope you aren't looking for me to help deal with one. I'm much too busy at the moment. Especially when there's always a crisis. Nothing new there. What is new, is the package I just got from Peitho! She's such a considerate girl. Sent me something from her new line of products. She's a fashion designer, you know," Ana yells down at me.

I lean against the wall and roll my eyes. Naturally, she's over here trying on new clothes that her equally irresponsible goddess partner in crime sent her. There might always be a crisis when it comes to her, but there are also always new clothes. Maybe Olly was right. I'm just not ready for a girl like this. Or maybe she's not ready for a real relationship.

"Close your eyes!" Ana calls.

I sigh and dutifully close them. "Come on, Ana. I'm not having the best day. Don't tease."

I feel her enter the room and come closer to me, her steps sounding light, as if she's skipping. I can't help but smile a little at that. She is rather carefree. It's nice that even with all of the craziness going on, she can still find something to be cheerful and happy about. Even if it is a new outfit. One I'll probably think is too revealing anyway.

"Open them!" Ana says, sounding breathlessly excited.

I open my eyes, quickly followed by my mouth. I feel my jaw just loosen and fall instantly. This cannot be an outfit. No. Not at all. At least, not for the public. She's in a fluffy white corset that pushes her breasts up high and needy. Under that is a pair of see-through white panties. On her head is a pair of velvety bunny ears, one bent coquettishly forward. Ana's hair curls sweetly under each breast, outlining them perfectly for my starving gaze.

"Neat, huh?" Ana asks cheerfully, coming closer and grabbing each of my hands gently. She turns in my arms and shakes her ass out at me. "Check it, there's even a little tail!"

"There is," I choke out, looking down. There on her perfect, lush ass is a fluffy, round tail to match the fur outlining the neckline of her corset.

"Cute, right?" Ana asks, lacing her hands in mine. She backs up until I'm against the wall, cupping her body with my arms wrapped around her. Then Ana gently rubs up and down against my growing dick, making me harden further. She lets go of my hands and steps away from me slightly, turning around to smile up at me.

I swallow hard. "Why did she send this to you?"

"Why do you think?" Ana rolls her eyes.

"But . . ."

Ana sighs. "Peitho heard from some of the other girls that I've started seeing a wild dog shifter. Exclusively. It's kind of a rare thing for any of us to agree to that. Maybe it was her way of congratulating me. Or joining the club of exclusive whores she's created. Most importantly, she wanted to spice things up, I'd assume."

An invisible weight lifts off my shoulders to hear her talking about our relationship like it's unique and important. It's nice to know that I'm not just one of thousands of other guys who have fallen under her spell. She's exclusively mine. Even her friends recognize the significance.

"I get that, but why a bunny?" I finally say.

Ana laughs and looks down at herself. "You don't like?" she asks, cupping her breasts at me.

My mouth waters. "I wasn't saying that. I just thought it was a curious choice . . ."

"Oh, silly me. I forgot to set the scene." Ana laughs, her golden eyes lighting up. She comes closer to me, pressing me back against the wall. In a breathy whisper, she says, "Imagine it. A dangerous predator out on the hunt. What is he? He's a wild dog, and he's so hungry. He's starving for a bite of soft, succulent, moist flesh. Suddenly, he catches a delicious scent. What could it be? An innocent little bunny just hopping in the woods. Instantly, the dog desires the bunny more than anything, but it hops away . . ."

With that Ana turns to bend over and rub her fluffy ass against my dick once more before playfully and quickly hopping away. Before I've realized what's happening, she's disappeared upstairs once more. I can't help but blink dumbly for a moment before my body, and cock, steer me in the right direction. I start charging up the stairs.

I can't help but become a predator on the hunt. My eyes flick over to the pupils of an animal, colors becoming brighter, sounds sharper, scents richer. I growl under my breath, feeling the canines in my mouth making the air whistle. It doesn't take me long to race up the stairs, following her scent to my room. I rip the door open, making it bang against the wall and bounce back.

There's my little bunny, waiting patiently for me on my bed. I growl my approval as she looks up at me saucily from under her ears. She bends forward on the middle of my bed, arching her back, displaying her ample cleavage to me as well as the sweet curve of her ass. Those delicious breasts that feel so right in my hands, my mouth. The ass that fits so perfectly into my hips as it rubs up and down.

Without thinking about it, I spring forward.

She lets out a joyous laugh full of adrenaline as she jumps out of the way so I bounce against the mattress instead of landing with her cradled in my arms. Mine, all mine. I growl low in my throat, the chase turning me on and making my heart beat faster. That, and knowing that I'll eventually get my way.

"You didn't think it would be that easy, did you? Max, you have to work for anything worth having, silly," she taunts me from the other side of the room, crouched and ready to spring as soon as I make a move. Her eyes are dilated from excitement, making them appear even larger and more animalistic.

I crouch low, like a predator. I stalk forward carefully, eyeing her as my nostrils flare, scenting the room. She smells strongly of power, magic, and lust. I want to bury myself in her scent and cover it with my own.

I gracefully leap off of the bed and move toward the door, blocking the exit. Ana watches me patiently, smiling slightly as she shrugs as if to say, "Oh well, didn't really want to leave anyway."

Ana lies down on my carpeted floor, belly up. She arches her back so only her ass and shoulders are touching the floor, letting her hand trail up her stomach to cup her breasts. She slowly lies back down, lying flat for a moment as she lifts her knees and lets them fall wide open.

I hadn't noticed myself slowly wandering closer to see what she'll do next, until I'm only feet from her. I watch her fingers slowly, oh so slowly, glide down the flat planes of her stomach . . . Suddenly, she springs up and over me, so she's directly by the door. As her hand closes around the knob, ready to leave me, I move faster than I ever have. My body directly behind hers, arms around either side of her, caging her in. With her back to my chest, I slam the door closed again.

I push her aggressively against the door with my body, nudging her legs apart so I can put one of mine between them. I breathe heavily against the back of her neck then give it a long lick, feeling her shiver against me.

She reaches around me, cupping my ass and pulling me more firmly against her so my hard dick grinds into her. I growl more darkly, feeling my control leave me. Which isn't a good thing. When you're half animal, control is crucial. Especially in this sort of situation. "Stop it."

"Make me," Ana challenges.

I grab a fistful of her hair, yanking it and pulling her head to the side for a deep kiss. A brutally impassioned kiss. I will make her feel everything I'm feeling. She will remember the feel of me around her and inside her and what it is to be completely conquered. She will never forget that she is mine. A predator never gives up what's theirs.

Ana gasps against my mouth as she pulls away to bite my lower lip. I groan, the taste of blood in my mouth driving me even crazier, even farther away from reason. I grind against her, pushing into her harder despite the layers of cloth separating us.

Ana turns around and starts yanking at my clothes. The sight of her heavy-lidded eyes and swollen lips make me ache with need. I let her lift the polo shirt over my head so she can run her small, soft hands down my chest and up my back. I keep my arms up around her head, keeping her in place as I kiss her deeply and push my dick against her. She doesn't seem to mind being pinned against my door.

He swiftly ducks under my arms, my passion-clouded mind barely following her movements as she leaps once again to my bed. This time I'm right behind her, and she has nowhere to escape. I rest my body atop hers and pin her down beneath me.

"You will not leave me," I tell her forcibly, voice low and guttural. The beast barely contained.

Ana gasps into my mouth as I rub my cock against her center, her legs wrapped firmly against my waist. She kisses my jaw and up to my mouth, her chest heaving as she breathes shallowly.

"Say it. You cannot escape!" I kiss her punishingly, searing my tongue and heat into her mouth as deeply as I can. I stroke my tongue against hers, mimicking sex. I kiss her hard and deep, then soften my mouth against hers. I rub my lips to hers, sweeping my tongue tenderly along her mouth. "You are mine."

"I'm yours. I cannot escape. I don't want to escape." She sighs, eyes open and looking at me as she says it. "I'm *yours.*"

"Mine," I growl approvingly.

I release her, and she instantly puts her arms around me, holding me even closer to her and urging me to move. I lift up enough to grasp either side of her costume and rip it down, until I can lift the entire front half of it off. The delicate fabric easily comes apart in my hands, Ana writhing beneath me at the sudden freedom.

She claws at the front of my pants, making me realize the long, sharp extensions her nails have become. They don't frighten me or upset me. Not even having them in close proximity to my manhood. Clearly she can be careful and manage not to hurt me. That she's so impassioned they've come out . . . how could that bother me?

When my pants hang in shreds and she sounds frustrated, I put her out of her misery. I reach down to pull my pants and boxers completely off, making her purr in satisfaction. She arches up into me, rubbing herself against my aching flesh.

I groan. "Stop that."

"Make me." She smiles evilly.

I hold her hips down with a tight grip, despite her wiggling. "Who's in control?"

"I am." Ana grins.

I frown. "You are mine." I roll her over until she's on her stomach again. I settle myself between her legs and kiss the back of her neck down to the middle of her back. I lift up until I'm kneeling behind her. "Who's in control?"

"Still me," Ana says, her voice muffled.

I bring my hand down to gently pat her full ass, before bringing it back to slap it with a sting. Ana lets out a hiss as she wiggles beneath me. I rub the newly reddened skin. Then I bring my hand back to slap the other cheek just as hard. She cries out beneath me at the pleasure with a bite of pain.

She moves her hips in a gentle rhythm, and I let my hand slide between her legs to rub against her. I let my fingers stroke her as I bring my hand back to strike her first cheek even harder. She cries out, and I feel a rush of moisture against my hand as she releases.

"I'm yours. You're in control," she gasps as she shakes beneath me.

I roll her over and watch her face as I let the aftershocks wear off. I smile as I rub my head lovingly against her neck, licking, kissing, and nipping against it. When she starts kissing me back I move my lips to hers and surge forward, impaling her suddenly and deeply.

"Max," she gasps into my ear—a sweeter sound than any I've ever heard.

"Mine," I growl in response.

"Yes, yes, yours," she assures me as I withdraw and surge inside her again, repeating the actions.

I stroke inside her again and again, her tight, wet hold on me driving me crazy. I close my eyes as I slow my strokes, making them long and deep. She grasps my ass, trying to get me to quicken my movements. I push deep inside of her and stay there for a moment, making myself ache to move. An ache I know she feels as well.

"Please . . ." she whispers into my ear.

That one word breaks me. Tears me apart until I'm raw. I would do anything for her. I pull all of the way out of her and slam back in, hard. She gasps and arches into my body, claws going to my back as she gently scratches down, making me burn so sweetly. I kiss her deeply, gently as I ride her sweet, heavenly body. Her fangs are out, biting into my lip so my blood mingles with hers.

"Going to—" She doesn't need to finish her sentence.

I feel her grip me harder inside herself as she spasms around me. She gasps and bites into the sensitive curve where my shoulder ends and neck begins. I slam into her as I finally allow my body to release. I feel it roll out of me, feeling such a sense of completion. As if my body is on a higher plane of sensations and understanding. As if she's touching something deep inside me as I'm touching something deep inside her. As if our souls have been bared open and raw to rub against each other in the most wonderful of sensations.

I let my body rest limply on top of her for a moment, completely spent and worn out. After a long moment of silence, I let myself roll off of her and pull her close to my side. She snuggles into me tightly, resting her head on my shoulder. I wince as her head rubs against the spot where her fangs dug deep into my chest.

My eyes widen with shock. "Ana?"

"Hmmm?" she murmurs with closed eyes.

"You marked me."

"What?" Ana opens her eyes with a snap and sits up quickly.

I point at my shoulder with a little smile. "You marked me."

She looks at the offending bite with horror. "What do you mean, marked you?"

"You know exactly what I mean."

Shifters mark their mates. With a bite, their scent integrates with their partner's so everyone knows that the person is taken. They are partnered and protected. They are not looking for anyone else. Marking is rare these days, but is most popular with pack animals, such as myself. Any supernatural with a heightened sense of smell will be able to tell I don't carry just my own wild dog scent. Hers is blended with mine now. I will carry it with me for decades, if not centuries.

"Isn't it the man who must mark a shifter woman? This is just a love bite," she tries to say.

I shake my head, feeling a little frustrated. I brand myself into her body, and she responds by branding me physically. Did she not hear herself as she said she was mine? How can she ignore the proof right before her eyes? I knew that her words were just the heat of the moment, but this act says a different thing entirely. This is not the sort of thing that can be excused by passion. It's one spirit choosing another in the most basic and fundamental of ways.

"You know that's not the only way it works. If you opened up your senses you'd be able to tell that. Smell me," I tell her, backing away slightly.

I feel Ana let down her guard, slowly closing her eyes so her senses can take all of me in. When she opens her eyes, they're completely black, her face blank of emotion. "Somethings happening," she says, her voice distant and detached.

"What's wrong?" I scramble closer to her.

Ana's body begins to glow a glorious red. The air around her feels electric with power, and it's like the world holds its breath to see what will happen next. Her head flings back with such force, I'm afraid that her neck will snap. The glow becomes even brighter as the electricity hits me, flinging my body back.

When my eyes open, the room is back to normal. I jump to my feet, finding her writhing in the middle of the floor, her face drunk with power. "Are you okay?"

Ana purrs, rubbing herself against me. "I've never been better, lover."

"What happened? Do you need anything?" I ask.

"You happened." Ana grins at me happily. "I never knew that it would feel like this to be worshiped."

"What do you mean?"

"Your love and acceptance of me fueled my transformation. You've done the one thing no one else could. You've helped me ascend beyond just a simple daimon from Olympus. Now I'm a true goddess, and my home is Earth. My powers will forever be bound to Earth now," Ana explains.

I shake my head. "I don't understand how that could have happened."

"Your love gave me the strength to see myself as something more than just a minor creature. I could have never done this without you, Max," she says, gripping me to her to kiss me sweetly.

"What does this mean for us?"

Ana smiles. "We were chosen to represent the Olympians on Earth, but we've had our own agenda too. Now we're one step closer to getting rid of their power over us for good. We'll stay here on Earth and discover our newfound power."

"I meant you and me," I clarify.

"Max, I would have never ascended if I didn't feel the love you have for me, and return it," she reassures me.

"So it's not a one-sided thing?" I ask, my heart starting to pound.

"Don't be silly. What we share is infinitely special. I've never felt like this or had a deeper bond with anyone. You're mine and I'm yours."

I can feel my face glowing. "Now I just need to bite you back."

She moans into her hands. "Dammit, the girls are *never* going to let me live that down."

* * *

"I knew this would work out in our favor!" Apate raises her arms in triumph.

"I'm trying to bask in the warm afterglow of my transformation," I complain, cuddling close to Max.

Nemesis sensed my ascension and quickly called a house meeting. I was trying to get a bit more alone time with Max, but she put a stop to that easily enough. I would much rather be cuddling my man and feeling the rush of my new powers than sitting around while the other girls eye me like a freak show.

"Max, you're one of us now. That means you're bound by the house rules. No telling any outsiders what we discuss here, including Ares," Nemesis warns him.

Max grins up at Nemesis. "Don't worry, dogs are loyal. I know to put Ana before anyone else."

"Oh my goddess, I know this is good for the group, but do we have to put up with this level of mushy grossness? It's even worse than the dragon, and I thought he was sappy." Dysnomia shudders. "At least he took her away for a majority of their courtship, so we didn't have to put up with this shit."

"Shut up, you annoying old prude. If you think finding the love of my life will keep me from destroying your ass, you're delusional. Do you feel how powerful I am? I could crush you before you even realized it," I hiss at her.

Max sighs happily at my side when I call him the love of my life. Really, how can I avoid calling him that? He's my ultimate worshiper—he deserves a little credit. Without him I would still be a lowly daimon. I'm in awe that he was able to give enough of himself to me to cause the change. I will never be more grateful for anything than I am that he saw something in me to cause such devotion.

"Since you've been extremely helpful during this mission and have been able to accomplish what everyone else has so far failed to do, we've locked in Australia for you!" Nemesis assures me, ignoring the moans from the others. "Ana, Ares has never been too observant, but try to stay out of his way for the remainder of our time here. I would hate for him to realize your power levels have risen. We don't need any questions."

Max raises a brow at me. "What does that mean?"

"Don't trouble yourself over it. When we all take over Earth, I've won Australia as my territory," I whisper back.

"All of Australia?" he asks in surprise.

I shrug modestly. "Even more worrisome, I still don't think we'll manage to get any privacy."

"This proves my hypothesis about Peitho and Hunter. It takes love to cause the ascension. You know what that means. I need each of you to be on the lookout. No more one-night stands or on-again off-again bullshit. You need to take this seriously and open yourselves up to the possibility of real relationships, and quickly. Now that more of us are transforming, the gods and goddesses might take notice," Nemesis says. "There's no time to waste. We need to complete the ascension before they step in and try to stop us."

"How could they stop us?" Enyo scoffs.

"We're on Earth as their representatives. They could easily order us back to Olympus for any reason they dream up. If we're back there, we'll never be able to tie our powers to Earth," Nemesis reminds her.

"I don't want to fall in love. I just want power," Enyo whines.

Lyssa pats her arm soothingly. "Remember, power comes with sacrifice."

"Did Ana's ascension affect you like Peitho's did?" Apate asks Nemesis.

"It felt different than Peitho's. Her ascension felt like wicked pleasure when the power struck me. Ana's felt exciting and electric when it hit my system, with just an edge of pain. I do feel stronger, but I haven't had time yet to discover what that means," Nemesis explains. "I'm clearly not nearly as strong as Ana in her fully ascended state, but it did fuel something in me."

"I wish it affected all of us like that," Dysnomia says, jealousy apparent in her voice.

"If we all stay focused, we will all be able to ascend. We know what it takes and how to accomplish it, now," Nemesis says confidently.

I look around at the other girls doubtfully. It's hard to picture any of them falling in love or forming lasting relationships. I don't know how Nemesis hopes to pull it off, but I'm glad I'll be there to witness it. Especially for Enyo and Lyssa. Who on earth will they convince to love them?

Out of nowhere, the house begins to shake, and we hear a bellow from downstairs.

Nemesis sighs. "Looks like someone is throwing another tantrum."

CHAPTER 16

W HAT DO YOU MEAN THE money was fake?" Ares
thunders at Reggie.

"What money? What are you talking about?"
Nemesis asks.

Ares shoots her an angry glare. "Reggie went to the bank to
deposit this week's profits into our account. The teller told her
that all of the money we had was counterfeit. Everything that
we've taken in these last few days."

I feel my stomach clench. Oh shit, you don't mess with an
immortal's spending money.

"I had to spend hours being questioned by police on where
the money came from. They were having a hard time believing
it was all revenue from the pub. They actually thought I was
dumb enough to try to deposit counterfeit money!" Reggie says,
offended. "I finally had to break out, or I'd probably still be back
there being questioned like a common criminal. If I knew it was
counterfeit, I obviously wouldn't have taken it there."

"I don't understand. How could this have happened? There's
no way all of our customers just happened to have fake money on
them. That's impossible. Especially without knowing," Darrel
says. "Are you sure it was all fake?"

"Every last dollar. Which did not help our case at all. They
thought/think we're the ones who switched it. That we have the
real money back here and traded it with fake money so it looks like
we have double the amount. I tried to explain to them that making

money would be way too much effort for us to go to in the name of making a few extra grand, but they didn't listen," Reggie says. "Money laundering is not something I've ever been involved with."

"It's true. It's highly unlikely. It must have been switched while it was either in the cash register or in the bag," Darrel says, thinking.

"Who put it in the bag for us?" I ask.

"Sophie, one of the cooks," Darrel says. "She wouldn't have done anything to the money. Besides, I can't imagine where any of them would have gotten the fake money. None of them would risk Ares's wrath. Especially when they know he hasn't been in the greatest of moods recently. If any of them were the ones who did it, they would have taken off with the cash."

"A few grand is hardly worth the risk," Apate agrees.

"I can't imagine any of them defying me. It had to be a fluke," Ares says, his anger having fallen to a low simmer. "It's that fucking Felicity again. She put someone up to this. It's one thing for them to keep me out of their community, but she's gone too far. She's encouraging her allies to make it impossible for us to do business. Through her actions, she caused the death of a human! She's unstable and needs to be taken care of, once and for all."

"I agree, she's taking it too far by intentionally provoking you. There's no excuse for this type of behavior," Nemesis agrees. "No, that doesn't mean you can kill her."

Ares closes his mouth with a mulish snap. "It would be easier. We could say her life is forfeit for the human's."

"She was indirectly responsible. She encouraged the coven to remove the spell, but I doubt she told them to remove it without warning while we had customers. I agree that she instigated the incident, but she wasn't completely responsible," Nemesis says.

"I wonder where our real money is," Darrel contemplates. "It had to be switched while it was being stored, before it was deposited."

Enyo says, "I shall kill the person dumb enough to betray us."

"Where did the bag go? Directly from the pub to the house? Where is it now?" Nemesis asks.

"They confiscated it as evidence," Reggie explains.

"You mean we have nothing? Not even any of the money to study for clues?" Darrel asks with disappointment. "We could have picked up a scent from the money, at the very least."

"That's exactly what I'm saying," Reggie sighs. "I did the best I could, but they pounced on that bag faster than I thought to take anything."

Apate starts coughing.

"We have nothing to go off of." Nemesis sighs. "There may not be anything we can do in this instance."

"I want retribution! This is not fair!" Ares growls. "If I can't punish the individuals who did this, then I demand that we confront Felicity now. This very moment. I don't want to wait for some stupid meeting to bring all of this damning evidence against her. Everyone will finally see the truth behind her actions."

Apate starts coughing harder.

"You okay?" Darrel asks her.

She gives a softer cough. "Ahem, well, we might have some of the money. I was able to sneak a bill or two away . . ."

Nemesis rolls her eyes. "Yes, yes, we get it. You tried to skim off the top and steal some of the revenue. Now, what do you have for us?"

Apate stands up slowly and brings her hands to her waist.

"You did not hide money in your panties. I'm not touching anything you pull out of there to analyze for clues. This shit is so not worth it," Dysnomia bursts out.

Apate gives her a dark look. "I didn't hide it in my panties, you idiot. I'd have to be wearing some in order to do that." She bends over and starts unfolding her knee-length socks down her leg. A few lone, larger bills start falling out of them.

"They might be a little sweaty, but they're better than nothing." I sigh. "Or at least better than crotch dollars."

"You're welcome," Apate says with some offense.

"Thank you, my dear. Ingenious of you to realize we'd need some of the money for proof, before you even realized it was fake. Truly, you never cease to amaze me," Ares says with an affectionate look.

Some days it's not funny. It's just sad.

"It looks like money to me," Darrel says, holing one of the bills with the very edges of his fingers, as if to avoid germs.

"Let's fingerprint it! I have a mini black light on me!" Dysnomia suggests.

We all give her an odd look. "What? You never know when a mini black light is going to come in handy. Like now, for instance."

"We need powder." Darrel starts and stops when, within moments, the table is full of every type of powder size and shade, all suddenly resting in front of him. We are girls, after all. We might be outwardly stunning, but that doesn't mean we don't powder our noses occasionally. Especially in this hot, hot heat.

Dysnomia carefully lines the dollar with a thin coat of powder and gets her little black light ready. When she shines it on the bill, she sucks in her breath with a whoosh. That's when I know two things: One, she's found something. Two, it's not something good.

"What? You can't tell me you recognize who did it just from a fingerprint," I say, trying to cut the melodrama.

"Nope. But the logo on the counterfeit sure does help," Dysnomia says, all of us crowding around her to see it. She points at the corner of the paper, and there, in tiny letters, too small for a mortal to even notice, the initials S+G and a little tree are visible.

"There's no way." Ares shakes his head violently. "They wouldn't dare do this."

Darrel bites his lip in the most troubled, constipated expression I've seen in years.

"Um, yeah, we can all see it. Plain as day. Clearly it means something to you two that it doesn't to us. What gives?" I ask.

Darrel runs a hand down his face. "There's a pair of local money launderers. One of them is a nymph. They're rumored to be good friends with one of the three counterfeiters."

"You're saying we've been had by a nymph?" Apate asks with horror. "There are some things even our amazing reputations can't come back from. I'm sorry, Ares, but you're never going to live this one down."

Ares moans in despair. "Don't tell the Olympians. Whatever you do, keep this little detail out of your report."

Enyo coos at him sympathetically. "Don't worry, Brother. They will never hear it from us that you were outsmarted by a tree hugger. Your secret is safe with us."

"Well, one nymph and her three bitchy, shifter friends. I imagine Savannah's husband, Gavin, wasn't totally kept out of it, but it was probably mostly the women," Darrel says. "He's actually not that bad. For a tiger. His sister, Mia, is one of the counterfeiters."

"Is everyone related around here?" Enyo scoffs.

"They *are* supernaturals," Dys points out, a reminder that all of us are pretty much able to trace our lineage back to one another.

With so few of us, it's hard to get an overly diverse gene pool going. We're lucky that most of our parents didn't get it on with their first cousins. Back in the day, I bet mimmortals weren't much better. Hard to digest that gross bit of truth, but it's a truth nonetheless.

"That's it! I refuse to take this any longer!" Ares thunders. "It's one thing to mess with my wine, my clients, and neighborhood, but it's another thing entirely to mess with my money! I won't take that!"

I watch calmly as his face becomes darker and darker red, making his dark brown facial hair stand out more. It does nothing to make him look less chiseled or handsome, but it also adds to his crazy factor. I wonder when he'll blow.

"I'm going to see that hag Felicity!"

"I don't think we should try to see her before we have the meeting," Nemesis says.

"It's time to take care of her once and for all!" Ares thunders. "I'm not concerned with pissing her off. She's made me right and truly angry now. Felicity is the one who should have been thinking about how her actions would anger me. Not the other way around. It's time to show her who she's dealing with, and that she should be the one being careful," Ares growls in his sexy, gravelly voice.

Apate brushes some imaginary dirt off her shoulders. "You heard the man. Assemble the mutts so we can step up to Felicity and her bitches in full hostile glory. Snap to it!"

Ares stomps away with Darrel trailing after him.

"All right, this is how this is going to go. Ares is going to storm over there and make our jobs even harder than they already are. I'm going to see if I can stop him and push the meeting up. The key here is not to let him realize that we're trying to appease him. Do not, for one moment, appear to sympathize with the enemy. You know how warriors can get." Nemesis rolls her eyes. "Temperamental babies."

Luckily with Ares's current mood, he's not likely to notice anything different about me. Especially since he's not the most perceptive immortal to begin with. My absence, however, would be much more obvious.

Enyo opens her mouth with a hiss. "Warriors are the foundation of society! And I will *not* go to great lengths to placate the enemy. Ares is justified in whatever he says or does to them. They should be feeling lucky they're facing his wrath and not the tip of his sword."

"That's what she said!" Apate shouts, high fiving Dys and me.

"That *is* what she said," Lyssa says, giving us a mystified look.

Nemesis glares at all of us, kicking Aergia's chair until she looks up sleepily. "I will once again repeat myself. Our goal is to smooth down as many ruffled feathers as possible. We don't want to create more waves. If you don't think you're going to be able to do that, it might be best if you stay here and wait for us to come back. Enyo and Lyssa? That means you."

"There's no way I would miss this confrontation. My brother needs me." Enyo glares angrily.

Lyssa just grins crazily. "You cannot stop me."

Nemesis taps her foot against the carpeted floor, furious. "If you fuck this up for me, and we end up having to stay here for weeks, possibly months longer, I will make your lives a living hell. I will paint your fingernails every day. I'll make you wear heels and dresses. I'll let Peitho set you up on blind dates. I'll make you study gossip magazines. You'll be forced to watch reality television with Dysnomia and Ana. Best yet, I'll make you adopt kittens. Am I understood?"

Enyo gasps out, "Not the kittens!"

Lyssa nods hastily. "Yes, yes, you're understood! No ruffled feathers!

Nemesis smiles evilly. "I'm so glad you agree."

CHAPTER 17

———❧———

F ELICITY, IT'S NEMESIS. I KNOW that we agreed to meet tomorrow, but I was hoping we could arrange for something sooner. We've had a few recent developments that we need to discuss sooner rather than later. Can the council meet in an hour?" Nemesis says into the phone.

I'm able to hear Felicity through the speaker. "It's entirely unprofessional to change the agreed upon time of the meeting. Why on earth would I agree to such a thing?"

"It's imperative that we see you now. There have been consequences to your actions, even the death of a mortal. These things need to be discussed immediately. This is urgent, not something that you can continue to push off," Nemesis responds coldly.

"I heard that someone died after you served them ambrosia. I had hoped it was a nasty rumor," Felicity states.

Nemesis frowns. "They would have never been served ambrosia if they hadn't made it into the pub in the first place. We've had many incidents with individuals in the community, and as the council head, it's your job to hear out our concerns, regardless of if we take an active role in your community. Others are affected by these situations, not just us."

Felicity pauses on the other line. "Fine, come to the bar in an hour. I'll have everyone who's available assemble to meet. I can't promise that everyone will be there, but I'll do what I can."

Nemesis hangs up without a response.

"I guess that's better than Ares storming into the place

unexpectedly," Max points out, trying to look on the bright side. I filled him in on the counterfeit money while we did our best to talk Ares down.

He wasn't completely off his rocker, but it didn't help when Enyo and Lyssa started egging him on to take care of Felicity in a permanent way. We should have separated them from the very beginning. They can't be trusted to look at the big picture, instead of their momentary amusement.

"Let's try to get Ares organized before we go." Nemesis sighs dejectedly.

* * *

"Don't worry, I'm here!" Ares barges through the front door of the bar with his usual drama.

I peek around his shoulder, noting all of the people we recently became acquainted with during the last week. The witches, drug dealers, and assorted other supernaturals we've recently had confrontations with. There are others that I haven't met yet, but I'm sure they're not innocent in this entire ordeal.

"Ares, why don't you take a seat?" Felicity sighs, motioning at some empty chairs to her right.

The leaders sit in the middle of the room, at a large table made of several smaller ones pushed together. Their associates sit around the room at large, like an audience. They eye us warily as we settle into the seats Felicity motioned at. Several of us continue to stand, Ares never one to miss the opportunity to bring an extensive entourage.

"We received your request for a meeting. You know very well that you aren't part of this community. You decided that for yourself when you went against our ruling. You continue to sell ambrosia, don't you?" Felicity asks him with a small smile of victory.

"You have no authority over me. Of course I continue to sell ambrosia," Ares scoffs.

Felicity's smile deepens. "You reject our authority, yet complain that we don't try to include you? You're a study of contradictions."

"I don't think you understand what I was saying. Why would I respect the ruling of a group of people who refuse to include me in their processes? If I have no voice to you, then you have no voice to me." Ares grins.

It might be a bit old and tired, but still a good move on his part.

"That's not exactly fair, is it?" Nemesis asks in a quiet voice, looking at Felicity pointedly, letting her influence help plant the seed of doubt to the other supernaturals in the room.

I see some of the other leaders look sideways at one another. Felicity has a personal vendetta against Ares for the whole Freddy mess. Plus, she doesn't want to lose her power in the community, and sees him as a threat. The others have no such vendetta. They don't have anything clouding their mind into forgetting what Ares is and how much they don't want to make an enemy out of him. In fact, if they played their cards right, he could be quite the asset. Some of them don't appear to be ignorant of that fact.

"It's completely fair, under the circumstances. Besides, you were there when we voted to deny you the rights to sell ambrosia. You knew about the decision, and yet you still sell it out of your pub," Felicity says.

"Yes, I was there when you all decided that. I was able to speak before you all and tell you why I wanted the right to sell it. I appreciate that most of you listened to me with an open mind. However, after that, I did not receive formal notice of the ruling from the council. I was also not offered the right to appeal the council's decision. Which, I believe, is the normal procedure," Ares says.

Felicity growls, visibly losing her cool. "We're not here to argue about what's right or how you've been wronged. We have supposedly serious concerns to discuss, if that was true."

Nemesis jumps in before Ares has a chance to talk. "We've recently had a series of offenses committed against us. Our ambrosia supply was replaced with mortal wine. I hope that whoever took it was careful with storing or disposing of the ambrosia. Our spell, which was fully paid for, to keep humans from entering the pub, was disabled. Drug dealers stopped selling in our territory. Profits from the pub were replaced with counterfeit money. It's all a great series of coincidences, don't you think?"

Everett, Felicity's second-in-command, clears his throat.

I take the hint. "I'm not sure where someone would have gotten the idea to commit these crimes against us. Or why they would think these crimes would go unpunished. Do any of you know why we've been having so many issues? What have you all been discussing at some of your most recent meetings?"

"That's none of your business," Felicity snaps, just as a rather pretty woman with long brown hair and green eyes speaks up.

"Ways that Ares has been ostracized and how he can continue to be punished until he no longer sells ambrosia," the girls says.

Felicity glares at her and snaps, "Savannah! That is privileged information!"

I grin at the woman, who I now know is the money-laundering Nymph. "You look familiar. Have we met before?"

She grins at me and the rest of the girls. "I'm Addy's younger sister. She told me you all were able to go to the shifter convention. I think I met some of you at a siren party or two."

Dysnomia laughs. "You brought the green whiskey to the St. Patty's day bash!"

Savannah gives a modest nod. "Yes, that would be me. If I'd known you guys were in town, I never would have wasted my time with those pranks. We could have been having way more fun than this!"

Felicity glares at her and snaps, "You all can go catch up now, if you want. I'm sure you all remember the way to the door. If not, Savannah seems fully capable of showing you."

Savannah glares at her. "Calm down. Just because I know the ladies doesn't mean I'm changing all my beliefs. I thought this entire feud was ridiculous from the beginning, not just because I'm friends with the ones we've all been attacking. On your command."

"Ah-ha!" Ares shouts. "You've been purposely attacking me! You admit it!"

Felicity gives him a bored look. "We weren't exactly trying to hide it. None of us have been pleased with your blatant disregard for the rules."

"I'm not sure why you think that gives you the right to plan a targeted attack toward us. We've never done anything to interfere with your business or anyone else's. We've certainly never deliberately put someone in harm in an effort to teach you a lesson," Nemesis states.

"What do you mean, deliberately put someone in harm?" Savannah asks with concern.

I see the witches turn away stiffly. I can't help but smirk at Jax.

"When Felicity ordered the coven to disable the spell, we were open that day. We didn't get any warning from Felicity or the coven before the spell was removed. Humans came into the pub, and we had no idea that they weren't supernaturals. We weren't aware that we needed to check them, since we had every reason to believe that the spell was still active. Six humans were served ambrosia. Five of them still live," Nemesis explains.

The others give us surprised, wide-eyed looks. "You mean a human died because of this feud?"

"Yes, because we weren't given proper service and consideration, a human paid with his life. We did everything we could to save him, but ambrosia responds differently to humans. There was nothing we could do to prevent his death once he'd had the ambrosia," Nemesis explains.

"You could have prevented it by stopping the sale of ambrosia altogether! You went against the council's orders, acted negligently, and that's why the mortal is dead! Not because the spell was removed or because we don't support your business," Felicity argues.

"You're stating that this kind of behavior is sanctioned? Turning on someone with pack mentality just because they don't agree with you is acceptable? If so, I think you need to revisit how your community is run," Ares argues.

Felicity turns to him with malicious eyes. "I told you all. He's wanted to change how we run our community all along. His goal has been to lead us, to take my place and make this a dictatorship."

Ares laughs. "You're kidding, right? I'm here to have some fun. I'm happy doing my own thing without you getting in my way."

A husky chuckle echoes around the room. "Ares, you haven't been behaving yourself, have you?"

"Damn," I moan, looking around for the source of the voice.

"What's wrong?" Max asks. "What's going on?"

"An immortal pissing contest. They sent his ex," I whisper.

Gaia, the Goddess of Earth, appears out of nowhere and struts to where we're seated. She swings her curvy, womanly hips, flinging her rich chestnut hair behind her. Her green eyes are vivid and sparkling, her mouth framed by delicate laugh lines. She appears earthy and womanly, irresistible to men everywhere.

"What are you doing here? Did they send you?" Ares asks, suddenly sullen.

"What did you think would happen when news of a human ambrosia overdose reached us? An investigation was needed. Who better to investigate a crime on Earth than Earth itself? All of my people are precious to me," Gaia says, eyes briefly landing on me.

I hold my breath, hoping beyond reason that she won't be able to tell that my power has shifted. Gaia, perhaps more than anyone else, would have a valid reason for stopping us from becoming goddesses on Earth. No immortal likes competition, let alone a goddess.

"How long have you been here?" Ares asks.

Gaia stops in front of him and waves away the questions dismissively. "I've been in and out for the last week or so, trying to get down to the heart of the matter."

"Gaia, it's such an honor to meet you," Felicity gushes with a startlingly fake, deferential smile. "I'm so glad that you're here to help us with our situation. Ares has been completely unreasonable and has put the rest of us at risk. This ambrosia matter only highlights the fact that he's unsuitable to be part of our community."

"I don't know about that." Gaia gives her a secret smile. "I mean, he's been almost as petty as you have in this matter. Surely he fits in just fine. After everything I've heard at this meeting, and your previous meetings, I'm forced to find that Ares isn't completely at fault for the young man's death."

Nemesis and Ares breathe sighs of relief.

Felicity glares at Gaia. "How can you say he's not at fault when he's the one who sold them the ambrosia?"

"That's an easy conclusion, but we both know there's more to the story than that. Ares took pains to make sure no humans would be sold ambrosia at his pub. You took pains to make sure nothing at his pub worked properly. It was a joint effort, if I've ever seen one. The death was unfortunate, but not deliberate. It was completely avoidable if the spell had remained in place." Gaia's eyes turn toward the coven.

"We offered to put the spell back in place!" Tess says quickly.

"Yes, after the human had already been poisoned. I'm surprised you don't have rules governing your coven to reduce the harm of innocent people. It's one thing to remove a spell or refuse business. It's another to give no warning when it's been done," Gaia says calmly.

"If you don't mind, I think I'll stay for the negotiations to make sure that a fair decision is reached. As it is, this has taken too much of our time and attention away from important matters. We want it resolved as quickly as possible, as is shown by our immortal representatives having been sent here." Gaia motions toward us before taking a seat in the back of the room. "You may proceed."

"I think the best course of action, as I've said from the beginning, is for Ares to discontinue the sale of ambrosia and the fights. He can continue to run the pub as a bar and restaurant only," Felicity states.

"I don't see what the big deal is. So we let him run his restaurant, sell ambrosia, and host the occasional fight. Before you asked us to start making things harder for him, we barely heard a thing about Ares. Besides the few random things like topless karaoke at the bar or something. Which, let's face it, any good shifter bar has at least once every few months," a tiger shifter says with grin. "It doesn't hurt us if he sells ambrosia. I wouldn't mind a cup of it here and there for special occasions."

"Yeah, if you want, we don't have to include him in the community, but I don't see what's wrong with giving him permission to do that at least," one of the foxes adds. "It wouldn't hurt us any. Or really affect us at all. We can just agree to stay out of one another's way. That's what we've done for the past several decades, and it's always worked for us. We're only having issues now because we're interfering with one another's business, and that's never a good thing. I think we all have better things to do than think of ways to run each other out of town."

"In fact, I don't see why we don't just let him back in the community," a rather reasonable witch asserts. "If we give him permission to sell ambrosia and agree to not hinder them, we could include him in full membership and have him pay his monthly fees. That would only benefit us in the long run."

"No, no, no! That is not something any of us should be contemplating. He has a disregard for everything we stand for! There's a reason we're organized now. It would be chaos if we weren't, and much less effective. Letting him back would go against everything we stand for as an organization!" Felicity bursts out angrily.

"Oh, give it up. All of us know why you're really mad at him," a wolf speaks up, making everyone quiet down.

None of us can quite see who said it, but all of us were thinking the same thing.

"I'm mad at him because he won't follow the rules," Felicity claims.

"Are you sure that's it? Or does it have anything to do with something you might be missing?" Emmett speaks up quietly.

She gives him a betrayed look. "How dare you? You're my second-in-command!"

"It's for your own good," Emmett tells her before turning to Ares. "You know what you did to create all of this hostility. Did you or did you not take Felicity's pet turtle? By the name of Freddy?"

Everyone looks at Ares with baited breath.

Ares shrugs nonchalantly. "I didn't take the turtle personally."

"He was a tortoise!" Felicity says angrily. "What did you do to him? Did you all really eat him? Savages! What kind of person does that? See, everyone? Clearly, this is not a man who can be trusted."

"It was an initiation task! I heard about your stupid pet tortoise and knew that it would be an epic prank. I don't see what the big deal is," Ares huffs.

"I had him since he was a hatchling, and he's over two centuries old! How dare you take a beloved pet and then not only steal him, but eat him? That's just sick on so many levels."

Ares shifts uncomfortably. Oh no.

"It was silly of you to keep a pet tortoise to begin with. I don't think someone who lets her judgment get so clouded over a simple pet should be making such important decisions for the good of the community," Ares says.

"I don't think a bloodthirsty pet eater should be part of this group," Felicity says, getting murmurs of agreement to go along with dirty looks now being thrown at Ares. If there's one thing a person shouldn't mess with, someone's pet is definitely on the top of the list.

"Well, actually . . ." Max begins, speaking up from nowhere.

"Shut up, Max," Ares growls.

Max says, "Sorry, Ares, but I can't this time. It looks like I need to clear up a few things. First of all, Felicity, I was there the night that Freddy was taken. I can promise to you that nothing bad happened to him. We simply put him in the jeep, after some maneuvering and fruit bribery, and took him back to the clubhouse. Ares looked him over in the morning. He was well fed and seemed healthy enough."

"Until you made soup out of him, if memory serves me right," she says bitterly.

"Ares actually kind of liked the tortoise. He ate out of his hand. Plus, he liked his shell. I'm not sure if you've ever noticed the small dent in the back right of it. Ares liked that Freddy came with his own shield," Max continues. "He liked him so much, he decided to keep him."

"Safely in his stomach," Felicity spits out.

Max frowns. "No, I mean *keep* him. Like, as a pet."

The blood drains from Felicity's face. "What do you mean, keep him as a pet?"

"I know Ares sent you that card saying that he made him into soup or whatever. The truth is, he turned out to like Freddy a lot. He wouldn't make soup out of him. Actually, Ares doesn't eat that much anyway. Nothing like turtle or tortoise. More like jerky and such," Max explains.

"Are you saying what I think you're saying?" Felicity asks.

"Max . . ." Ares warns.

"Yup. Freddy is still alive," Max says, causing everyone in the room to gasp with amazement.

"I definitely wasn't expecting this," someone in the back mutters.

"Right. This is so worth missing my soap opera. Someone go make the popcorn."

Felicity's eyes narrow. "You're just saying that so I'll have them all agree to reinstate Ares's membership to the council of organized crime, along with the rights to sell ambrosia at the pub. Or at least a revote on the issue."

Max says, "Nope, not at all. It's the truth. And if it's the truth, there's no reason why he shouldn't be a member or have the rights of a member. There's no crazy vendetta between the two of you."

"You have no right saying these vicious lies," Ares tells him.

"If they were lies, you'd just laugh at them," Felicity counters, some hope showing in her eyes. "Well, what do you want in exchange for Freddy? Tell me where he is, and I'll do what I can to get you your membership back."

"You think I'm that stupid? You get me my membership back, and then I'll tell you where Freddy is," Ares counters.

Two women stand and move to the head table. One is long and lean with short black hair and yellow eyes. She smells like a panther and seems just about as lethal. The other has long blonde hair and dark brown eyes. A lioness. The two of them are a combination I would rather avoid if possible.

"I think the two of us might be able to help you, in this situation," the woman with black hair says silkily. "I'm Angelica, and this is Christina. We're part of Purrfect Perpetrator. The legal group."

"Lawyers?" Ares backs away in horror.

"That's right. I think the two of us could be a great help to you. We can draw up the necessary contract to make sure both of you achieve what you hope to in this negotiation. Think of us less as lawyers and more as mediators, for the time being. Sound good?" Christina asks.

Felicity sighs. "Fine, I suppose so. But you're footing the bill. You're the one who started this mess by taking Freddy in the first place."

Ares sniffs regally. "I will agree to this, but only because I'm less petty than you. Plus, I clearly have more money."

Angelica whips out some paper and a pen from a briefcase by her recently vacated chair. "Ares, you'd like to regain membership as a leader to your faction of organized crime, correct? Along with the full benefits that membership should provide you, including but not limited to a vote equal to the other crime ring leaders, invitations to monthly meetings, invitations to local functions, and a pass to the shifter fun gym/park?"

"That is correct," Ares confirms.

"You would also like Felicity to stop suggesting the other crime groups make doing business harder for you. You will instead work together, since you'll once again be part of the same community," Angelica says.

"That sounds about right."

"Now you, Felicity, would have to agree to those terms. In return, you'd like the whereabouts of your pet tortoise, Freddy, to be disclosed," Angelica says.

"Yes, I want my pet back." Felicity nods curtly.

Angelica scribbles some things down and says, "I believe that's all you need, correct?"

"Yes, as well as cooperation in group decisions," Felicity adds after a moment, probably trying to seem more group-oriented instead of admitting this entire fight has very little to do with the common good and is mostly about her being pissed off for personal reasons.

"Great, I think this document puts those terms into writing for you. Felicity, you agree to reinstate his membership, grant him membership privileges, and stop leading the attack against his pub and sale of ambrosia? This includes fixing any previously led attacks. Such as the witches giving back the spell they recently took down, to make sure mortals don't notice the pub. Ares, you agree to share the location of Freddy in return for your membership to the club and peace with the other criminals," Angelica says.

They both nod in consent.

"Does anyone disagree with the terms I just listed?" she asks.

A money launderer asks, "Does that mean we have to return the things we've taken?"

"Yes, you must make your previous actions as right as possible now that you'll be neighbors in the community and belong to the same organization." Angelica nods. "Any other questions? No? Then I need you both to sign here and initial here, here, and there."

All of us watch with held breath as Ares and Felicity sign where indicated.

"Now tell me where he is!" Felicity demands as soon as the pens hit the table.

"First, tell everyone to stop working against me!" Ares counters.

Felicity gives him a dark look and says to the room at large, "Since Ares is now a member of our criminal organization, we will offer him the cooperation expected from comrades. That means the witches will reinstate their spell, the dealers will sell in the area, and we won't steal or otherwise mess with his product or business. Is that understood?"

There's a murmur of consent around the room. Some people look bored. Others are openly irritated about all the to-do just because of one small personal incident. I'd like to say this sort of immaturity is unusual and probably won't happen again any time soon. But, I know the reality. The older you get, the less stable.

"Thank you very much. Now, to answer your earlier question, I would first like to start with a small story," Ares begins.

"Oh, goddess," I hear Apate mutter.

He glares at us and continues, "Once upon a time, a few weeks ago, I set a task to some of my pack. Some would call it an initiation task. Others, hazing. I, however, like to think of it as a show of their dedication to the pack. What would be a better form of loyalty than to have them infiltrate a neighboring pack and steal from them?"

I can't help but shake my head.

"I had them take something of little value. Just a pet turtle. Then they brought this large beast home. With his dry, scaly skin, big gaping mouth, and eyes full of wisdom, and personal protection system, I knew what had to be done. First, I made him a salad. Then, I set up a sanctuary for him. I ordered a greenhouse online—it's surprisingly simple—and had my minions set it up. I've got the heat turned up, veggies growing, and a lawn chair set up. The two of us often spend our evenings together. I'll feed him carrots from my hand," Ares explains.

Everyone looks at him in open shock and ridicule.

"You're saying you built him a greenhouse?" Felicity asks.

"Yes, it's much roomier than you would assume at first glance. The point is, I couldn't just return him to you. You had him in filthy conditions! He just had a penned-off corner of the room. With me, he has wilderness and open space and all the fresh food he could ask for," Ares explains.

Felicity's face turns red. "There is no way I'm letting you keep him. You can just throw that idea right out of your mind.

He has a perfectly fine home here with me. Clearly he's doing well or he wouldn't be over a hundred years old. Why don't you leave well enough alone?"

"Ah, yes, have you ever given Freddy the opportunity to procreate? He's getting a bit old if you ask me. I was wondering if he had any young who could take his place in Freddytopia once he passes on. I wouldn't want it to go to some stranger, you understand," Ares says.

"You think they understand it's a tortoise, not a puppy or a prince?" Dys asks me in a hushed voice.

The two of them pause to glare at her.

"No, of course Freddy has never had any children. That's an insane suggestion. Why on earth would I breed him? Do you know how many eggs the female lays at a time?" Felicity scoffs.

He gives her a condescending look. "Yes, I could see that being a problem for you, considering you barely have enough room for Freddy on his own. Freddy is of superior genetic stock. If you had made sure he'd have offspring, you could have kept a Freddy from his line every generation. You do plan on being here a while, after all. Don't worry, I can always have some of his DNA frozen for future use."

"Did he just suggest what I think he did?" I turn to the others with wide eyes.

"Oh yeah, I think he had that cow milked." Apate nods.

"His DNA belongs to me, and I didn't agree to you taking a sample. Now I'm going to head to your house and collect my Freddy!" Felicity says, standing.

"But he has a better home with me! You have to think of what's best for Freddy, not you!" Ares protests.

Felicity glares at him. "Being with the person who raised him since he was a hatchling is what's best for him!"

"Can you give him everything that I have to offer?" Ares asks.

Felicity just stares him down, quietly contemplating the murder of a god.

From the other side of me, I hear the two lawyers talk quietly to themselves.

"Custody agreement?" Angelica asks Christina.

"Yes, that might be just the thing. Divorced parents and a child caught between. It's been a while since I've done the divorce court thing, but I can certainly think of something. Mediation, at the very least," Christina agrees.

She tilts her head in consideration. "We can start negotiations. We're going to make a fortune off of these two and their alliance."

"Play your cards right, and you could probably make a need for them to have a contract for just about anything." I wink at them.

Felicity glances up at me with a smirk. "Mind your own business, Immortal. Don't you have a little mortal immortal puppy mate to keep you busy? Now, that doesn't sound messy in the least. Nice mark—it still stinks of a fresh bite."

"First of all, it's mimmortal. Get with the lingo, Grandma. Second, I would thank you not to sniff my mate. It's bad form. Though you should probably already know that," I huff at her.

"Mark? Mate!" My girls turn to me in shock.

I groan and give Felicity the finger. "Shit just got real."

"Before we end the meeting, I would like to bring one last vote to the collective group," Emmett speaks up.

We all turn to him in surprise.

"What are you doing?" Felicity hisses.

Emmett ignores her. "I would like to remove Felicity from the head of the council. The pack had a meeting earlier today, and it was decided that it would be best to remove Felicity as the alpha of our pack. I was chosen to replace her."

"Oh no he didn't!" Apate says in a stage whisper.

"You can't do that!" Felicity shrieks.

"You've proven yourself to be an unstable leader who's more concerned with your personal agenda than that of the collective whole. I'm sorry, but we can no longer let you lead us. Does anyone approve of the motion?" Emmett asks.

"I second the motion!" Savannah quickly agrees. "I would like to vote immediately for a new leader. I nominate Emmett."

There are murmurs of agreement from around the room. Ares

gives Felicity a condescending smile. "Don't worry, Felicity, you're still welcome to come to the pub any time you like."

Gaia stands up from the back of the room, gaining everyone's attention. "Excellent work, everyone. I'm glad that you were all able to come to a peaceful resolution."

"As always, a pleasure to see you." Ares gives her his most charming smile.

Gaia's look is full of seduction as she says, "I should hope so. We'll have to make it happen more often."

Gross.

She slowly makes her way to us immortal representatives, and I do my best to rein in my power and fade to the back of the room. I try to seem as unnoticeable as possible. Dysnomia and Apate dutifully step in front of me, hoping to distract from any noticeable changes. Ares may not have realized anything changed, but Gaia is certainly wilier than that.

"Another successful mission, Ladies." Gaia inclines her head at Nemesis.

"We're happy to assist with any task assigned to us. It's our goal to properly represent the immortals," Nemesis states. "We're happy to take care of any tasks so that you may see to higher responsibilities."

"Indeed, you do your jobs well. I can't wait to see what you're assigned to next," Gaia agrees, her eyes falling on me with a small frown before she disappears back to Olympus.

* * *

"Well, we've been outed." I smile cautiously at Max.

"I heard. Well, I literally heard her say it, then got messages from various friends and family members asking when the formal wedding is." He grins back, but it doesn't go up to his eyes. "Sophie is freaking out and talking to all of the family and pack back home.

I finally just turned my phone off, so they're bugging her now. Who knew a little mating bite would turn into so much chaos."

I sit next to him in the backseat of his car, parked a few blocks from the house, where he's been hiding out for some time it seems. Everyone else is either at the meeting or over at the pub celebrating. Ares and Felicity have worked out the Freddy situation. Ares is going to have him weekends in the beginning, and possibly more often further down the road. They're also going to see about breeding him.

"That's awful, making your little sister take the heat like that. I admire your strategy. Almost makes me wish I had a little sister I could pawn things off on," I say.

Max nods. "She comes in handy."

"Yeah, she can blow that formal wedding suggestion to shreds," I agree, shuddering at the thought of putting on a big, white, poofy wedding dress.

"How did yours take the news?" he asks.

I settle in my seat, thinking back to my phone call with Peitho, where I got to confess that I'm happily mated. She was pleased for me, but was pretty adamant about using protection. She let me know she'd be sending me a gigantic box of monogrammed condoms with overnight shipping.

I smile at him. "It went well."

"Right." He laughs. "So, what are we going to do?"

"Honestly . . . I don't know."

"We have to decide pretty quickly here. I heard Nemesis on the phone already making travel plans. Sounds like you guys are going to be out of here pretty soon," Max says.

I nod. "We never stay in one place long."

"So, what do you want?"

"Well, the thing is, I'm not sure if I'm ready to settle down in one place. I know that Peitho decided to stay with Hunter at his home when they mated, but I think a lot of that was due to starting a family. She can't really travel with the rest of us, or be in danger while she's expecting. I doubt that will change once they have a young child. I, on the other hand, don't expect to have children anytime soon. But I know that you prefer pack life; plus your sister is here," I tell him.

Max nods at what I've said. "I've traveled a lot—the only reason I'm here in one place at the moment is because of Sophie. I think she'll understand if I travel with you and the others for a while. I don't need pack life. I just want to be with you. I can't imagine us being separated."

"I can't imagine that either." I smile. "I would love for you to travel with us. It's always an adventure. I know the other girls can get out of hand, but we'll find a way to deal with it, I promise. First on the list will be to get our own living space. Or at least our own bedroom."

"I would definitely like our own bedroom." He grins his wild dog grin.

"We don't have to live this way forever, but I don't think I'm ready to give it up quite yet. Eventually, though, I would like to settle down with you. You ground me, somehow. You calm me down and make me feel like it's okay not to do anything. No, I don't mean it like that. You make me feel like I don't have to do something. The pressure to figure out my purpose or travel or find . . . something. Anything. That pressure is gone. It's like you're an anchor or something. I feel like you've helped me to fulfill my purpose."

Max smiles. "Maybe you've found something in me?"

I smile back shyly. "Maybe I have." I move across the middle seat until I'm against his side. He naturally puts his arm around me, and I sit like that for a moment, blissful. "When I'm in your arms, everything feels right. I'm perfectly and utterly content."

"I know exactly what you mean," Max agrees, holding me tight for a moment before loosening his hold. "I really want to stay with you. I enjoy your company so much, and I feel driven to be with you and protect you. Like a mate. I want to make you happy, and I love your crazy randomness. There's always something going on with you or the other girls. It's insane and I love it. You're like your own little pack, in a way. I want to be part of that pack. I want to lay my kill at your feet and sleep cuddled against your chest."

I grin. "Are you asking what I think you're asking?"

"Will you be my mate?" he asks.

I relax into him, melting into the contours of his body. "Doesn't the bite already make me your mate?"

"I'd rather be the one to do the biting, this time," Max says.

I smile softly, my blood already boiling at the thought of being claimed.

"Is that a yes?" he asks.

"How could I say no? You're offering to put your life aside and travel with me and my crazy sisters? I will never find another man insane enough to do that. Yes, I'll be your mate. You're my mate. We're firmly mated." I smile happily.

Max pulls me close and kisses me deeply, searing my mouth with the taste and feel of him. He makes my heart speed up, the thought of kissing my mate making me smile and feel like I'm going to burst. Where is this coming from? Is this what being in love feels like? Is this my something in life? My happiness? My ever after?

"Stop thinking," he commands, biting my lip. Exactly what I need.

I grin. "Mine."

"And you're mine," Max tells me firmly, holding me close once again. I bask in the comforting sweetness of feeling perfectly right and completely worry free. One day at a time. "Let's go see where Nemesis is planning to take us."

"Oh, right, you can be the one to tell the girls. I think they were kind of hoping you and I would stay down here for a while, until the honeymoon period wears off. I'm sure they won't mind dealing with both of us. We're not even that lovey-dovey. Tell you what, while you tell them we'll all be traveling together, I'll start packing our bags!"

Max raises a brow. "You think I'm that dumb? I might be a dog, but I'm not a wolf."

EPILOGUE
———∽∾———

FIVE MONTHS LATER

"I can't believe Peitho still isn't married yet. She's taking forever planning that goddess-awful wedding of hers. Plus, she's like a million months pregnant. Hasn't she popped that baby out yet?" I ask Dysnomia as she helps me fold some of my things.

"You're just bitter because of the fight you two had." Apate laughs from the other side of the room, trying on a pair of my shorts.

I frown. "That was no little fight. She told me that my claws make me look like a gargoyle and my fangs give me an unattractive lisp."

"You told her that her gold skin makes her look like she's wrapped in tacky tinsel," Dys points out. "I believe something about a Vegas showgirl was also thrown out there. You know how much she hates being compared to others."

"On her side again, I see. Just because she's pregnant and soon to be married doesn't mean that you all have to take her side on everything! It does not make her right about all of the stupid things she says. In fact, if anything, it probably clouds her judgment for the worse!" I announce. "You all should take my side, since I'm not forcing you to parade around in ugly ass dresses for my own sick amusement. At least I'm not having some huge formal wedding!"

"You know, for once, you're actually making some sense," Apate says.

"I'm sure I have no idea what you're talking about," I huff. "I'm always the voice of reason around here."

"Oh, come on, Ana, you know it makes sense that she's pissed," Dys says.

"Well, it's not my fault she didn't think of something as amazing as Max and I did. She has no reason to blame me for her jealousy," I say.

Apate and Dysnomia exchange a glance.

"Peitho is marrying into a royal family. To dragons, that's kind of a big deal. Plus, she's going to be giving birth to the newest dragon prince in centuries. Once again, that's kind of a big deal. They can't agree to just bite each other, call it good, and take a honeymoon just for the hell of it," Apate explains.

"Once again, I fail to see how that is my problem," I tell them.

Sure, Max and I recently agreed to make this thing legit and agreed to the whole life partner thing. For the foreseeable upcoming eternity. Not all that big a deal. I don't know why people insist on a wedding and rings and big parties, where they invite a bunch of people, half of whom they don't really like. Or even worse, all the family who show up.

It's a lot of time, effort, planning, money, and annoying traditions all to get to the good part. The agreeing to be one another's for the rest of their lives. Which doesn't take a ceremony or ring to do. The only good thing that comes from a wedding is the honeymoon. A great excuse for a fabulous one-on-one vacation including tons of lingerie, embarrassing photos, hot sex, and exotic new foods.

Max and I decided to be smart about all this. We'll end up with pretty much the same results. We're going to be each other's forever, minus the ceremony and giving of rings. We'll have a yummy cake, without the big show of cutting it together and such, or goddess forbid, having to share it with others. Then we'll have our amazing honeymoon. It's like happily ever after made simple.

"I still think they could have managed a small, private wedding. I'm not saying they should elope, but it could have been just him and his parents. I guess we could have gone too, if she insisted. Then they could have spent their time planning an amazingly kickass honeymoon instead of looking at a bazillion different table arrangements," I say.

"You know they couldn't have," Dys says.

I continue as if she didn't speak, "I still don't think it gave her any right to tell me I'm no longer in the wedding. I mean, I'm practically her sister. If I'm not there, you know she won't walk down the aisle. Besides, I was the one who was supposed to bring the booze while we're all getting ready, to do a shot together before we go out in those hideous dresses in front of hundreds of people."

"Ahem. I've already been told I'm in charge of bringing the vodka now," Apate says with eyes downcast.

Dys says, "Don't worry about it. She'll change her mind soon anyway. Just don't have her look at your honeymoon album anytime soon, okay? You'll come back, she'll have the baby, she'll get her body back, and we'll have the wedding of a millennium. As long as you play your cards right, your invite will still come in the mail. If you're lucky, you'll be a guest instead of a bridesmaid."

"Fine, fine, I won't brag about my amazing honeymoon minus the stupid wedding," I finally agree.

"Stupid wedding, huh?" Max asks from the doorway, giving me that wide doggy smile.

I drop whatever I'm folding to skip over to him and throw myself in his arms. "You're alive!"

Dysnomia and Apate quietly make an exit from the room, shutting the door behind them.

"Yes, of course I am. I was only gone a week, love. They just wanted to see me and find out how I'm doing. Plus, I'm much more popular back home now that everyone knows an immortal chose me as her mate. You might be surprised, but that doesn't happen all that often. Especially since there are few immortals floating around. Or, you know, socializing with wild dogs." Max smiles sheepishly at me.

I kiss at his neck, saying, "One week is long enough. I don't know how we managed without our horny nighttime cuddling. I don't sleep nearly as well if I'm not cuddled up against your side. Not to mention if you're gone then the girls feel very free to just walk right into my room, wake me up, and make me go out to do awful things with them. Like put blue hair dye in Aergia's conditioner."

"Is her hair blue?" Max laughs.

"Goddess no. She's too lazy to actually use the conditioner, not that we realized it at the time." I roll my eyes. "So, how's your family?"

Max left me for an entire week so he could go see those other people who steal my time with him. Granted, it was some big family reunion type thing back in Australia. So he kind of had to go. But still, I don't see why they needed him for an entire week. I think he could have stopped by, said a quick hello at the airport, then gotten on a plane right back home to me.

I never thought I'd be one of those women who needs their man around all the time, but it's still so fresh and new. I didn't like having him gone at all. Beyond just missing him, there was no buffer between me and the girls while he was away. I mean, sure, he offered to take me with him, but as if I'd agree to that. I had valuable packing, shopping, and planning time with him gone.

After two days I was done with that and quite ready for him to come back.

"They're all doing well?" I ask politely.

"Yes, they're all doing well, and I told them that it will be a while before I can visit again. I know we'll be busy with our travels and appointments. We have the baby, the wedding, all sorts of things to do. Not to mention the honeymoon and all the *us* things we have planned," Max says, kissing the top of my head gently.

"I do rather adore us things," I agree.

"Me too," Max says. "How's your chest doing? Any regrets?" he asks, brushing his hand along the side of my left breast.

I shiver lightly. "Doing just fine, thanks for asking. Besides, regrets are for mortals."

Since we decided to do the honeymoon thing and whole life together bit, we thought he might as well mark me too. Before he left, in the heat of passion, he chose to mark me there. It didn't really hurt. It was exciting and thrilling to be claimed so completely. If it didn't come along with his annoying wet dog scent, I would be completely content with it.

"They haven't noticed yet?" he asks in surprise.

"Nope, I think because I spend so much time with you and wear your clothes sometimes anyway, they didn't notice that your scent is on me in a new way. I'm hoping they don't notice until after the honeymoon. I so don't need to deal with that round of teasing again." I roll my eyes.

He chuckles. "They only wore fangs around you for a week."

"They threw holy water on me," I point out. "They drew bite marks on themselves and said I'd wandered in and marked them during the night. They put a fire hydrant lamp in my room. Must I continue?"

"I'm pretty sure it wasn't really holy water," Max tries.

"Still, I'd rather wait to deal with that again, if it's all the same to you," I say.

"Fine with me. It's not like they won't find out eventually either way. We're mates, we're both marked, and we're both in love," Max says.

I hold him tightly. "Yes. Perfectly in love."

He leans down to kiss me deeply, plunging his tongue into my mouth.

A loud alarm goes off in the house, sounding like a fire alarm. The door opens up, and suddenly all the women come rushing in. They have on camo, boots, and have smudged soot under their eyes. They're also holding . . . muzzles.

"The alarm has been sounded! We're at risk of attack! Squad one, you hold down the first target. Squad two, on standby!" Nemesis announced.

I roll my eyes. "Really, guys? Muzzles?"

"Come on now, Ana. Didn't think we'd notice the new tit tat? Or should we change your name to Chew Toy?" Dys asks.

"What are you going to do without me?" I ask with a shake of my head.

Dys and Apate smile evilly at one another.

"Don't worry, Ana, I'm sure we'll think of something," Apate assures me.

"Besides, we'll be focused on our cameo at the Goddess Academy. I'm sure the Olympians have missed us these last few months." Dys smirks. "They'll be sure to invite us back real quick after this trip."

Their cackling laughter begs to differ.

"Oh, yeah. We're so in need of a honeymoon." I cuddle back up in Max's arms, knowing there's really no other place I'd rather be.

ABOUT THE AUTHOR

Victoria C. Johnson lives in Michigan with her husband and two daughters. She became serious about her passion for writing shortly after having her first daughter. As someone who strongly believes in doing what makes you happy, she decided to follow her own advice. She loves writing almost as much as she loves reading. Victoria adores happy endings, heartfelt characters, and extraordinary situations. She hopes to bring a little more of that to life every day.

To find out more about Victoria C. Johnson and her books, please visit:

website: www.victoriacjohnson.com
facebook page : facebook.com/victoria.c.johnson.author
twitter: @V_C_Johnson